THE SPLENDID TICKET

# McSWEENEY'S

SAN FRANCISCO

McSweeney's and colophon are registered trademarks of
McSweeney's, an independent publisher based in San Francisco.

Cover illustration by Masha Krasnova-Shabaeva

ISBN 978-1-952119-49-1

10  9  8  7  6  5  4  3  2  1

www.mcsweeneys.net

Printed in China

# THE SPLENDID TICKET

A NOVEL

BILL COTTER

McSWEENEY'S

SAN FRANCISCO

*For Krissy, the One.*

# PART I

# CHAPTER ONE

# The Red Monster

ONE TUESDAY AFTERNOON IN the early spring of 2012, Angie Grandet was driving I-68 West on the high overpass that arched over a knot of surface roads north of McCandless, Texas. McCandless was like many old oil-boom communities in the center of the state, its glory days long gone, many businesses boarded up, but signs of life here and there: a diner, a couple filling stations, an Elks Lodge, a barbecue joint with a statewide reputation, an anemic bookstore, reckless children on Huffy bicycles figure-eighting in the middle of idle intersections. A resplendent turn-of-the-century town hall, painted inside and out in brilliant jewel tones, dominated the main drag. An operational MoPac spur ran north-south through town. Poker and bridge and bourré flourished on kitchen tables on any given evening. That time of the year, storms would roll in from the west every afternoon around four, tear the fresh leaves from the budding sycamores and pecans and live oaks, and leave roadside drainage ditches bloated with racing torrents of grayish water that kids would swim in till their mothers called them home for dinner.

It was raining, hard now, harder than usual, the kind of deluge that overwhelmed windshield wipers, and the traffic on the overpass had come to a complete stop. Angie waited. Just to her right, barely visible through the sheets of water, was a sign on a sixty-foot pole, high enough that drivers could see it, a blue and crimson billboard she had not paid any attention to before. It was dominated by a number: 324. And to the right of the number, a letter: M. Angie puzzled over this message while the rain fell hard on her car, so loud she could not even identify the song on the radio.

Oh. Of course. The lottery. The current jackpot was $324 million.

The rain began to let up a bit. Lucinda Williams resolved on the radio—

*I ask about an old friend that we both used to know*
*You said you heard he took his life about five years ago*

—and the traffic picked up. The rain stopped, some demigod twisting a faucet, and by the time Angie exited for McCandless, the meridian sun was out and high and the world steamed.

On the passenger seat next to her was a small zinc bucket filled with coins, change she had rescued from her husband Dean Lee's coveralls, from her daughter Nadine's jeans, and from Angie's own pockets whenever she did laundry. A couple times a year the bucket filled up, and she would cash it in. Most banks would no longer count that much loose change—they insisted it be in rolls. So it had to be taken to the grocery store, which had a counting machine, a big red monster like a Coke machine that rapidly tallied even buckets of change, keeping an outlandish percentage for the service.

Today, after its take, the machine counted an even $324. A meaningless coincidence, of course, but when she brought her paper voucher up to the teller at the business center, Angie decided to get a lottery ticket, the only one she'd ever bought. Dean Lee was the gambler in the family. Angie had never shown any interest. Neither had Nadine. Their youngest, however, had had the gambling bug. Dean Lee taught Sophie two-card poker—Texas hold 'em—as a four-year-old, and winning a few pennies from her father would put her in a glittering mood that only losing a few pennies could extinguish.

*Sophie.* The star of a slideshow of fading images that played against the inside of Angie's forehead when stuck on overpasses in cloudbursts, in grocery lines, or maybe in bed, the cracked and stained popcorn ceiling pushing down on her like the platen of some great press, whenever and wherever the labors of domestic tedium were at pause.

"How do I do it?" Angie asked the clerk, a teenage girl whose right earlobe was tattooed with a tiny, greenish-black ouroboros. Except for the tattoo, the girl—Misty, according to her nametag—looked much like Angie had in high school—warm green eyes, black hair whose natural part zigzagged unmanageably, a slightly crooked mouth that some boys found weird, others irresistible.

"Just fill out the dealie," said Misty, giving Angie a hard look, maybe sensing she was being closely observed. "Pick the numbers you want and give it to me."

A line was rapidly forming behind Angie, every last person holding a lottery ticket form and craning to see what the goddamn holdup was.

"Or," said Misty, tweaking her inked lobe, "just let the machine pick your numbers."

"Won't it pick losing numbers, though?"

"Most winners are picked by computer. It's like, random."

"All right, let's do that."

"Two dollars."

"When's the drawing?"

"Tomorrow night."

Angie forgot about the ticket.

A week later, while looking in her purse for a dollar to tip the girl at the new drive-thru coffee kiosk in McCandless, Angie found the lottery ticket again, folded in thirds and tucked behind the emergency $20 bill in the zipper portion of her old billfold. When she got home to their little house on Fawn Street, Angie dragged her laptop out from between the mattresses in the master bedroom, where she kept the house valuables. You never knew when Lolly Prager, the local bookie who Angie's husband was forever in dutch to, would drop by to look for household stuff he could turn into cash to settle a portion of Dean Lee's gambling obligation.

Angie gave the neighbor, Mrs. Anand, fifteen bucks a month for the use of her Wi-Fi. She stretched out on the unmade king bed and, with both her ticket and coffee cup held in one hand, she checked the lottery website. When Angie discovered she was the only winner of a $324 million jackpot—$206 million if she took the lump sum—she calmly finished her coffee, checked the numbers again, and again, and, with a shivering, metastasizing thrill, she picked up the telephone to call her mother, Adeline Bigelow.

Adeline did not have voicemail, or even an old answering machine, so Angie, positively vibrating with enthralled impatience, let it ring. Adeline's habit upon hearing a ringing phone—Angie had witnessed this countless times—was to lie on her couch at a self-satisfied angle of repose, like some Hill Country Madame Récamier, and wait for the ringing to either stop, start again, or to not stop at all, at which point she would demurely swing her legs to the floor, slide on a pair of cerise marabou slippers, saunter over to the Pepto Bismol–colored landline, and answer with some variant of the following:

*Adeline Marjorie Mikoselic Bigelow speaking on the telephone, whom may I ask is calling at this demonic hour?*

It was on the nineteenth ring that Angie Grandet remembered that her mother had died six weeks earlier.

Angie hung up. She checked the lottery numbers one more time. She took a deep breath, then prepared herself to tell Dean Lee, who would be her husband for only a few more months. The divorce proceedings had been civil so far, and would be final on the twenty-third of July. Angie pictured Dean Lee sitting in the front yard, watching the sparse traffic, his blued .357 revolver oily in its shoulder holster, all the world with its dead and living things bearing down upon him.

Angie stood. In the kitchen of their little house on Fawn Street, she peered out of the valance curtains over the sink, and spied Dean Lee sitting with a can of Pearl beer in an old lawn chair, the collapsible sort whose seat and back are made of broad strips of synthetic material loosely woven together and riveted to an aluminum frame—the everlasting kind found folded up and leaning against garage walls all across the country, waiting for the Fourth or Labor Day to be hauled out and scattered on driveways and patios, ready to be stretched open like mouths and fed the asses of the day's celebrants. Or remain outside year after year, like Dean Lee's chair—colors bleached out, nylon embrittled, metal corroded with the whitish frost of aluminum oxide—daring its owner to outlive it. Dean Lee's back was to her. It seemed to be his regular disposition—it seemed she only ever saw the double-arced piping of his western shirts, the warm, shiny, honey-brown sash of his shoulder holster, his muddy black ducktail, the wrinkled sunburn on his neck beneath it. She could not recall the last time she had looked her husband in the face. She was not entirely sure what he looked like, even though she had once known his face like the blind know the counting numbers in Braille.

Angie let the valance fall. She stared down into the dirty dishwater. She took the lottery ticket out of her pocket and held it over the sink. She loosened her grip so that mere friction kept it from fluttering into the tepid water. Outside, Dean Lee sneezed, then again. The man suffered from terrific cedar fever, the scourge of Central Texas.

Angie found a couple pseudoephedrine tablets and a fresh can of Pearl and went outside. "Here, Dean Lee," she said, coming up behind him.

"All right," said Dean Lee, reaching for the pills and the beer. It was one of the minor human kindnesses that blossomed like a tiny fern in the cracks of the concrete.

"Got your phone on you?" said Angie, hands on her hips.

Dean Lee looked up at her.

"Yeah, why?"

Angie studied the face staring up at her, remembering now its angles and subtle asymmetry around the eyes and roughneck squint, wondering exactly what had happened to the man she married, where he had gone. He looked more or less the same, a cross between Scott Glenn and a sunbaked brick, but something had been subtracted from him, or maybe something had been added, some smothering agent. It was not something that kept her up at night, but it nagged at her when she pulled the tabs on his beers or peeled the foil back on his allergy tablets or poured ice cubes into the baby pool. Of course she knew what it was. He would never, ever talk about it. Had he mentioned Sophie's name, even once, in the last six years?

"I want you to look something up for me," said Angie.

"What?"

"March 29th MegaMillions."

"Why?"

14

"Just humor me."

"You win or something?"

"Oh sure, I won the lottery. Just do it, Dean Lee."

With a great sigh, Dean Lee put both cans of beer down in the dirt and dug his phone out of the pocket of his coveralls. With some difficulty, he found the number and showed it to her.

"Okay?"

Angie took her lottery ticket out of her pocket and handed it to Dean Lee without a word. He studied it for two solid minutes. Angie tried to crack her knuckles, but they'd been recently cracked, so instead she counted the teeth in her head that she was going to get fixed when the money came rolling in.

"This a xerox or something?"

"What do you think?"

He studied the ticket some more. He turned it over and over in his big, callused hands, held it up to the setting sun, blew on it, read every word thereon out loud, checked the numbers a dozen times against those on his phone.

"God almighty, Angie, I think this is a fuckin' winner, you know that? I think this is the real deal."

"I *know* it's the real deal."

She plucked the ticket out of his hand like a mother taking matches away from a toddler.

"Here's what'll happen," she said. "The divorce is eleven weeks away from being final. Right? So we're going to cash this ticket, take the lump sum, split it right down the middle, and not contest a penny in the divorce. You heard me? Then we're going to move on, in new and separate paths. We will not meet again. You will take your burdens, stand on your platform, and wait for your train to take you away from here. And Nadine and I will stand on ours, going in the opposite direction. And there you have it. The end."

They were still married, so it was technically *their* money, not hers. But the ticket, at least, was in her possession, so she called the shots for now. Nine-tenths and all that.

Angie did not see redemption in this ticket. She would *eat* it in an instant if she felt like that would be the easiest way to handle the complications. Angie liked the taste of paper, always had. She had chewed on Post-it Notes as a child, marveling at the possibilities of a cure for world hunger. Paper was everywhere!

Dean Lee regarded his wife.

"How long have you known about this? Without telling me?"

"Oh, Dean Lee."

Angie slumped. She wanted to sit down in the front-yard dirt and comb her hair over her face and disappear. How many times had she felt like this over the past six years? Was it this feeling she was trying to escape in divorcing this man?

No. It was Sophie. That was all, that was everything, that was the only thing.

"You've been hiding it," said Dean Lee, looking around in the dirt for his beer. He picked them both up, tested relative coldness by touching one, and the other, to the apples of his cheeks.

"I wanted to be sure of it, for it to be a surprise, for—"

"You—"

"Be happy, for chrissake. You're rich, Dean Lee. This is your way out."

She waved the ticket under his nose like smelling salts. He grabbed at it, once, but Angie was far too quick—she snatched the ticket away, folded it in thirds again, and tucked it into the watch pocket of her jeans.

"Rich, huh," he said.

"Rich."

"For real?"

"*Yeah*, for real. You can pay Lolly Prager back and play poker every day for the rest of your life."

"I want a new truck."

"Have it then, Dean Lee. Have one hundred new trucks."

Dean Lee acquired a faraway look. He sipped from the colder beer, then the warmer one. Both beers finished, he crumpled the cans into balls and pitched them into a fallow baby pool at the end of the driveway near the mailbox.

"With zebra stripes."

"Hell, get some zebras."

"And I wanna move."

The faraway look was suddenly gone, replaced by one of acute focus. Dean Lee sat up straight in his lawn chair and stared at his wife of eleven more weeks.

"Me too," she said.

"Austin, on the lake," he said, sticking a rigid index finger in her face as exclamation.

"Okay."

"I wanna go to Hawaii."

"So go," said Angie. She didn't care where he went. She had cared for an awfully long time, then she didn't. Now she wasn't sure. "Anything else?"

"I'll think about it."

Dean Lee sat back in his lawn chair, ran his hands through his hair. Angie could not guess what he was thinking. He did not look like a man who'd just won a hundred million dollars. He did, in a way, look like a man who'd been snuck up on and told he had one daughter, not two, and to get used to it.

He sneezed mightily, once, twice, three times.

"What you want, Angie?" he said, searching for Kleenex in his coveralls. "What'll you do with your money?"

"Oh, I don't know."

This was not entirely true. She had been thinking about it.

"C'mon."

Angie blushed. Dean Lee never asked her about herself. At least he hadn't in years. He looked genuinely curious.

*I want my—*

"Well, I want to see if a really expensive bottle of wine is really all that much better."

"How much?"

"Twenty thousand."

"Gonna drink it all by yourself?"

*—daughter.*

"Maybe I will."

"What else?"

Angie looked up. A neighbor, Ladye Carlisle, was driving by in her old Volvo. Her husband had died the year before. Sometime after the burial, Ladye Carlisle had come over to borrow some baking soda and had told Angie, out of the blue, that her husband Eddie had been having an affair for years with Callie Ng, the florist in Chamberlain. Callie had come to the funeral and jumped into the grave with Eddie's casket when they started pitching dirt in. Ladye had related all of this very evenly, and left Angie's house dry-eyed with a box of Arm & Hammer.

Angie waved, but Ladye Carlisle didn't wave back. The Volvo disappeared around a corner. Angie thought she might give Ladye some money.

"There are a lot of people I want to give money to."

A thick, pinkish bolt of lightning pitchforked across the northwestern sky, followed six seconds later by a peal of thunder. Dean Lee licked his thumb and stuck it in the air.

"Only about a mile off and heading thisaway."

"Let's watch."

"Why these storms always come from the west," said Dean Lee. He was talking to himself. He was alone.

A few fat raindrops exploded in the dirt.

"Mind you don't let that ticket get wet now."

"Don't worry."

"I could use another beer, babe."

While fetching another can of Pearl, Angie looked around and imagined, for the first time, saying goodbye to the house and its meager chattel. She studied the north wall of the living room, which she had started repainting a robin's eggshell blue some eight years ago, then ran out of paint, and there had been no money to buy more, the remaining walls dingy from years of children scraping by with peanut butter and jelly sandwiches. The mélange of buggy, dented thrift-store furniture, solid IKEA acquisitions, and one or two genuine antiques that were heirlooms from her mother brought a complexity of feeling so overwhelming that Angie had to turn away.

Outside it had begun to rain steadily. Dean Lee had not moved. She popped the tab on the Pearl, opened the screen door to the approaching storm. Angie walked the brick walk to the edge of the yard and handed Dean Lee his beer.

"You know what else?" she said. "I want the perfumer Jacques Cavallier to design a scent for me. My own fragrance."

"Well, all right then." Dean Lee closed his eyes and turned his face to the rain trickling through the boughs and leaves of the magnolia spreading over them. "What about charity? Gonna give any away?"

"Yeah," said Angie. "Eventually. Probably most of it. But not right away."

"I'm giving it all to the Dean Lee Grandet Foundation for Beer and Poker Foundlings."

Angie laughed. An unexpected flush came to her cheeks, her neck, fell down her spine. She wasn't sure what was happening. She hadn't loved—or even liked—her husband in years, and just like that he wasn't so bad. As if a telescopic wormhole had opened up, and she could both see him as he was a decade ago and see herself as she had once loved him. She saw him as he was before Sophie had been... *subtracted*. That was the word on her headstone. Subtracted. Angie saw Dean Lee Grandet before Nadine had been halved into two child soldiers on opposing sides of a ranch-house civil war. Before Angie's very soul had been shooed away like a mayfly trapped behind a windowpane. Before Dean Lee had begun accelerating across the watery littoral dividing guilt from the final relief of it.

Angie reached out to touch her husband's shoulder, thought better of it.

# CHAPTER TWO

*How we weep and laugh*
*at one selfe-same thing.*

IN MID-MAY OF 1997, Junie-June and Leroy Prager, ages five and six, somehow convinced their babysitter, Angie Bigelow, that they did not need baths that evening. They also successfully argued that it was newly customary in the Prager household to eat popsicles before bedtime. Kathleen and Lolly Prager arrived home at 10:30 to find their dirty, blue-mouthed children still up, sitting on the couch with Angie, watching a man selling fake katana on the Home Shopping Network. The Pragers found the whole business hysterical. Lolly gave Angie her pay and a big tip, and Kathleen gave her a bear hug and a doggie bag from the restaurant.

"Let's get you home," said Lolly, delicately biting off the end of the last blue popsicle. "Mind if I pause once or twice along the way?"

"Okay with me."

Lolly smiled, his leather face wrinkled like the sweet spot in a catcher's mitt. He was vain about his exceptionally white and perfect teeth, and as a child he had done a print ad for toothpaste that had run in *Better Homes and Gardens*, for which he had been paid.

Lolly usually made a few "business" stops when he took Angie home.

They drove awhile through the moonlit Hill Country, past stands of mesquite and cedar and scrub oak, taco joints that never seemed to open, roadhouses that never seemed to close, theirs the only vehicle on the road for miles at a stretch.

On Fawn Street in McCandless they stopped before a whitewashed tractor tire laying on its side in front of a decrepit ranch house. From a breast pocket of his western shirt, Lolly removed a small notebook, made a mark in it with a golf pencil, then honked his horn.

"Whose house is this?" said Angie, not sure if she really wanted to know. Lolly was a bookie, a poker player, a chicken fighter, a fringe citizen. It was well past eleven, and any "business" visits Lolly made at this hour were not likely friendly ones.

"Just a fella owes me a sum."

A chill crept into the cab of the truck. Angie hugged her knees and listened to the *cuk-cuk-cuk* of the engine as it cooled and the soft scratching of Lolly's golf pencil on paper. Angie wanted to ask *how much?* but didn't. Gamblers and gambling didn't appeal to her very much. She had gone to the racetrack regularly with her father as a child, and had loved to watch them parade the horses, but that was the extent of her interest. Watching her father either grinning, red-faced, as he counted his wad of cash, or chewing on his fist and screaming at the windshield as he drove them home, broke, had been all the same to her as a seven-year-old.

Thinking of her father, Caspar Bigelow, in the cooling dark of the pickup opened up a hole of loneliness in Angie's solar plexus that nearly took her breath away. Lolly honked again, a bit longer.

"Them kids give you much grief?"

"No sir. Charmers."

She meant it. Even with the popsicle prevarication and the

anti-bath-time theatrics, Angie loved Leroy and Junie-June. Angie loved all children. She had wanted a child of her own since she was three. Someday she would have that. She would have two children, exactly. Girls. That was what she wanted. Angie Bigelow did not often get what she wanted, but she would get this.

Lolly leaned on the horn and did not let up. Lights began to go on in the neighborhood. Then, a bare, dim bulb illuminated the porch of the house in question. Finally, a man pulling on a T-shirt emerged from the front door. Lolly let up on the horn and rolled down his window.

"Hello, Dean Lee."

"Lolly."

"Dropped by to discuss your obligation."

"I know that."

Angie suddenly got goosebumps on her arms and legs, substantive ones, little moguls. It was either the cool country air or this man's voice, low and staccato.

"So," said Lolly. "What you got for me?"

"Who's that?"

"Babysitter," said Lolly. "Just giving her a ride home, over to Chamberlain."

Angie stared straight ahead, ignoring the men. It felt as though thousands of tiny expert skiers were navigating her goosebump mogul fields.

"That right."

"Try to focus here, Dean Lee. I visited with your boss at the bottling plant, Nelson Kallendorf, a little while back, and he said—"

"What's her name?"

Angie froze like a tuna on a Japanese fishing boat.

"Never you mind," said Lolly, waggling his notepad at Dean Lee.

"Now look. Nelson is thinking about turning half your paychecks directly over to me until that $5,935 is paid in full, unless—"

Dean Lee left Lolly talking to himself and walked around to the passenger side of the pickup. He knocked on the glass, startling Angie. She unfroze and rolled down the window.

"'Lo," said Dean Lee. "Lolly yonder mentioned that you on your way to Chamberlain."

"Yeah," she said. "So?"

"I'm going that way."

"So's Lolly."

"He'll likely be making more stops along the way, like he just did here. But I'm express. Straight to Chamberlain, no stops."

"I don't know you."

"Dean Lee Grandet," he said, reaching into the cab with his right hand. She took it, giving it a firm squeeze.

"Angie. Bigelow."

"If I may interject here," said Lolly, pointing the dull end of his golf pencil at Dean Lee. "This man is a debtor and a profligate."

Angie glanced at Dean Lee. All acute angles and blasted sandstone, a dimple in his chin, a broad clavicle peeking out of the collar of his T-shirt. It was dark, though, and the night can tell tremendous lies. He leaned into the cab and smiled. His breath was sweet, like English breakfast tea. She had never known a man with pleasant breath before— in her experience, they all smelled like blowtorched taco meat and carious molars.

"Thank you, Mr. Prager. Maybe I'll go with Mr. Dean Lee from here."

What was she doing? A part of her actually was in a hurry and didn't want to make more debtors' stops with Lolly Prager, and this part was aligned with a part that wanted to spend a little time with Dean Lee

Grandet. These two parts overwhelmed the puny competing part that knew it might be best to stay put in the chilly cab of Lolly Prager's pickup truck.

"Are you sure, young lady?"

"Sure."

Angie climbed down out of the truck. Lolly drove off. Angie and Dean Lee stood next to the tractor tire, which was faintly illuminated by a lawn jockey holding a cracked yellow lantern.

"Used to have a buncha crocuses in there," said Dean Lee. "My old-time-used-to-be planted 'em. But some blight took 'em over one day, and that was that."

Angie realized she wasn't sure what crocuses looked like. She didn't know her flowers. She liked the idea that Dean Lee did.

"Now it's just a skeeter farm," he said.

Angie was dressed in cutoff jean shorts, and just the mention of mosquitoes made her legs itch.

"Who's this old-time-used-to-be?"

Angie had been in the company of this man no more than a few minutes and she was already experiencing minor but still unmistakable pangs of jealousy concerning some long-ago ex. How could this be? What was happening? She had not expected to fall for some guy in the middle of the night, in the middle of the Hill Country, during the middle of the week. But she never knew when she'd get those *I-like-him* butterflies, so why not now? After all, she'd fallen for men in weird places before. Helmont, her first boyfriend, she'd run into in a pet cemetery; Jonny Rae, her third, she'd exchanged glances with in the dirk booth at a knife show in Austin; Galt, her last, she'd met on a tour of writers' houses in New Orleans.

"Ah, that woulda been Delilah, good ol' girl. We had the same birthday, born the same hour even, we're both twenty-five years old now, but we didn't see eye to eye on occasion, and she was a little bit of a mystery, too. She rented two U-Hauls and got her brothers to move all her shit over here one weekend, then rented the same two U-Hauls—I recognized 'em from the dents and the Alaska plates—and got her brothers to move all her shit out the next. That Monday to Friday I swear to you I can't say what happened or what I done wrong, hell, I was at work most of the time and you can bet I treated her right at night. You know, I'm still chewin' that mystery over, Angie."

Hearing her name uttered low in the misty dark made the blood thrum in her wrists. Dean Lee kicked at the caliche with his old sod-busters and shook his head, clearly perplexed by the arcane treacheries of Delilah.

"Might not have had anything to do with you," said Angie. "Some women are complicated, weird, driven by non-Euclidean geometries."

*I am.*

"All right."

They were quiet for a while, listening to the mosquitoes and the whir of the bats swooping after them. Though it was way too late for birds, some species Angie had never heard before soon began to chirp, a plangent *tso-whee-oh, tso-why*.

"Any idea what that is, Dean Lee?"

"Don't know nothin' 'bout birds, I'm afraid. I'd recognize a cardinal, and a vulture, and a pigeon, I guess. Reminds me of a book I'm reading, though."

Angie was a little surprised the man was a reader. She had considered asking him earlier what he was reading, expecting a *nuthin*, or maybe a *Louis L'Amour* at best, then decided to keep quiet.

"Oh? What's that?"

"*El obsceno pájaro de la noche*," he said. "You know that book?"

"*The... Obscene... Bird of Night*? In English, yeah. You're reading it... in Spanish?"

"Yeah."

"You're kidding."

"No, why'd I kid?"

"I don't know, you—"

"—don't look like a reader. I know."

"No, it's—"

"It's all right."

They listened to the birdsong. Far away, a potential mate answered, the call nearly swallowed by the mist and the distance and the night.

"You like it?" said Angie. "The book?"

"It's all right," said Dean Lee. "I read it before. Listen. I grew up in the valley, little town called Pharr. Daddy was white, Mama was Mexican, from Mexico City. When I was fourteen the next-door neighbor, woman called Aintzane, got sick, I don't know what, but she was bedridden, alone. She went blind. Daddy made me go over and sit by her bedside every day after school and read to her from her walls of books, all Spanish stuff. I remember Adolfo Bioy Casares's *La invención de Morel*, Gabriela Mistral's book of poetry, *Desolación*, Roberto Bolaño's novel *Estrella distante*—that one was brand new at the time—the Spanish translation of João Guimarães Rosa's *Grande Sertão: Veredas*, and all the big names, Neruda, Paz, Márquez, Borges. Took Aintzane four years to die. I read 317 books in all. She didn't talk once, except at the very end, she took me by the wrist, and she said, real fierce, in a voice that sounded like what spiderwebs must sound like to bugs caught in them, 'Eres un buen hombre como tu padre,' and I realized Daddy and her, they'd had a thing. I ain't read a book in English since, and I know

now English is a big, ugly language of too many words, a language for fools and greedy folk, and Spanish is a slender, perfect language, God's tongue. Anyway, I read *El obsceno pájaro* for the first time back then."

In the dark Dean Lee looked like he might be blushing, a little ashamed of his monologue. He began contemplating the lawn jockey, which gave Angie an opportunity to contemplate Dean Lee. After a moment, she realized her mouth was hanging open. She had grown up in a literary, bibliophilic household—her mother was a book restorer, her father had been a voracious reader—but everyone read in English. Now here was a man who read, but could hardly put a sentence together. She simply didn't know what to make of him.

"You're not interested in books in English at all?"

"No ma'am."

"There are some good books in our language."

"Ain't my language. Ain't that clear? From how I talk? I can't talk Spanish much better, I can just read it. I was reading it with my mama when I was four. I read Cervantes when I was ten. I still have the copy I read, it has pictures and definitions of the hard words at the bottom of the pages, it's all ratty and falling apart now, a treasure of mine. You wanna come in and see it?"

*Yes, I do.*

"No, I better get home. My mother's expecting me."

"Oh goddammit, your *mama*? How old're you?"

"Twenty-three."

"Jesus Christ, you scared me, I thought I'd gone and picked up a goddamn teenybopper, though you sure don't look like one."

"Wow, thanks."

"Shit. What I meant was—"

"It's okay, I'm teasing. Better take me home, though."

Angie punctuated the command by reaching behind her and slapping at a mosquito on the back of her thigh, much harder than was necessary to neutralize the creature. The smack set a couple unseen backyard hounds to barking.

"You take care of that skeeter?"

Angie suppressed a smile. She yanked on the passenger door to his pickup till it finally opened. Dean Lee climbed in. Before starting the truck, he stared at Angie for ten solid seconds while she scratched at her mosquito bites. She didn't look at him, but it felt like the left side of her face was blistering from sunburn.

"Drive, please."

"Where to?"

During the entire sixteen-and-a-half-minute journey from McCandless to Chamberlain, Angie waffled over whether to allow Dean Lee inside her apartment and permit him to take her clothes off and let him have her. Every single time the dark night threw a shaft of light on Dean Lee, whether from the headlights of a passing car, from the dome light of his truck, or from the flare of his Bic when he lit a cigarillo, the man proved startlingly attractive in just the ways Angie liked: Comanche cheekbones, prizefighter nose, dark, wide-set eyes, rockabilly pompadour, crooked, Elvis smile. And even well past midnight, he appeared clean-shaven. Angie Bigelow liked her men smooth. In general, she liked her men quiet, too—for the most part she didn't approve of naughty rhetoric in the bedroom; it distracted her from the fantasies in her head. But in Dean Lee's case, perhaps some sweet Spanish nothings might accelerate the fun.

"Your mama was Mexican, but you don't have an accent."

"Daddy was the talker in the house. And besides, most of my friends were Anglo kids. That's where people learn to talk, their friends.

Ignorant, too, them kids, so that's how I sound, I guess. I turned eighteen, went to work offshore, them people even dumber, no lower class of persons than what work offshore."

He stopped in front of 1251 Corrigan Lane in Chamberlain.

"No lights on in there, Angie Bigelow."

"I live in the garage, round back."

"That right?"

"That's right."

"Maybe I could come in for a nightcap?"

But she decided against it. For one, it was late and she had to work in the morning. And two, she truly hadn't appreciated the teenybopper remark. She explained her thinking to Dean Lee.

"Now, you can't hold that against me. What twenty-three-year-old grown woman wants to look like a teenybopper? Answer me that."

"It was the way you put it, as though I was so far removed from teenybopperdom as to be an old, doddering fishwife."

"A what? Look, we don't have to bother going inside. Plenty of room in the old F-150 here."

Angie opened the door.

"Angie..." started Dean Lee.

"Be a gentleman, Dean Lee. Get my number from Lolly and give me a call. Take me on a date. I want to go to Entrecôte in Austin and eat escargots."

"Snails. Goddamn, Angie. Well, all right then."

Angie shut the door. Dean Lee waited till she got inside her garage apartment, then drove off.

Angie undressed, showered, sprayed Bactine on her mosquito bites, fell onto her futon, and tried to get some reading done—a third edition of Florio's *Montaigne* her mother had restored for a customer who had

30

never returned to collect it—but Angie could not concentrate. She turned off the lamp and stared hard at her bumblebee nightlight in the wall by the bookcase. Was Dean Lee going to be her next boyfriend? Did she want another one so soon after Galt, that towering, dirty-blond disappointment? Galt, who wrote ten hours a day and slept twelve; helpless, sexless, obsessive-compulsive, terribly cute Galt Dugan, whose poetry made her cry? Dean Lee seemed the polar opposite: highly sexual, like an adolescent gibbon, and, though well-read in his narrow way, he seemed aliterate, as though he might write only when he needed to kite a check for a twelve-pack at the convenience store on the corner or maybe communicate his telephone number on a cocktail napkin to a brunette in a roadhouse. Angie had, historically, been incautious in choosing boyfriends, and had never managed to hang on to one for more than a few months before he self-destructed in one way or another. Dean Lee, in spite of his debt and what Lolly had said about his being a profligate, did not necessarily seem to be on a path to destruction. He appeared to have an awful lot of confidence in himself.

Angie turned the lamp back on and opened Montaigne up, at random, to chapter thirty-seven. As she tried to think of something that had the power to make her both laugh and cry, she fell asleep.

It was after Angie's third date with Dean Lee that she decided to introduce him to Adeline. Following a 5:25 p.m. showing of *Trainspotting* at the Alamo Drafthouse that featured jalapeño poppers and five-dollar milkshakes, the couple went back to Angie's garage apartment, where they finally discharged the thumping lusts that had been accumulating like quarters in the belly of a slot machine. After a while, Angie interrupted the debauch.

"My mother's going to bed soon," she said, pressing a cold can of RC Cola to her sweat-soaked ribcage. "I want you to meet her."

"Aw, hell, really?" said Dean Lee, peeling open another condom wrapper. "We're just gettin' going here. Say, ain't that cold?"

He gently thumped the can of RC Cola with a fingertip.

"Feels good. Adeline lives forty feet away. Get dressed. Won't take long. She'll love you."

"I don't know..."

"Do it."

There's no foolproof way to mask the signs of recent sexual activity in a human being, and if both parties are present, they tend to highlight each other. Angie and Dean Lee were like a skywritten ad for premarital fucking, and Adeline might as well have been in her backyard on a bright sunny day, looking up, reading contrails.

"Would you two like a cigarette?" Adeline said, the corners of her mouth tinted with the remains of Kremlin-red lipstick and the beginnings of a knowing smirk. "I might have some of your father's Camels from before he died."

"Funny, Mom. This is Dean Lee. Dean Lee, this is my mom, Adeline."

"Hm," said Adeline, holding out her hand, limply.

Angie studied her mother's gaunt, angular pose, looking for something of herself in her. Where Angie was cushiony and feathered at the edges, her mother was a study in elbows; where Angie moved with economy and gentle caution, Adeline clenched and shook; where Angie was a study in dusk, her mother was a garish spasm of saturated reds. For God's sake, had Angie come from this? Was it in her somewhere?

"Pleezameetcha," said Dean Lee.

Dean Lee and Angie stepped inside Adeline's house. The complex musk of old books, horsehide glue, coffee, and bergamot came at the couple like infantry. A trio of shaded lamps illuminated walls of books bound in calf and vellum and alum-tawed pig, a few bound alla rustica or in wooden boards, most hundreds of years old, a half dozen or so produced before printing with movable type had been invented. Angie had grown up with these shelves, the books on them. Many had been Adeline's father's. Some were Adeline's.

"What's your line, Deanie?"

"Ah, that's 'Dean Lee.' Bottler."

"I see. And what is it that you bottle?"

"This and that. Liquids, for the most part."

Dean Lee looked around the living room. His eyes settled on Angie. He winked at her, out of sight of Adeline.

"Here's the part where you ask me what I do," said Adeline, whirling around, clearly catching her daughter in a private moment with this new... person.

"Uh, what do *you* do? Adeline?"

"I am a bookbinder, book restorer, occasional collector, and custodian of an important inherited library."

Angie watched this interaction between her mother and her new lover, and saw in it nothing but a future of wrath and dolor. What had she been thinking, bringing him over here?

"That's very interesting."

"Really? Angie, is he telling me the truth? Does he find my work— my books—interesting?"

"I don't know, Mom, I've only had a few conversations with him, about poker and reading. We're just getting to know each other. I can't tell when he's lying yet."

"Well, I'm going to assume you're just being polite, and spare you a tour," said Adeline. "Do you have family, Deanie?"

"Folks are gone. Got a sister."

Angie listened intently. She had not known Dean Lee long, but long enough to have asked him about his family. She realized now, with some shame, that she hadn't. "What happened to your 'folks'?"

"Mom!"

"It's okay, Angie, I don't mind. Mama died of cancer, pancreatic. It took her fast. Daddy killed himself."

"How old were you?"

"Nineteen. They died the same week."

"I see. Cause and effect?"

"Guess you could say that."

There was something about Dean Lee that appeared to disallow sympathy in Adeline, even for such synchronized tragedy: her face remained hard. It pissed Angie off. Yet there was something in Adeline, too, that did not permit Angie to speak up. She felt, all at once, like a child, alone at the children's table at a family picnic while the adults laughed and gossiped, a force field of alcohol and DEET surrounding them, insulating them from the concerns of children.

"You must be very close to your sister, Deanie. Older?"

"Younger. And no, Suzanne and me don't get along."

"Shame."

"Not really. She's a bitch. Worse. A monster."

Dean Lee stood up and took a random book off the shelf, a thick calf-bound folio without title or decoration of any sort. He opened and read the title.

"*Anatomy of Melancholy.*"

"It's pronounced MEL-an-CHOL-y. Do you know Burton, Dean Lee?"

"Can't say I do," he said, handing the book to Adeline.

"Pioneer of psychiatry and depression," she said. "This is a cheap fourth, lacking an internal leaf. What's your last name, Dean, uh, Lee?"

"Grandet."

Dean Lee reached for another book, evidently thought better of it, and instead smoothed his hair back.

"Any relation to Eugénie?" said Adeline, mirth in her eyes.

Dean Lee turned and stared at Adeline.

"You know my aunt?"

Adeline shelved the Burton, then stared back.

"You really have a relative named Eugénie?"

"My mother's sister."

"That's hysterically brilliant."

"Why?"

For the first time since she'd met him, Angie saw in her lover's eyes a trace of fear.

"It's the title and main character of an old French novel, Dean Lee," said Angie, gently. "I'm sure your aunt knows."

"She might not," he said. "She's not exactly all put together right."

"'Not exactly all put together right,'" said Adeline. "Can you explain that?"

Adeline plopped down on a corpulent divan. A visible cloud of dust plumed up around her, mushrooming toward the ceiling in the dim light. Dean Lee and Angie took a few steps back, bumping into the dining room table. They sat.

"Mental wards, since she was around twenty."

"What's her diagnosis?" said Adeline, looking around at her bookshelves, as though searching for her shelf-worn DSM-IV. Then she crossed her legs and put her head in one hand in a very hippie-therapist way.

"How would I know?"

"She's your aunt."

"I met her once. I was nine. She stole my shoes."

Dean Lee looked down at his boots, cheap, wrecked Tecovas.

"Mom, Dean Lee reads Spanish literature. *In Spanish.*"

"Angie, dang, come on," said Dean Lee, trying to pluck a whisker out of his neck that he'd missed shaving.

"You don't say." Adeline yawned.

"Right now he's reading... what is it again?"

"*Extracción de la piedra de la locura.* Alejandra—"

"—Pizarnik." Adeline interrupted her yawn to laugh. "That old suicide. She was a bloated, stuttering speed addict who couldn't finish anything she started."

"She was a brilliant poet is what she was, Mrs. Bigelow."

"Well. I beg."

It was true Angie did not know Dean Lee very well, and every day revealed some new side of him. This was the first time Angie thought she saw between the blinds a horizontal sliver of real anger. But Adeline could inspire that in people. *Real* anger.

Adeline leapt up like a surprised fawn and disappeared into the kitchen.

On the dining room table an ancient linen tablecloth supported two bronze candelabras and a bowl of pears. Dean Lee and Angie looked at each other.

"Dang, she don't like me *at all*," whispered Dean Lee.

"Shh."

Adeline reemerged with brie and crackers and a bottle of wine.

"Deanie, honors?" she said, handing him the wine and a restaurant-style corkscrew. Dean Lee, an inveterate beer-from-a-can drinker, turned the contrivance over in his hands, then handed it back. Adeline feigned astonishment.

"What, a professional bottler, stumped by a cork? Angie, who have you presented me with this evening? All the other boys you've brought over have been able to handle a cork in a cheap bottle of Tempranillo. Here, dear, you do it."

"Mom! God!"

Angie was fairly sure her mother would mention her other boyfriends as a kind of test of mettle for Dean Lee, but was more than a little surprised she hadn't waited till later in the evening. Angie took the corkscrew and opened the bottle.

"This is triple-crème, I hope you like, and these are almond crackers, I'm gluten intolerant, they're delicious, try."

"Ain't it your bedtime?" said Dean Lee. Menace, like a gas, began to seep into the room through the gaps in the floorboards.

"But I have guests," said Adeline, pouring glasses of wine. "And I also feel like I have some investigative work to do. Now. What do you see in my daughter?"

"Oh, Mom."

"Well, Mrs. Bigelow—"

"Call me Adeline."

"Well, Adeline, I think what you'd like to hear is that your daughter has a charming personality, and that she's real super-duper smart, and that she's sweet and kind, and great with people, worldly, devoted to her friends and family, a beacon in her church, a light in her community, willing to help a stranger in need. And all of that may be true and verifiable—I just don't know her well enough. But what I've found most interesting about your daughter, so far, is that she looks damn fine getting fucked from any and every angle."

Dean Lee, with one eye on Adeline's dropped jaw, drained his Tempranillo in three peristaltic gulps. Then he left.

\* \* \*

Angie broke it off with Dean Lee as punishment for his disrespectful treatment of her mother. But he pestered Angie over the phone, begging, and after a promise to send Adeline a handwritten apology on handmade Griffen Mill paper, she decided to see him again, which was a relief to both the lovers, and their reunion was not one interrupted by movies or dinners or other outings—it was spent in either her futon or his bed, and occasionally, in the cab of his truck or the back seat of her Celica.

One could almost see the crystals of frost growing between the main house and the little garage apartment. Adeline, as a rule, didn't usually approve of Angie's boyfriends—they were never smart enough, except for that one, Beaufort Charles, a really beautiful boy, brilliant in a Rhodes scholar kind of way, but so distant and uninterested was he the day he came to the main house for coffee, not once did Adeline catch him looking at Angie, and yet he showed such curiosity about a book Adeline was restoring, a 1499 *Hypnerotomachia Poliphili* in which the phallus in the woodcut of the sacrifice to Priapus at mvi had been crudely excised by some prude of a bygone age. Adeline had cunningly drawn a new phallus in ink on sympathetic old paper and inserted it in place, also drawing in the missing text on verso. Beaufort examined the work with a jeweler's loupe and announced it perfection. Adeline had later told Angie that she had thought at the time, *This is the man for my daughter*. But a week later Beaufort Charles moved to Newfoundland to WWOOF. Then came Jonny Rae. And Darren. And Kyle. And Brill. And Corning. And Strad. And Bracchus. And Homburg. And Galt. Shameless, helpless man-children all. But none so odious as Dean Lee.

\*   \*   \*

After he and Angie had been together about six months, Adeline knocked on her daughter's door.

"Is that man here?"

"You know he's not, you can see his truck is gone. What do you want?"

"Why do I have to want anything? Can't a mother visit her daughter?"

"After you ignore me for more than half a year, won't even wave to me from your kitchen window? What have you got there?"

"I brought you a lasagna."

"Oh. Well. Thank you."

"No ricotta, just sweet Italian sausage, whole roma tomatoes, authentic, lots of parmesan, mozzarella—delicious."

Adeline presented the lasagna as though it were the head of Holofernes in a basket and she Judith, all business. Poor Holofernes was covered in multiple layers of recycled foil, scorched and veined in thousands of old wrinkles.

"And the cost?"

"Why, there's no—"

"You know what I mean."

Adeline opened her eyes wide, the whites seeming to grow whiter with ingenuous incredulity. Then she narrowed them to slits and glared at her daughter as through a medieval war helmet.

"You've never dated anyone this long. Are you going to marry this man?"

Angie said nothing. She placed the lasagna on top of the half-finished, 2,500-piece jigsaw of Max Ernst's *Europe After the Rain*, which occupied the entire kitchen table.

"What *is* it? The sex?"

"I don't want to talk about it with you."

"It *is*. Your father was a tiger in the sack—"

"Mom."

"—so I understand your position, but Caspar Bigelow was also a good man in many, many ways, except perhaps for the occasional wagering issues. You have to ask yourself what this Deanie has to offer besides mattress finesse and an iron backside."

When Adeline wanted Angie's attention, she would sometimes resort to subtle sexual crudeness, and it usually worked. But Adeline could see Angie wasn't going to let it this time. Adeline knew it especially bugged her daughter when she spoke of her father in a sexual context. Angie had mentioned this to a therapist once when she was fifteen and it prompted a call to Child Protective Services, causing a major brouhaha—they both got into trouble. And Angie announced, in that moment, not to discuss anything of a sexual nature with her mother ever again.

"Mom. I'm not listening."

"If in fact he's that good. Maybe he's not even all that. Maybe you're settling. For a substandard lover and a subpar human being. Six *months?* Think about what you could have done with that time, who you could have spent it with. Remember Beaufort?"

Adeline crossed her arms and stared at a mark in the linoleum of her daughter's kitchen floor that looked like a koala cub smoking a meerschaum. She had never noticed it before.

"Beaufort was asexual, Mom."

"He was?"

"Yes."

"What about Corning? He was okay."

"Corning was in love with his childhood babysitter. I told you that story already."

"Oh, yes," said Adeline. "Yes. The incomparable Giselle."

Corning Murtaugh's dad had been a long-haul trucker, and so young Corning had spent equally long stretches with sitters, one of whom had made an impression when he was seven. In the dead of summer, he had woken from a long nap and looked out his bedroom window, only to see the sitter, Giselle, fully naked, rubbing herself down with kerosene under the mottled noonday sun filtering through a light-ning-splintered Shumard oak in his backyard. The mental cinema of the occasion—replayed ad nauseam against the scrim of his prefrontal cortex, along with the thousands of narratives he had manufactured to explain Giselle's actions—were the central figments of Corning's psychosexual life. As appealing as Angie was, and as much as he liked her, Giselle would brook no competition. When Corning brought over a red metal gallon-tank of kerosene and some shop rags, Angie sent him away for good.

"What about Brill?" said Adeline.

"Didn't read."

"Oh, that's right. Math."

Brill, it's true, had been interested only in mathematics, the biogra-phies of pioneering mathematicians—the more sordid and pathological the better—and winning a Fields Medal. One evening, when Adeline and Angie had finished off two bottles of Prosecco, Angie confessed that Brill had once interrupted a fairly prodigious session of cunnilingus because he had an idea for shortening Andrew Wiles's proof of Fermat's Conjecture by two lines. Both Angie and Brill were left unsatisfied, and broke up not long after.

"Oh dear. I had forgotten that. Strad?"

"Addicted to cosplay pornography."

"I do not even know what that is. Homburg?"

"Went abroad to study semiotics."

Homburg had actually gone to Milan to stalk Umberto Eco. Rebuffed by the great man in the Bibliotheca Ambrosiana reading room, Homburg reacted by stealing a moped and mopeding to Beirut to join Hezbollah.

"What about Darren? Jonny Rae? Bracchus? Galt?"

"Prison, raw foodism, black metal, death by overturned golf cart, writer. I've told you all this. You're not remembering on purpose."

"Poor Bracchus," said Adeline. "But that last one, Galt, what was he writing?"

"Poetry."

"My."

Adeline loathed poetry like some people loathed the Ohio State Buckeyes.

"And he was hopeless romantically," said Angie, clearly enjoying having an answer for every one of her mother's assays. "I tried everything. We read books, watched videos, went to seminars, even hired a spotter—nothing. A cold, dead, glassy-eyed mackerel."

"But such a sweet, polite, well-read boy."

"It's not enough, Mom. Don't you get it?"

Angie crossed the kitchen to the oven, set it to 375°F. Adeline made very good lasagna, and she could tell Angie was hungry.

"But does it have to be Deanie Grandet?"

"Come on. He's not so bad."

Adeline began pacing the kitchen. All she could see now was the koala and its meerschaum.

"Tell me more."

"He has a pretty good job."

"Liquid bottling expert. Yes."

"It's true he's interested in target shooting, pickup trucks, state politics, but he makes me laugh, Mom, like no other man has. And I don't know anyone who has read the modern Latin American canon. I bet you don't either."

"Don't be too sure about that, dear. And what about his other interests?"

The passerine way Adeline tilted her head and twittered the word *other* seemed to get Angie's attention.

"What?"

"Women and gambling."

"Poker, sure, but…"

"Why, I just happened to mention in passing to one of my clients, Carey Ratchko, who was over picking up a nice early *Emblematum Liber*—a third edition—that I'd restored, that my daughter was dating a new young man with an interesting, literary last name. And Carey said he was distantly acquainted with Deanie as a problem gambler and a frequenter of whores and strip clubs."

"Dean Lee is a *professional* poker player," said Angie, disregarding the blaring term *whores*. "He is so good he actually earns money playing."

"Your father was a gambler. Are you going to marry your father? Most girls do. I did. We don't all regret it, though I think you would."

"And Dean does not frequent strip clubs anymore," said Angie. "He quit. He told me so."

It was starting to get hot in the kitchen. The thermostat on Angie's oven was a little off, and it tended to get very hot very fast. Baking was a challenge. Adeline had once offered to buy her a new stove, but Adeline attached strings to the deal, and it never happened.

"Oh did he. Whores, too?"

Adeline opened the door to the oven, then stepped back dramatically, as though she'd just glanced into a glowing high-tech kiln at a secret government test site. "I want you to leave."

"Oh do you?"

"And I don't want you to come back."

"I'll change the Wi-Fi password," said Adeline, who grew exceptionally petty when she felt like she was losing, be it at Scrabble, bridge, or discourse. "You'll have to get your own signal."

"You're so small. Go away."

"Rent just went up fifty dollars, too."

Adeline was starting to embarrass herself. She would have to leave if she didn't want to do permanent damage. She did love her daughter, after all. She didn't really *like* her, but she did love her, in her way.

"Go to hell, Adeline."

Adeline left, and Angie slammed the door after her. Then Angie opened the door and threw the lasagna onto the driveway. The casserole dish shattered. Glass, cheese, tomatoes, pasta, and foil everywhere. The mess stayed that way for a week until finally Dean Lee divided a tendon on a shard of glass that went right up through the sole of his mule-hide boot, and Angie went out and cleaned everything up. That was it, for Adeline and the young lovers, for a long, long time.

As it turned out, Dean Lee's principal drawback as a boyfriend was that he was unavailable two nights a week and all day Sundays. Lolly Prager's poker game started at 6:30 p.m. sharp on Mondays and Thursdays, and Sundays at noon was when Joy Callum launched his game, a down-market affair of sots and scratch-ticket addicts where even Dean Lee had a fighting chance.

But the rest of the time, Dean Lee was an enjoyable date. He took Angie to Austin to hear live music, to the movies, to restaurants, though often on her dime—Angie was slowly coming to realize that maybe Dean Lee was in fact not such a skilled card player, relying much on luck and arcane systems, and his three days a week at the tables usually drained his already meager coffers.

Among Dean Lee's many efforts, beyond poker, to maximize the spending power of his wages at the bottling plant was to consistently vote or otherwise militate against tax increases and the politicians who supported them. He was aligned with a group, many of whose members he played cards with, who believed that the federal income tax was constitutionally illegal, and, as a talisman of support for this position, Dean Lee had taken to keeping on his person at all times a .357 revolver. The weapon resided in an old split cow shoulder holster, worn smooth and sweat-aged to a burnt caramel. Angie did not like this weapon at all but was slowly getting used to it. After ten months of dating Dean Lee, she couldn't imagine him without it.

Over the course of that first almost-year together, the frequency of outings to Austin declined at approximately the same rate that the sexual ferment increased: Dean Lee was very good in bed. Or, more correctly, Angie and he were very good together. Angie was beginning to think that maybe it was the foundation of their relationship. And that there was not much getting built upon this carnal bedrock.

After an especially aerobatic session on a humid Sunday afternoon in early March of 1998, Angie and Dean Lee lay in bed at his little Fawn Street house, panting, discussing what had just happened.

"What was *that?*" said Dean Lee.

"I don't really know. You okay?"

"Yeah. You know, we got a pretty good thing going here."

Even though she was hot and sweaty, Angie rolled on her side and threw a leg and an arm across Dean Lee.

"Yeah. Not bad."

Dean Lee even made her laugh sometimes. No one had ever made her laugh, except her father and her old boyfriend Galt. And her father didn't really count, because she was eight when he died and any idiot can make a child laugh. And Galt, well, he wasn't trying to be funny. So, in a way, Dean Lee was the only person who'd *ever* made her laugh. And this business in the sack…

"Loud, though," she said.

"Yeah. Think we'll hear from the Bjornboes?"

"Who?" With some effort Angie sat up and drank from a warm ginger ale on the bedstand.

"Neighbors, yonder."

"Why?" said Angie, turning and staring sharply at Dean Lee. "Have they complained before? I mean, before me?"

"No, never," he said, quickly. Angie was fairly sure she had just caught her boyfriend in his first lie. Maybe not his first, but her first catch.

Angie had jealousy around Dean Lee's exes. She couldn't help it. He had a lot of them, too, and he could not resist talking about them, even though she stuck her fingers in her ears and made babbling white-noise sounds whenever they came up. One ex in particular, Leslie, "looked *just like you*, Angie, 'cept littler bazooms" and was also a little "roomier"—information Angie thought Dean Lee imparted to make Angie feel good, meaning Dean Lee thought Angie must think ill of herself, which she did not.

"Sure about that?" said Angie. "Maybe Leslie uttered some window penetrating squeals? Alyssia some wolf howls? Janelle some sow grunts?

Maybe your headboard slapping against the drywall all night made your neighbors' cavities ache?"

"No, no, no," said Dean Lee, taking the ginger ale bottle out of her hand, arranging a mound of pillows in the center of the bed, and pitching Angie on top of them. He slapped her once on the behind and began whispering in her ear.

> Ay que no se quebrante tu silueta en la arena,
> ay que no vuelen tus párpados en la ausencia:
> no te vayas por un minuto, bienamada...

Angie shuddered.

> porque en ese minuto te habrás ido tan lejos
> que yo cruzaré toda la tierra preguntando
> si volverás o si me dejarás muriendo.

The afternoon thundered on.

Their combined ardor created a kind of blindness to other aspects of their life together, in particular Dean Lee's gambling, Dean Lee's continued disrespect for Angie's mother, and Dean Lee's wandering eye. This last was so flagrant; Dean Lee had developed a habit of scanning, from instep to eyeliner, every female from sixteen to sixty who came within a thousand yards, a kind of damp, curious, livestock-auctioneer's half-smile pasted on his face. Angie had become practiced at slapping off this half-smile.

"You may ogle women your own age and older, Dean Lee, but that is all, you heard me?"

"Ow. I heard you."

They were sitting in the parking lot of a Home Depot in Austin. A teenage girl had just walked by with her mother.

"She's not more than seventeen, for God's sake."

"I was just fixing to ask you something real important when you slapped me, Angie."

"Oh, really? What, Dean Lee?"

Dean Lee quickly produced a ring from his shirt pocket. A microscopic fleck of diamond caught a late-spring shaft of sunlight and reflected it around the cab of the pickup. "Will you marry me?"

Angie's mother had predicted this moment. She also predicted Angie would say yes.

"Yes."

Angie hadn't mentioned that she was seven weeks pregnant. While Dean Lee was in Home Depot shopping for ten-penny nails, Angie had been two doors down in the bathroom of a CVS peeing on an e.p.t. wand, waiting, watching it turn blue, a thrill rising through her like a free diver coming up for air.

Almost two months before, Angie had lost her Ortho-Novum packet over a long weekend and missed three pills. The packet simply vanished from her purse, no explanation. On the third day, she remembered. Angie had been on I-35 just south of Austin, in some of the worst stop-and-go traffic she could remember, struggling to stay awake after a sleepless night with Dean Lee, when in front of her a dirty, windowless van without operational lights of any kind jammed on its brakes. Angie stomped on hers and just avoided hitting the monstrosity, but her purse, sitting on the passenger seat, vaulted forward and emptied itself onto the floor. When she finally got off at Slaughter Lane and was able to pull over at a gas station, she hastily refilled her bag, except, of course, for the Ortho-Novum, which had slipped unnoticed under the floor liner. Three days and three missed pills later, when she finally found the pill packet in the car, the damage had been done. She never told Dean Lee. She found herself in thrall to her own deception.

There was no money for any kind of a serious wedding, so Dean Lee thought it would be fun to elope, right now, and get married in Las Vegas—during Binion's World Series of Poker. Somehow Dean Lee had scraped together enough cash to enter the main event, and even paid for the plane tickets and hotel room.

A week before they left, Dean Lee visited Egulph's Epic Dermis Tats on Airport Boulevard in Austin. When he opened the barred glass door to the studio, a recording of the Civil War rebel yell actuated. A Confederate rebel yell was, in its many variants, always a blood-freezing squall, intended to make Yankees shit their pants. Despite the outcome of that four-year sociopolitical American distemper, the yell was probably pretty effective, and the results of that unpleasantness between the states may have been even less favorable to the South had they not employed the yell at all.

A shirtless man illustrated with vivid irezumi tattoos emerged from a back room, holding an electric kitchen knife and a plastic bottle of squeeze mayo.

"Hep you?"

"Ah," said Dean Lee, not often intimidated. "Getting married. I need a tattoo."

"Have a look at them books," said the man, whom Dean Lee presumed to be Egulph. "Holler when you're ready. You got cash, right?"

"Yeah, fifties."

Dean Lee sat and started leafing through the binder labeled "Pin-Ups" on the spine. It wasn't long before he found what he wanted.

"Okay."

Egulph emerged again, stuffing the better part of a turkey sandwich into one side of his mouth. He arranged Dean in the reclining chair and set to work drawing and inking an uncannily photorealistic pinup girl in four colors along the length of the inside of Dean Lee's left forearm. It took five hours.

"Louise," announced Dean Lee, admiring his swollen arm.

"Who dat," said Egulph, still sucking on the remains of his sandwich. "Fiancée?"

"I don't know. But she makes me feel homesick. Homesick is a feeling I like."

"One thousand eighty-two dollars and fifty cents. Take this little booklet and read it. Aftercare. Do what it says. That ink'll scar up and look shitty if you don't."

Angie hated Louise. Louise seemed to be watching her, making fun of her. Louise was *with* Dean Lee, more deeply and more permanently than Angie could ever be. Louise's perfect body would never age, fade, distort.

After they landed at McCarran International in Las Vegas, Angie and Dean Lee hailed a cab and drove straight to the Suspicious Minds Wedding Chapel at the decaying end of the Strip. Dean Lee handed the chaplain $450 in fifties, combed his hair in the reflection of a seven-foot papier-mâché Elvis's aviators, and held out his rental-tuxedo-upholstered arm for Angie to take. She hesitated long enough for even Dean Lee to notice.

"What?"

"Is that your tattoo arm?"

"Yeah, but it's covered up and don't hurt no more."

"That's not my concern."

"What then?"

"Doesn't matter."

"Come on, now," said the chaplain, a man in his fifties dressed like Colonel Tom Parker in a polka-dot ascot and buckram stingy-brim. "Weddings should be pulled off cat-quick, like Band-Aids."

It was over in ninety seconds. Angie Bigelow had married Dean Lee Grandet.

And then Dean Lee was gone, off to play in the greatest poker tournament known.

It so happened that on the third hand of the main event of the World Series of Poker, Dean Lee got dealt a pair of black eights on the button. He threw in a bunch of money after suspiciously modest action, got called by two players, reraised by a third, and, with calls all around, flopped 8♥ 3♣ 2♣. After the shocking acceleration of bets reached him, Dean Lee threw in all his money, got two calls, then turned over his hand.

"Fuck y'all," he said, then crossed his arms and waited.

The turn came K♥, the river A♥. The seven seat turned over a 4–5 of clubs, and the eight seat pocket aces, leaving Dean Lee in a cloud of third-best poker dust. With that, he was handed the inglorious honor of being the first person knocked out of the tournament. His name and photo appeared on a few internet poker chat sites, appended by mocking and sympathetic comments in equal measure.

After he busted out of the tournament, Dean Lee wandered around Las Vegas, kicking mailboxes and clenching and crying. He tried to hail taxicabs, but they avoided him, surely sensing trouble. Eventually he forced himself to calm down, finger-combed his hair, studied himself in the window of a drugstore, took a few deep breaths, then casually hailed a cab. It pulled over.

"Chicken Ranch," he said in a voice he hoped did not give away the anxiety he felt at his pending betrayal. Even if it did, the cabbie appeared not to care.

"Hour away, brother, ninety-dollar fare one way, yonnastan?"

Dean Lee put three fifties in the plexiglass tray.

"Yeah. Come on, before I change my mind."

"Before you chicken out on the Chicken?" The cabbie laughed, a sound like Isaac Hayes gargling Sue Bee honey.

As the considerable desolation of Highway 160 slid by outside the greasy windows of the cab, Dean Lee contemplated what he was about to do. He'd been married less than twenty-eight hours. He had $800 in his pocket. Given the circumstances, Angie would understand. If she ever found out, that is.

At the Chicken Ranch, the girls regarded him with some interest, and he them. Cara, Chiquita, Felicity, Doe, Alien, Chesti, Lizzibel, Françoise, and Xenon. In the end, he selected Felicity and Xenon, the former because she looked like his ninth-grade social studies teacher, Mrs. Arrowsmith, on whom he'd pinned a great crush many years ago, and the latter because she was dressed like a waitress—Dean Lee found waitresses wholly off limits and therefore sexy and desirable. The trio retired to a room decorated with bamboo and tiki gods and artificial palm fronds hooked up to hidden oscillators that made them wave gently, keeping the stagnating air from becoming actually poisonous. Dean Lee stood in a corner by the bed while Felicity and Xenon smiled at him and tugged at his clothes.

Dean Lee was excited about the prospect of two women at once, the founding American dream as far as he was concerned, but something was getting in the way. It was a sensation coming from his body. He couldn't quite put his finger on it. He gently pushed the two women aside and began to examine himself, feeling his stomach, his ribs, his thighs, his throat, the crown of his head. Finally, his hand settled on the region of his heart. The central organ felt like it was trying to elbow its way out of his chest. Dean Lee stood up straight, neatened his clothes, smoothed back his hair.

"Ladies, I can't do this," he said, and promptly took his leave.

Dean Lee hiked out to the highway and stuck his thumb out. After about four hours a highway road crew picked him up. He climbed into the back of a spectacularly dented Dodge Ram. They dropped him off at the Luxor. Dean Lee took a jitney up to Binion's. He found Angie in their hotel room, hysterical. He confessed everything. She hit him with a telephone receiver a few times, then calmed down.

"I'm sorry, honey, I wasn't myself," said Dean Lee, rubbing his head where Angie'd clocked him. "But I didn't do nothing, I swear."

"Is this what I'm going to be dealing with now?"

"No—"

"Louise and hookers? I have to tolerate looking at your arm porno every time we make love and maybe smelling vagina on you when you come home at night?"

"No, like I said, I wasn't myself, I lost big, huge, worse than ever—"

"I'm pregnant."

"Oh for chrissake. For real?"

"Yes."

Angie had been getting her nerve up to tell Dean Lee, sensing he wouldn't be happy about impending fatherhood, even though he'd never expressed an opinion one way or another, but the recent developments had completely numbed her. She felt nothing. She sat on the hotel room bed, where she'd slept alone the night before. She didn't care what Dean Lee thought, not now. "How pregnant?"

"About eight weeks, that's how."

Angie was suddenly furious again. She had been ecstatic to be pregnant, absolutely psyched to be a mother-in-the-making. It was all she had ever really wanted. And Dean Lee was fucking it up.

"Well…"

Angie recognized that "Well…"—a semi-interrogative that half-asked whether she was going to get an abortion, a semi-demand that half-ordered her to.

"No."

"'No' what?"

"No, I'm keeping it, that's what. I want it. And you're going to promise me, solemnly, that you're done with that hooker nonsense."

"Done."

"Good. Because you're going to be a daddy to my baby. You know why? Because I lost my daddy when I was eight, and no child should have to grow up without one. You heard me?"

"I heard."

Angie got off the bed, found her purse on the floor, and rifled through it for a moment. "Now," she said. "Here's twenty dollars. I want you to take a taxicab to the grocery store, buy some vinegar and Easy-Off, come back, and take a three-hour tub, not one minute less. You are to use every drop of those and scrub your body clean of poker, the Chicken Ranch, and its denizens."

Dean Lee looked at his wife with some alarm. Angie was gratified to see it.

"But Easy-Off—"

"Count yourself lucky I don't make you buy a cheese grater and grate Louise away. You heard me, Dean Lee?"

"I heard."

Dean Lee unconsciously folded Angie's money into sixteenths, stuck the tiny green rectangle into his billfold, and skulked out of the room.

Angie threw herself on the bed and buried her face in a pillow, which smelled, faintly, inexplicably, of jet fuel. Her tears amplified the musk considerably, which made her cry all the more, because jet fuel reminded her of the Braniff airport lounge in Houston, where she spent time as a child with her father, who was already heavily on her mind. Caspar Bigelow had died when Angie was eight years old. He was the victim of a freak crime: kids firing flare guns at cars on the highway, for fun. Angie still got an apology letter from one of those kids once a year, the same text, as though he never aged. Angie had been in the car. They were on their way home from Kid Kwon Do class, where Angie, the youngest, excelled. Her father stayed the whole time, the only parent who did, watching, clapping, cheering her on. They had stopped at Amy's Ice Cream for scoops of toasted praline and were just finishing up their cones when a flare sailed into the open driver's side window and struck Caspar between the eye and ear. Angie was unhurt, though the car rolled several times and was hit by a careening fish truck. Angie unbuckled herself, but their car, a Chrysler New Yorker, had folded up in such a way that she couldn't get to her father to help him. She climbed out through a window and lay in the grass of the median. A stranger cradled her until EMTs arrived. She never found out who that stranger was.

Of the funeral Angie remembered nothing but a red Infiniti that drove slowly by, playing gangsta rap so low and so loud it made fenders and bumpers chatter like the teeth of the frostbit. The hole in her life left by the death of her daddy was unfillable—by her mother, by friends, by men. Angie wanted a child more than ever now, a real child, not some walking, talking, blinking, tinkling Hasbro effigy that sucked the life out of twenty-five dollars' worth of D-cell batteries every thirty minutes. She wanted a child to talk to, to listen to, to hold, to comfort, to clean and dry, a child whose hair she could shampoo with No More Tears and rinse clean with warm water poured from a measuring cup, like Adeline used to do to Angie.

Then she grew up and became pregnant. And she realized she now had the power to essentially *manufacture* not only a child, but also another father (though, granted, not her own), one through which she could witness the machinations of fatherhood as they should be performed.

Dean Lee was going to be that father.

Angie and Dean Lee left Las Vegas and went home to the Texas Hill Country. Angie would never go back to Nevada. Dean Lee would, but many years later.



Dean Lee's debt to Lolly Prager had risen to $9,875, a highly problematic number, at least for Lolly: too large to have any real hope of collecting, too small to send a persuader over to administer a hospital beating—it was Lolly's policy not to use violence unless a debt exceeded $10,000. But Lolly charged hefty interest, and if Dean Lee was not careful, the failsafe point could easily be reached, and he might get paid a visit by the likes of Colonel Vogter or, worse, Ron DeGroot of Muskogee, who liked to flog his marks with jumper cables and then drink all their liquor and woo their women—Ron looked like a winning union of Steve McQueen and a redwood stump. So Dean Lee made trifling payments and managed to keep his debt under the $10,000 mark. Still, Lolly paid weekly visits to the Grandet household on Fawn Street to seize items of potential resale value, a chore that pained and embarrassed him, because he was still highly fond of Angie, his old babysitter. But business was business. He took furniture, lamps, toaster ovens, blouses in dry-cleaning bags, steaks out of the refrigerator, and once, the refrigerator. He had never threatened to take the bed, possibly because Lolly was something of a prude—the monstrous California king was never made and always looked like it had just been fucked in. Because the bed seemed safe from collar, Dean Lee was always careful to hide his precious .357 and Angie's sickeningly expensive laptop between the mattresses when he saw Lolly's pickup coming down Fawn Street.

A neighbor, Mrs. Shaamaa Anand, had recently given Angie a kitten, a little tuxedo that Dean Lee named John Deere. He slept with them in the bed, used a litter box in the bathroom, played with parrot feathers on a long stick, ravaged felt bananas filled with catnip, purred like a two-stroke engine, and sat on a windowsill in the kitchen, watching the blue jays and mockingbirds harass the squirrels in the yard.

Angie was about four months pregnant when Lolly stopped by on a search and seizure one blazing late-summer afternoon.

"Angie, my dear, I'm sorry once again," said Lolly, stepping inside the Fawn Street house and taking off his hat, a ten-gallon affair that had the appearance of having been carved from a block of milk chocolate. He held the hat against his stomach as a kind of gesture of regret hard lined with fiduciary resolve. Dean Lee owed him a lot of money.

Just then John Deere raced across the kitchen floor, chasing an especially fleet palmetto bug.

"Oh, who have we here?"

"I don't know the bug," said Angie, "but the cat was a gift from a neighbor. John Deere, we call him. The cat, not the neighbor."

Lolly's face darkened. He stood there a long while, thinking, his face growing stormier, evidently trying to remember something.

"How far along're you, Angie?"

"With the baby? Seventeen weeks."

Lolly tucked his hat between his knees and dug a new phone out of the back pocket of his coveralls. Fifteen minutes later, he found what he was looking for: an article about how some microbe in cat poop was bad for pregnant women. They could contract something called toxoplasmosis. He handed his phone to Angie to read.

"We're gonna take ol' John Deere off your hands, Angie. Just till the baby gets here. We'll reunite the whole everybody when the time comes. Me and Kathleen got eight cats, one more won't make a difference. This'll be the only one we got with a name, though. C'mere, John Deere."

And with that old Lolly scooped up John Deere, dropped him in his hat, and replaced the Stetson on his head, cinching it down tight over the old roughneck wrinkles in his forehead. Lolly looked around briefly, maybe seeing if there was anything he could take along to bite into Dean Lee's debt. But finally, there was nothing left to take.

Dr. Katie Rodrigue, the physician at Brackenridge Hospital who delivered Angie's child, remarked to the new mother that of the 1,121 children she had ushered into the world in her thirty-six years on the job, none had slipped so effortlessly from the aqueous to the pneumatic as Nadine Grandet.

"She practically fell out of you," said the doctor, her fingers on Angie's pulse, her eyes on a clock over the television. "She was not there, and then she was—no neonatal shenanigans, just a big yawn and a nap."

"When can I have her?"

"Soon. They're just keeping her toasty downstairs for now."

Nadine may have had an easy time of it, but Angie felt existentially spent. A nauseating emptiness kept her from sleeping. In her wakeful discomfort, Angie thought hard about her family of three.

# CHAPTER THREE

# The Vanishing

EVEN THOUGH EACH MEMBER of Fawn Street had their peccadilloes—Dean Lee spent evenings trying to find poker games that would not turn him away; Angie suffered postpartum insomnia that left her alert twenty-two hours a day; the infant Nadine pitched mellow colic whenever she was left in her crib by herself; the recently returned John Deere had developed a habit of gnawing on whatever bit of cord or cable that was exposed to him, and had narrowly escaped electrocution no fewer than three times—the quartet still managed to form a kind of peaceable kingdom, and together lived in what no one could really mistake for anything but a strident, restless harmony.

Every cord in the house was now wrapped in flexible plastic tubing designed to defeat the needle-like teeth of John Deere, and so the little cat had taken to chewing the eraser-ends of pencils, including the metal ferrules, a relatively harmless occupation that Angie endorsed by purchasing six dozen No. 2 pencils and scattering them around the house—sticking them in houseplants, placing them in empty water tumblers, jamming them in the pansy garden outside. The house and yard began to fill with damp pencil stumps, dead wooden soldiers.

Dean Lee, on the nights he couldn't find a game, stayed in and sat at the kitchen table and dealt hands of cards to himself and told poker stories to Angie while she nursed Nadine.

"At Lolly's one night, I never told you this, sweetie, so don't get upset, now," said Dean Lee on a frosty mid-December evening about two weeks after Nadine was born. "I was sitting there looking at some pretty ugly cards and there was not much action anyway and everybody was being real quiet and all of a sudden there was some rolling thunder way off in the distance, to the west, and old Chris Hebert, you know old Chris, with the neck gout? Anyway, he said, 'What was that, thunder?'"

Angie shifted in her chair and adjusted Nadine. She looked at her husband. She didn't know what he was going to tell her that was possibly going to upset her, but she didn't care. She felt at peace. Something about the distribution of her child's weight in her arms balanced the chemistry in her body, and the alchemy of the world enveloped her and her little family in a warm equilibrium.

"Then Grip Wheedle stands up," said Dean Lee, standing up himself. "And he throws his cards on the table and starts waving his arms around. Now Grip Wheedle—I don't believe you know him, sweetness—is a seventy-five-year-old man who never says a word, ain't said so much as howdy since 1986. Anyway, he stands up and shouts: 'Thunder? Hell, them're cannons! It's the French! Run for your lives! Run for your lives!' Then Grip grabs his coat and his stacks of poker chips and runs out the door, forgetting his old Ditch Witch gimme cap."

Nadine was awake now and had one eye on her father.

"So we're all remarking on the sudden change in Grip Wheedle, switching out the decks of cards, and taking side bets on whether Grip would be back and how fast, when there's a knock at the door. Gouty Chris Hebert opens it, and wouldn't you know two men in black ski masks and Uzis bust in. They were there for the money. And they got it."

"Dean Lee!" said Angie. Instinctively, absurdly, she covered Nadine's ears. "You never told me you got hijacked."

"They only got about $200 outta me. I was already losing, but poor ol' LuLu Hulch got took for about $28,000."

"My heavens. Who were they?"

"Don't know. They didn't say much—New Orleans accents, Irish Channel, took the cash and guns and phones and left. All over in three minutes."

"Dean Lee," she said, seeing if her daughter had sensed the change in mood in the room. "When?"

"'Bout three months back."

"They didn't take your gun?"

"Nope, it was under my coat on the floor. They didn't see it."

Angie observed her husband across the table. She tried to imagine him with a submachine gun pointed at his head. She began to cry.

"Aw, babe. Naw. Aw. Okay now. It's all right. Okay."

Then Nadine began to wail.

"Oh brother. Here, Angie, hand 'er over."

Mother and daughter wept together and did not move. Dean Lee placed his deck of cards on the table, removed his holster and gun, hung it on his chair, walked around the table to his wife, and took Nadine in his arms. He began walking around the table, singing quietly.

> *"Goodbye, Joe, me gotta go, me oh my oh.*
> *Me gotta go, pole the pirogue down the bayou.*
> *My Yvonne, the sweetest one, me oh my oh.*
> *Son of a gun, we'll have big fun on the bayou."*

Nadine stopped crying.

*"Jambalaya and a crawfish pie and filé gumbo*
*'Cause tonight I'm gonna see my ma cher ami-o.*
*Pick guitar, fill fruit jar, and be gay-o,*
*Son of a gun, we'll have big fun on the bayou."*

Angie stopped crying.

*"Thibodaux, Fontaineaux, the place is buzzin',*
*Kinfolk come to see Yvonne by the dozen.*
*Dress in style they go hog wild, me oh my oh.*
*Son of a gun, we'll have big fun on the bayou."*

Dean Lee handed Nadine back to Angie, sat down, put his gun back on, dealt himself out a new hand of cards.

"LuLu Hulch ain't been back."

"You have, though," said Angie.

"That's right, I have."

Angie stared hard at her husband. She stared so hard that she began to see through him. Then he began to vanish. Soon, he was gone. There was no one in the room but Angie and her daughter and John Deere asleep on the divan, dreaming of erasers and zip cord. So this was what it would be like, just the three of them, if someone pointed an Uzi at her husband's head at a poker game and fired. She closed her eyes, waited.

Just the three of them.

She opened her eyes.

Dean Lee Grandet was back. Dean Lee Grandet smiled at his wife.

* * *

When Nadine was fifteen months old and Angie became pregnant with Sophie, Lolly again volunteered to take John Deere for the duration. The day Angie came home from the hospital, Lolly brought John Deere over in his big Stetson and left both the little cat and a Hallmark card on the kitchen table.

The household was so preoccupied with baby matters that no one thought to open the oversized lavender envelope for a week. When Angie finally got around to it, Lolly had included a "coupon" worth $1,000 off of Dean Lee's gambling debt as a baby shower gift. The gesture pissed Dean Lee off—he thought his debt should've been wiped out altogether. But Angie called Lolly immediately and, to show her gratitude, informally dubbed him the girls' godfather.

"I love those children," said Lolly weepily.

Angie knew he did; she knew he felt partly responsible for their existence, after having saved them both in utero from the dreaded litter-box microbe.

But Dean Lee quickly built up his debt again, mostly by accruing interest. Lolly had largely banned him from his own card games except under special circumstances: her husband was permitted to play only when he brought cash and used exactly half of what he had to pay down his debt; the rest he was free to gamble with. There were plenty of other games around, but Dean Lee was either not welcome at them, or they were too penny-ante, or too big, or too something. So Dean Lee decided he would start his own game, acting as dealer. He decided on Mondays and Thursdays, and it was to be strictly no-limit hold 'em. He spent $300 on a flimsy mail-order poker table and $60 on lawn chairs, set everything up in the den, contacted every poker player he knew, and managed to get commitments for the first game from Dard Fanshaw, Frank Slide, Coburn Metlow, and Quality Sanchez. Dean Lee drove over to Lillie's Auto Shine and talked one of the employees he habitually flirted with, Sassy Krilik, into putting on a skimpy outfit and working the game as a cocktail waitress, which meant opening cans of beer and serving them to the players whenever they looked thirsty. The first Thursday night was a success, and Dean Lee raked nearly $1,500 out of the game without playing a single hand. But Dean Lee was aching to actually play, so the following Monday, when the same players showed up along with Sandy Nubbins and Gouty Chris Hebert, Dean Lee dealt himself in. He was broke in about two hours and found himself back to only dealing.

The house on Fawn Street was tiny, the game big and raucous. There was no room for a mother and two little children except to retreat to the master bedroom. Little Sophie slept in her bassinet in the corner by the bathroom, and Nadine lay on the big bed with her mother, leaning against the headboard, watching kitten and puppy and baby videos on the laptop. Nadine would eventually fall asleep, and Sophie would wake up and need nursing. Angie would buy one episode of *The Sopranos* at a time on Amazon. Angie was not married to a mob boss, but she was married to a man with not entirely foggy connections to the underworld, such as it was in McCandless, Texas, and so she identified strongly with Carmela and felt that she shared her struggles. Angie would watch episodes that starred Edie Falco two or three times in a row, studying them, looking for clues to her own life.

After a few months, Lolly Prager broke up Dean Lee's game by simply paying everyone who played in it $500 to never play in it again, and that was that. Angie had her house back. By this time, Sophie could crawl rapidly enough to get a rug burn, and it seemed as if the death of Dean Lee's poker game was the first time he realized he even had a second child. The comically fast crawling delighted Dean Lee, and he would laugh hysterically as the child sped across the den floor like a battery-operated toy. Little Sophie routinely entertained her father with giggles and squeals and obscure expressions and goofy looks and her very being. Simply put, Dean Lee adored his younger daughter.

He took her to work with him to show her off to Nelson Kallendorf and the rest of the bottling crew.

"Y'all, this is Sophie," said Dean Lee one morning in the break room at NEK Bottling, where everybody gathered to smoke and chew on whatever came out of the old vending machine by the coffee maker, and generally bitch about bottles and lids and wives and children and state government. "My daughter."

All the men took turns grinning back at Sophie's cherubic glow, and all the women took turns holding her, even old grouchy ever-disgruntled Maisie Barlittle, who, reluctant at first, finally accepted the child. She carried her around the break room, whispering in her ear and showing her the OSHA and CPR posters and *Employee's Must Wash Hands* sign in the bathroom, and letting her put nickels in the vending machine. When 8:30 rolled around and it was finally time to get busy bottling, it seemed for a moment that Maisie was not going to give Sophie back to her father. It took Nelson Kallendorf himself to crowbar the child out of Maisie's embrace.

"You bring her back next week," Maisie said, fierce, pointing with both index fingers at Dean Lee's head. Sophie reached out and grabbed both fingers, squealed, and old hidebound Maisie melted.

Dean Lee even brought her to a poker game and had her sit in his lap while he gambled and drank beer. She cooed and gnawed on the old, dirty poker chips and licked the condensation off the beer bottles and otherwise charmed the crusty, uncharmable old poker players around the table. Dean

Lee even won $1,250, half of it with a deuce-seven offsuit, and decided he would be 1) bringing Sophie along to card games with greater regularity, and 2) playing deuce-seven off every time he got dealt it from now on.

Maybe if Sophie had been a more difficult child, Dean Lee wouldn't have been as fond of her—if she'd been colicky, petulant, slow, or morbid, but she was none of those things. She was cute, beautiful even, putto-like, good-natured, kittenish, and she belly-laughed at everything anyone said.

Nadine was nothing like her little sister. Where Sophie was all rounded-off and soft, Nadine was subtly burred; where Sophie was the wink in a jest, Nadine was the glare in an argument; where Sophie was the yellow-green tracery of fireflies at dusk, Nadine was the arch of darkness on a foggy night. The sibling rivalry started immediately. Nadine dumped a bowl of cold oatmeal on Sophie in her bassinet on her second day home from the hospital; on her fourth day, Nadine hid her sister's Huggies in the shed in the backyard, obliging Dean Lee to go to the store for more. Over the next few years, the rivalry became more pointed, focused on getting Mommy's attention.

Dean Lee did his best not to play favorites, but everyone knew who it was. Nadine was not damaged or even bothered by any of this. She had, for one, the indivisible love of her mother, as well as the bright-eyed admiration of her little sister, in spite of the rivalry. And, given Nadine's independent constitution, she could have survived perfectly well without either. Sophie, however, needed constant attention and care; she could not easily pass a moment alone.

One evening when Sophie was nearly three, Dean Lee was out playing cards, Angie had taken Nadine to the Alamo Drafthouse on Koenig

Lane in Austin to see *Bambi*, and Sophie was home alone with Randi, a babysitter recommended by a neighbor.

"Sophie baby!" Angie called out when she and Nadine got home. "Sophie? Randi?"

Nothing. Angie dropped her purse, the remains of her popcorn, and she began running through the tiny house.

It was Nadine who found her little sister, dressed in her orange nightie with embroidered caterpillars around the neckline, alone in the empty bathtub in the back of the house. Sophie was a child-shaped block of panic and abandonment. Her tears had actually pooled around the drain. Nadine climbed into the tub with her little sister, held her tight, and sang Hank Williams in her ear as gently and as best she could.

Dean Lee was called and was home in less than ninety seconds—the bourré game he'd been at was being dealt at the Bjornboes', next door. Randi arrived at the front door at about the same time as Dean Lee. Unlike Dean Lee, though, Randi was in a state of semi-dishabille—no shoes, evidence of bralessness, a McCandless Glee Club T-shirt turned inside out.

It so happened that Randi's boyfriend, Gerry, had come by to visit while Nadine and Angie were at the movies. Randi wouldn't let him in, so she left Sophie in the house by herself and went outside to pay Gerry a friendly visit in his car, which was parked at the curb.

"Goddammit, where's Gerry now?" thundered Dean Lee, Randi cowering in a corner.

"He just drove off, he's gone, we didn't do anything!"

"Never," said Dean Lee, shivering with rage, "never, never, never..."

"I'm so—"

"Angie will drive you home."

CHAPTER FOUR

# Recoil

ANGIE AND SOPHIE PLAYED slapjack on the floor of the den while Dean Lee sat in his lawn chair in the front yard, home from work, a victim of bronchitis. He was reading Víctor Montoya's *Días y noches de angustia,* which he'd gotten on interlibrary loan from San Antonio Public. Now and then an arid hack could be heard, along with the moist *fltsch* of a can of Pearl being depressurized. The household was awaiting the arrival of two people: Dean Lee was expecting a visit from Lolly Prager, and Nadine was due home from school at any minute.

Whenever Sophie slapped a jack, she would scoop up the cards, carefully jog them until they formed a little deck, then stand up and perform a dance intended to both entertain and lightly taunt her mother. She was good at poker for her age, and she liked it well enough, but slapjack was her game. Today Sophie was wearing her pink straw cowboy hat, secured in place by two pink leather thongs tied in a bow under her chin. Angie glanced at the door. Nadine was a little late.

A cluster headache began to immobilize Angie. When Sophie slapped a jack, the reverb echoed around her mother's head, above the soft palate and behind her eyes.

"Honey, my head hurts. I'm going to go lie down."

"No!"

When Sophie protested something, she threw down little conviction, and because of it seldom ever got her way. Her method of dissent was offered up without the persuasive nasal whine her older sister had mastered.

"Just for a little bit. We can finish later."

"Five minutes?"

"Thirty. Tell Nadine to come say hi when she gets home. Otherwise, I don't want to be disturbed, okay?"

"'Kay."

Sophie sat down and pretended to shuffle. If there was one thing Sophie wanted more than anything in the whole world, it was to be able to shuffle like her mother. Angie could take a deck of cards, divide it perfectly, like a machine, into two identical halves, bend them into flawless rainbows, and with a sound like the purr of a jungle cat, merge them together, slowly, so Sophie could see the individual cards slipping between one another, then push the decks into a whole, square it with her fingertips, and perform the whole show again, over and over, Sophie watching, her little heart throbbing, climbing her throat, threatening to appear in her mouth.

"Okay by yourself?"

"'Kay."

"Daddy's right outside, you can see him, see?"

"'Kay." She let the cards fall out of her hand and spill on the floor, face up, Sophie's approximation of a tantrum.

"Okay, Sophie, I'm going now."

On her side of the bed Angie put a pillow over her face. She listened to Sophie playing slapjack by herself in the other room, marveling at the capacity of children to entertain themselves. She listened to Dean Lee's cough, to the creak of his old chair as he shifted around. The autumn cicadas. A telephone rang in a neighbor's house. Then another, and another. She listened to the sparse traffic on Fawn Street, trying to identify the owners of the vehicles by the sounds they made. There, the whistly whine of Mrs. Anand's old Honda Accord, and there, Jodo Kreutz's diesel Mercedes. And... what was that? Some vehicle she didn't know, a wayward stranger, a visitor, somebody's aunt from Dripping Springs maybe, or some pizza delivery boy in his mother's Escort. Then, silence.

Lolly's truck now. It sounded louder than usual, angry. The engine rose in pitch as it shifted into park, then a moment of quiet. A slamming door. Lolly, shouting.

*Dean Lee, I'm just about finally done with you, sir.*

He yelled something else, but Angie couldn't make it out. She strained to hear, then got up, ran into the living room. Lolly had four men with him, all from Dean Lee's various card games. She didn't know them well—Karl Beery, a skinny antique cowboy from Oatmeal; Batman Vasp, a bodybuilder from Vidor; Chris Hebert, the gout-stricken pipe threader from Temple; and Dyman Barrande, an overgrown Apple genius from Cedar Park. Lolly stomped around the den, the kitchen, pointing at this and that, lamps, sofas, the new TV set, the throw rug, the side table, the painting of the gray kittens on the wall, the fake cuckoo clock; then the men with their strong, tattooed arms began scooping everything up and carrying it off down the hall, all this stuff that for years Lolly had declined to take, he was now taking, wholesale. Angie felt frozen, unable to speak, pushed herself up against the dirty wall in the den to stay out of the men's way. Karl and Dyman were on their knees in the kitchen, unhooking the leads to the gas stove,

Batman was scooping spices out of the cabinets and into a paper bag, Chris was under the sink loading cleansers and tools into a dirty vinyl basin, Sophie leaning over him, asking, *"Whatcha doin', whatcha doin'?"* Angie ran to the bedroom, where she found Lolly trying to upend the vast California king mattress by himself, failing, then screaming for Batman to come and help him. Angie followed them as they carried the mattress down the hall and outside, past Dean Lee sitting in his lawn chair, buried in his book, insensible to what was happening around him. Angie screamed in his ear, but he seemed not to hear. Lolly and Batman loaded the mattress into one of five trucks parked on the lawn. The men streamed in and out of the house with furniture, boxes, bags, loading things into the old pickups.

A school bus stopped in front of the house. Nadine got off. Batman walked up to her, picked her up, and put her in the cab of a green Silverado. At the same time, Karl came out of the house carrying Sophie, three decks of cards filling her tiny hands. He put her in the cab of an extravagantly rusted Dodge Ram. Angie screamed. She ran up to Lolly, who was standing in front of Dean Lee in the front yard.

"Angie, take off your clothes, now, we need them clothes, bra, panties, all."

Then Lolly kneeled down. He drew Dean Lee's revolver from his shoulder holster. Dean Lee closed his book and placed it against his heart. Lolly fired once into Dean Lee's forehead.

Angie woke with a violent start. She sat up in bed, looking around the bedroom, replaying Lolly's voice in her nightmare, telling her to take off her clothes, then raising the gun to her husband's head and firing, seeing the bullet, strangely made of dented iron, emerging from the muzzle, entering her husband's forehead, bloodlessly, like a dirty finger pressed into Silly Putty, until it disappeared, and he opened his mouth to protest, and no sound came out, and she woke, tangled in sheets...

Angie listened, but there was nothing but silence in the house.

Then a moan, graduating to a scream.

Nadine later told her mother and the police that on the short bus ride home from school she had sat next to her friend Rhonda Prynne. Rhonda was the only girl her age who brought a purse to school. It was a small, olive-green sling bag with a long, fake-gold chain strap, just large enough to hold a few items of her mother's makeup, none of which she was allowed to use.

"Look what I have," Rhonda had said, undoing the latch on her purse. "Money."

"How much?" said Nadine.

Rhonda removed six one-dollar bills from a pocket in her purse. She fanned them out and presented them to Nadine.

"I'm going to the dime store. You know Barbie broke up with Ken, right?" Nadine hadn't known. Rhonda had the most significant Barbie collection that Nadine knew of—dozens of dolls, still in boxes, even some Gold Label Barbies, rare dolls limited in production to one thousand and very hard to get.

"So I'm gonna buy a Ken doll, because he'll probably get really rare. You should get one too, before they're gone. How much money do you have?"

"I don't know, lots," said Nadine, who had a dollar forty-five, all in pennies, which she'd won playing poker with her father. "How much is it?"

"Five dollars and twenty-nine cents. More with tax, but six dollars is enough, and you'll get some change for Swedish Fish. Look, here's your stop. Go home and get your moolah and meet me at the store in like, mm, thirty-four minutes. Okay?"

Nadine exited the bus. She walked the half block to her house, scheming on where she could get the money. She wasn't above pilfering a few coins from the laundry bucket or the top drawer of her parents' dresser, but four dollars or more was pushing it. Her dad wouldn't give her anything, and her mother would say she didn't have it. There was a chance she could talk Sophie out of whatever she had, but it was unlikely she had much—she usually spent or lost her quarter allowance within minutes of receiving it. Look, there's Dad, sitting in his dumb chair in the yard, reading some dumb Spanish book as usual. Who's he talking to?

Lolly! Nadine liked Lolly—something about the smiley wrinkles in his face—even though he took stuff out of the house sometimes, making her mother cry, and sometimes her daddy, too. Anyway, if he didn't take away anything this time, he might be good for as much as a dollar.

"'Lo, sweetheart," said her daddy. He didn't have his gun. For some reason, he never wore his gun when Lolly came by. Maybe he was afraid Lolly would shoot him with it, or that Daddy would shoot Lolly. Her father was looking awfully glad to see her.

"Hi, Daddy. Hi, Lolly."

"That's *Mister Prager*, honey," her father said gently, closing his book and setting it down in the dirt.

"You can call me whatever you want, baby," said Lolly. "Where's your little sister at?"

"I don't know, inside?" Nadine said. Everybody always wanted to know where her little sister was. Charming, beautiful, delightful Sophie. Nobody ever asked Sophie where Nadine was.

Nadine waited expectantly. She wondered how transparent her need was but didn't care. "Well, when you see her, you give her this," Lolly said, handing her a dollar folded once lengthwise. "And one for you, too."

"Say thank you, young lady," said her father.

"Thank you." Nadine couldn't believe her luck. She would be more than halfway there if she kept Sophie's dollar. She darted inside the house, stuffing the money into her pocket. She found her sister playing slapjack on the floor in the den.

"Where's Mom?"

"Napping, go say hi," said Sophie, without looking up.

"How much money do you have?"

"I have nine quarters that are mine."

Nadine wasn't entirely sure how much that was, but it sounded like a lot.

"Can I have it?"

"No way, José. Mine."

Nadine started in the laundry room. There was only a dollar and three cents left in the laundry change bucket. Nadine took it. In the living room, she went through the couch cushions, deep, coming up with combs, bobby pins, antique Sucrets, a pocketknife, nail clippers, Mom's yin-yang necklace, and a whopping twenty-seven cents. Nadine's six-year-old logic dictated that there could be money between the mattresses of her parents' bed, so she snuck into their room, and, careful not to wake her mother, stuck her hands in the California king on her daddy's side. There was no money, but she did come away with his greasy .357. It was so heavy she could scarcely hold it in one hand. She pointed it at her mother, who was sleeping soundly with a pillow over her face. Nadine got an idea. She went into the den. She watched

Sophie play slapjack for a few moments. Then, with both hands, she leveled the gun at her sister.

"This is a stickup! Gimme all your quarters!"

Before Sophie could look up, the gun went off. A single bullet struck Sophie in the chest and knocked her backward. The weapon recoiled, splitting Nadine's upper lip. She dropped the gun and screamed. The world became very bright and very red.

Then all was black.

# CHAPTER FIVE

# Satellites

DEAN LEE GRANDET DID not like to walk. He drove where he needed to go, even if it was down the street to the Valero for beer. He didn't even like to walk from the driveway to the front door of his own house or from the kitchen to the den. But when he dropped by the McCandless police station to pick up his revolver—Chief Duhamel told him that no crime had been committed, to come and get his weapon—Dean Lee walked down the steps of the station, past his old F-150, and out onto the shoulder of Doerling Road, a street he had driven down nearly every day of his life.

Dean Lee walked. Whenever he came to an intersection he would stop, think about which way he wanted to go—left, or right, or straight—then head in the direction that seemed most uncertain, or that would lead him farther from the epicenter of his crime. Dean Lee kept his head up. He stared down oncoming drivers he felt were staring at him in judgment, even if he could not see through their windshields. Dean Lee felt like he could walk a thousand miles.

He turned left onto a road he did not know. The setting sun shone straight down into his eyes. In the past few miles, he had lost the feeling in his hands. His feet were beginning to grow numb. Dean Lee walked into the sun, clutching at the fabric of distance with his teeth, while all sensation left his body at the same rate the vermilion ball of the sun dropped toward earth. By the time it had disappeared below ground and dusk had come to reign, Dean Lee was largely anesthetized, moving west along the unknown street like an object on a conveyor belt, the only corporal sensation the feeling of his tongue falling back in his throat, the only smell the puncturing blare of mercury fulminate, the only sound the hollow underwater *pup* as his elder daughter fired at his younger daughter while he sat in his own front yard arguing with the town crook, the only taste the taste of another's blood on the roof of his mouth, the arch of sycamores in the dying light the only thing he could see. Dean Lee moved west, only to find that he was not approaching the oblivion he sought.

More than four hundred people attended Sophie's funeral, half of them strangers, a third of them Dean Lee's poker buddies. Adeline put in an appearance, the first time Angie had seen her mother since the lasagna incident, almost seven years before. She looked like Miss Havisham in a crinkly Victorian getup, and kept her distance. She spoke to no one and vanished like a hummingbird the moment the formal rite was concluded. Angie wondered if the next time she would see her mother would be at *her* funeral. No, of course not, thought Angie, furious, I will never outlive Adeline Bigelow, a biblical Sarah who will outlast everyone in Chamberlain, Texas, and probably the town itself.

The sight of the men from Angie's recent dream—Batman Vasp, Karl Beery, Chris Hebert, and Dyman Barrande—standing together in their rumpled brown suits, hovering over the King Ranch chicken, nearly caused Angie to suffer a violent panic attack, the first of her life. She ducked into the ladies' room at McCandless First Baptist. There were other women in there, chatting, but the room hushed when Angie came in. She leaned over a sink, waiting for a purgation, or something. A young woman, beautiful, like Sherilyn Fenn in the original *Twin Peaks*, came over to Angie.

"I'm so sorry for your loss, Mrs. Grandet."

Angie couldn't speak, but nodded, staring at the drain. She felt helpless, unmoored, outclassed. This woman was *more* than she was. Who was she? Angie wanted what she had, her stability, beauty, poise. Angie wondered if she had living children.

"My neighbor, Ginny?" continued Sherilyn, turning and hoisting herself up to sit on the vanity. "Her little girl, Beryl, fell into an empty swimming pool and died. Of a broken neck. A few years ago? So. I really, really know what you're going through right now."

Angie turned and looked at Sherilyn. She was extraordinary. Angie smiled at the young woman, leaned toward her, as if to say something. Sherilyn bent forward to receive her words. There was no sound in the bathroom. As quick as an asp, Angie kissed Sherilyn on the mouth, hard, a vampiric kiss, meant to extract, not to impart. Sherilyn gasped, leapt down from her perch on the vanity, and fled, wiping her mouth. The other women in the bathroom stood aghast. Angie studied her mouth in the mirror. She never wore lipstick, but now had traces of a pale, opaque shade of salmon smeared on her face. She tasted it—a balsamic semi-sweetness that reminded her of junior high school dances. The nausea and panic she'd felt earlier began to dissipate. Somehow she had gained something. She had taken, as she had been taken from.

Angie rejoined the crowd. So many she didn't know. So many men. There, Rhonda's mother, Gabriella Prynne.

"Angie, how you holding up, honey?"

Angie still found it difficult to speak, so she nodded. She could sense Gabriella looking at her lipstick-smeared mouth.

"Rhonda told me that when Nadine failed to meet her at the dime store, she knew something bad had happened, that's what Rhonda told me. She's psychic I think, my little girl. Oh, I can't imagine what's going on in your little household right about now."

The "little" qualifier irked Angie, even in the state she was in. Gabriella Prynne and her husband Willie were well off from a score of ancient, inherited oil leases in Arkansas that had been yielding major fracking revenue, and the couple liked to spend their money on bespoke cowboy boots, one-of-a-kind aircraft, and vanishingly rare dolls. They had the kind of money Angie would never see, living as she did in the long, black shadow of Dean Lee's debt, even if Angie was to get a part-time job somewhere. Gabriella could afford to strew her hallways with lilies, sprinkle gold leaf on her salads, fly to Hong Kong for single-malt scotch auctions, find gray-market pre-Columbian artifacts for her bathroom shelves, buy out a Girl Scout cookie drive for fun, rent an island for a luau-themed bridge tournament, donate six digits to a mighty good cause. Angie's rage came to just below the surface, and sat, like a U-boat.

"You just can't imagine, huh."

Angie was aware of the eyes turning toward them, the eyes turning away from them, all the attention she was beginning to command by raising her voice, by being tall and strong and small and busted all at once. Angie licked her lips, tasting the waxy remains of the kiss of a few moments before, drawing strength from it.

"What I mean is," said Gabriella, taking half a step back, "that feeling that's around like maybe being partly responsible for what happened, you know?"

"I see. My fault. I killed my daughter."

"No, not you, honey. Dean Lee."

When Angie was a junior in high school, she'd had a friend, Arla, a grade younger, who was terrified she was going to die of cardiac arrest. To reduce the risk of being killed by her own malfunctioning body, Arla kept her hand on her heart at all times, monitoring irregularities. This had been her practice since the age of eight. She claimed she was so sensitive to the engine of her own heart that she could predict up-and-coming bodily events such as colds, acne outbreaks, menstruation, depressive episodes, cavities, and even, given the right circumstances, external events such as extreme weather and the outcomes of University of Texas football games.

Once, though, Arla's heart fooled her. In Mrs. Gold's pre-calc class one Friday morning, Arla's heart began to flutter like a monarch in a mason jar, a miniature violence brushing against her ribs. She jumped up, upsetting her desk and scattering books and pencils and papers, and demanded an ambulance *now*. Extensive emergency room diagnostics found nothing amiss and sent her home. The next day, Arla's mother, Exelette, came to her daughter's room.

"Arla."

"Mom! Knock next time."

Exelette sat on the end of the bed and began to smooth out creases in the quilt. Arla's right hand went to her heart. She pressed one ear to her shoulder and stuck a finger in her other ear. Damping the sounds of the world allowed her to hear both her heart and her mother at the same time.

"Arla. Listen. Do you remember Jacob Hiram?"

"Dad's old mechanic?"

"The auto magician. Yes."

"He's weird. That lump on his calf. I thought Dad fired him."

"Yes. But Jacob and I remained friends."

Arla's heart beat regularly, a steadfast *th-thka* that betrayed nothing.

"I will be spending the rest of my life with him."

*th-thapuh    th-thapuh    th-thapuh*

"Your father will be moving to Butte. That's in Montana."

*th-thapuh    th-thapuh    th-thapuh*

"You will go to live with my sister, your aunt Verle, in Shreveport. That's in Louisiana."

*th-thapuh    th-thapuh    th-thapuh*

The following Monday, Arla told her friend Angie that her heart could warn her of everything, anything, except for her own blindness, her own blinkered disregard for the real world around her.

Angie studied Gabriella, wondered briefly if Arla was still in Shreveport, then closed her eyes. Angie placed a hand on her heart. She felt nothing, no beat, as though she were a birch tree or one of those uncannily lifelike sex dolls. Or a fresh corpse. She opened her eyes. Gabriella was gone.

Angie desperately wanted a drink. She wasn't much of a drinker, but she was dying for something strong, something that would sear. *Puncture.*

Angie pushed through the crowd and went outside into the October morning sun. In the parking lot stood a man she recognized, Carrollton DeGolyer, a guy she'd gone to high school with but hardly remembered. Carrollton, a pharmacist at Dotteridge Apothecary in Chamberlain, had developed a great crush on Angie about the time she met Dean Lee, but his timing was off by a few hours, and he got left in the dust.

"Hello, Carrollton."

"Angie."

"I need to get out of here. Take me to Bain's."

Bain's was a roadhouse next to a defunct pig stand out on FM 1321. It was one of the few places in Travis County where one could get a shot of tequila and a twenty-ounce steak at nine-thirty in the morning, and that was what Angie felt like she needed, minus the steak. Populating the roadhouse was a scatter of bikers, a couple of professional drunks, a lone businessman, two Japanese college kids playing 501, and a few spent truckers. Angie and Carrollton, in their black mourning attire, stood out.

"Y'all look like y'all just come from a funeral," said the bartender, a squat and powerfully built man in a tank top who looked like he was coated in WD-40.

"Six tequilas," said Angie. "I don't know what he wants."

Carrollton ordered a margarita, got laughed at, ordered a glass of red wine, got laughed at, ordered a Miller High Life, and got it.

The barkeep had measured off Angie's six tequilas and poured them all into a mayonnaise jar. She drank half of it immediately. Angie glanced at Carrollton. He had become slightly jowly but was still attractive.

*What in the world am I doing?*

Just hours before she'd met Dean Lee, Angie had come into Carrollton's apothecary to fill a script for insulin for her perpetually ill and diseased cat, Browne. It so happened that Carrollton also had a cat with diabetes. He took her into the toy aisle of the store and demonstrated on a stuffed armadillo how to give insulin injections in the scruff of the neck, quick and dirty. He gave her the armadillo, then asked her if she'd like to go to dinner.

Angie recalled the conversation with pellucid accuracy. She remembered she had been mad at Adeline about something at the time. What was it? Boys? Probably. She had broken up with Galt, the sexless poet, a few months earlier. Angie had felt like she was channeling Adeline in her conversation with this pharmacist fella.

"I like expensive restaurants," she said, holding her armadillo like a football. "Good ones."

"Okay," said Carrollton, carefully breaking off the needle of the syringe, removing the plunger, placing the needle fragment inside, replacing the plunger, and dropping the now-harmless shot in the pocket of his pharmacist's apron.

"And wine by the bottle, not the glass."

"Okay." Carrollton smiled.

"But on the other hand, I'm pretty easy to get into bed."

"Okay." Carrollton stopped smiling and acquired a look of studied attention, like a child being tutored in geometry.

"As long as you're smart and funny and entertaining and don't talk about yourself too much."

"Okay."

"Do we know each other?" said Angie.

"I was a year ahead of you at Chamberlain High. I was not memorable. I was that kid who broke the pole-vaulting pole and nearly got impaled. Remember?"

She did. That was all that she knew about the guy. Angie was curious about the scar.

"Shit, yeah. You okay?"

"Like it never happened."

"Well, how wonderful for you."

Angie remembered hating Adeline in that moment, interfering in her dalliance.

"Not really true about the sex," said Angie, not knowing what else to say, fighting Adeline. "I'm a challenge to get into bed. Are you confused yet? What's your name?"

"Carrollton."

"You're named after a street in New Orleans?"

"I'm named after my great-great-great-grandfather, a horse thief hanged from a scrub oak by Leander McKelly, Texas Ranger."

Angie became preoccupied by the distance between Carrollton's eyes. They seemed to be exactly one eye-width apart. This symmetry appealed to her in a deep and meaningful way, and she had a powerful urge to lick him between the eyes; more than that, to suck him there, give him a 'twixt-the-eyes hickey, a throbbing red one that would get him sent home, or to the walk-in clinic for balm and a poultice. Even Adeline wouldn't think of that.

"Am I keeping you from your labors?"

Fucking Adeline. Only *she* would utter a sentence like that.

"I don't care."

Basically blowing his face was probably out of the question, but maybe she could touch him there under some other pretense.

"I don't know why," she said, though she did know, "but I'm tempted to write my number on your forehead. Backward, so you can read it in the mirror. May I?"

Angie produced a ballpoint from her purse.

"No, I don't think that'd be a good idea."

"Oh, you're married."

Angie smiled like marriage would be no impediment whatsoever.

"No, no, I—"

"Embarrassed."

"No, I—"

"What?"

"I don't want anyone else to have it."

"Good answer! Hold out your hand."

Angie tucked the stuffed armadillo between her legs and wrote her number on Carrollton's palm. Holding his fingers in hers she found highly erotic and did not let go right away. They were cool, smooth, and dry, the loops, arches, and whorls of his fingerprints pronounced. She closed her eyes and "read" his index fingertip with her thumb.

"Better call me soon."

"Can I have my hand back?"

Carrollton did call her soon, that evening in fact, but she was out babysitting Junie-June and Leroy Prager, the night of the blue popsicles. Carrollton called again a few nights later, but Angie had her phone turned off because she was entertaining Dean Lee Grandet in her garage apartment. When she finally answered when he called a few days after that, she had to inform poor Carrollton that she was dating someone.

"These things don't often last with me, though, Carrollton, so chin up. I've got your number, I'll give you a call when things go belly up with this guy."

Angie never thought about Carrollton DeGolyer again. She drank down the rest of her mayonnaise jar of tequila.

"You know, I had quite the old crush on you, Angie Bigelow," Carrollton said, swirling his mostly undrunk beer around the inside of the clear bottle. "It never really flagged, either. I didn't know what to do with it, so I transferred it to one of my manic-depressive pharmacy customers, Chandra Loos. You might know her, she used to be in the news a lot for various excesses of public insanity."

"Don't remember," said Angie, thinking about the mayonnaise that used to be in the jar, if the bartender had made turkey sandwiches for his children with it. She wondered briefly what his children looked like. If he had boys. Or girls.

"Then, I retransferred my Angie crush to Jessamyne Sparks, another pharmacist at Dotteridge who got busted for stealing animal tranquilizers. She was the one with that weird oval patch of hair on her forearm that she refused to cover or depilate and which freaked everybody out. Do you—"

"Don't recall."

"And then I used Harper what's-her-name as reliquary for my Angie crush. Remember her? She was in your class in high school, I think y'all were friends, the cute one that dressed like she was in a '40s movie."

"Yeah. Harper." Angie remembered. A red-haired beauty who moved away just when Angie really needed a friend. Angie wondered if Harper ever had a child, if the child was alive. "So, Carrollton, what finally happened? Get married, divorced, any kids?"

"Nope," said Carrollton, fishing in his back pocket for his wallet. He opened it up, and a clear plastic accordion unfolded, revealing photos of women in every slot. "Just keep shifting my Angie crush to various women. Like transferring balances to new credit cards when the interest rates get too high. You see this last blank photo slot?"

"Yeah. For me."

"You're married."

"That photo thing is a little creepy, Carrollton. A little serial-killer-y."

"I don't care."

Carrollton hadn't drunk past the neck of his beer bottle. The bartender came over and picked the bottle up and peered at it thoughtfully.

"Not thirsty today?"

"Did I pay for this?" said Carrollton, folding up his photo accordion and putting his billfold back in his pocket. "Did I motherfucking pay for it?"

"Calm down, Carrollton," said Angie, wondering if there would be a fight and a bouncing.

"If I wanna spend two fucking hours drinking it, I will, if I wanna pour it on the floor, I will, if I wanna piss it down your greasy shirt, I will, if I wanna baptize your retarded triplets with it, I—"

"Carrollton!"

The bartender placed a baseball bat, magnificently cratered and caked with what looked like blood, on the bar.

"Let's go, Carrollton."

Carrollton, a slight, bespectacled, ginger-bearded man with a bit of a limp, pointed at the bartender, and then at Angie, and said: "I am here with a grieving mother, and nothing, but nothing, you can say or do is gonna budge me."

Carrollton stood up, crossed his arms, and waited. The bartender picked up his baseball bat and came around the end of the bar, headed for Carrollton. Carrollton didn't move.

"I'll give you my Jeep and ten thousand dollars if you can even make me blink, you spineless, roid-rage shop rag."

The bartender feinted convincingly with the bat. Carrollton did not blink. The bartender screamed, *"Get out my 'stablishment!"*

"Pussy."

Carrollton unzipped, put his thumb over the lip of his bottle of Miller High Life, stuck the bottle in his open fly, business end out, then let his thumb up. He drained the bottle, shaking off the last few drops. He placed the bottle on the counter, zipped up his fly, and stomped in the beer puddle, flinging beer here and there, including on WD-40's ankles.

"Let's go, Angie."

In the parking lot, Angie decided she needed to do a cartwheel, an act of abandon she had not accomplished since she was twelve. Her daughter Sophie had been a cartwheel machine, perfect rotations and landings every time. Sophie had told her mother once that she would trade her cartwheel talent for her mother's card-shuffling talent in an instant.

Angie got gravel shards stuck in her palms, but other than that, she did a nice smooth cartwheel which got some applause from a few bikers. It occurred to Angie, absurdly, that maybe somehow Sophie had inhabited her mother, some trick performed by agents of heaven.

"You're my hero, Carrollton. I want you to run me by Dotteridge so I can buy three packs of cards." Angie was going to put them in a flat-rate box from the post office and address it to *Heaven* and see what happened.

"Hero, ha. Sure, let's go to the apothecary."

"You are a hero."

"I'm just an idiot. Why'd you go and marry that guy, Angie? I would've married you in an instant."

"Dean Lee asked me, Carrollton, and I was pregnant. Plus, it is true that I experienced at the time a purely physical sexual attraction to the man. Still do, I guess. But now we have lost a child. Together. That's permanent."

She wondered: *Who was she?* She sounded like a fucking therapist or a member of some cult of psychically anesthetized mothers.

"He's a bad man," said Carrollton, looking at the gravel like he was thinking about cartwheeling too, but deciding against it. "Divorce him and marry me. I'll take care of you and Nadine. I have a lot of money. I make a lot of money. And I'm going to inherit a lot more."

"Oh Carrollton. How could you take care of me? Nadine?"

"I love little kids. I have six nephews and nieces and I'm the favorite uncle, out of four. Nadine would have a little family of cousins. And— you want me to say it? I love you. I have since the day I met you."

"You don't love me. You had a crush. A crush is not love."

Angie was pushing him, testing him. Kind of. She knew Carrollton didn't really love her. She knew he wanted to rescue her. The urge to rescue was not the same as love. It was a temporary thing, much like sex. A rescue was an orgasm, over in the time it took to sneeze. Love was the long game, and Carrollton, she was sure, did not have it.

Not that it mattered now.

"I'm serious," he said. "In fact, why don't you move in with me. Today. I'll even go beat the shit out of ol' Dean Lee. I'll kill him. Not really."

Angie suddenly reeled, took a step back, and sat down hard in the gravel. A mayonnaise jar with six shots of tequila in it was a substantive commitment, and consumed, as it had been, on an empty stomach, was going to take its time metabolizing. In the twelve seconds that separated marginal sobriety from bona fide inebriation, Angie wondered what she was going to do today that she would later regret. In those twelve seconds, she understood, at least, that "regret" was a relative term. She regretted many things, many things. Today, though, now that all was upended, all gravitation removed, the edges of the world pushed back into the heliopause, it was hard to imagine doing something, anything, that would really cause her regret such that it would eclipse the regret she already felt at allowing her daughter to kill her other daughter. Angie could steal, murder, rob a train, carjack a teenage student driver, shoot heroin in her eyeball, mow down a sidewalk lemonade stand run by Brownies. She could fuck Carrollton DeGolyer.

Carrollton sat down with her in the glass- and bottle-cap-pebbled gravel.

"I'll call a moving van," he said. "We'll leave Dean Lee Grandet in the dust. What's your maiden name again?"

Angie had to think about it for a moment. *Her maiden name?*

"Bigelow."

"Leave your married name there, too, become Angie Bigelow again. Flee that fucker. Everybody knows he's trouble. Gambling, the gun, disrespecting your mama—"

"How the hell do you know so much?"

"People talk."

"And you listen, your big conch ears taking it all in, believing every word. You must think I'm just some dumb, meek little scab-kneed mouse-wife to put up with it. Well, there's plenty you don't know, will never know. I'm not moving in with you. I don't want to see you again, Carrollton DeGolyer."

Angie got to her knees, to her feet. She made it to the road and began to walk back toward town. She made it about a hundred yards when Carrollton drove up beside her in his old Jeep.

"Angie, get in. Please."

"No."

"I apologize for meddling. Now please get in."

She stopped. Carrollton reached over and opened the door. She climbed in.

"You're a nice person, Carrollton."

"So—"

"Let's go to your place."

The tequila began to divide Angie's consciousness into two distinct personae, one dominant, one submissive, each engaged in constant dialogue over exactly how to conduct their central host's behavior from moment to moment. And as Carrollton unlocked the front door to his house and ushered Angie inside, the binary nature of her tequila personality argued over whether she should drink more, whether she should sleep with Carrollton, whether she should stay overnight, whether she should leave her husband and be with Carrollton. How could she ever leave her only living daughter alone for so long? What the hell was she doing here, what the hell was she *doing*?

"I have a great reposado," said Carrollton. "Fifty years old, if you'd like to continue your theme of the morning."

"Yeah, sure," said Angie's submissive persona, whom she had decided to call Glenda. "A double."

Carrollton poured her the drink from a bottle shaped like a saguaro.

"I'll be back," he said, and disappeared into the bathroom.

Angie looked around, her tequila-vision doubling the dirty clothes in almost fecal mounds all over the floor, the crusty dishes colonizing the counters. Pulp paperbacks piled everywhere, Jim Thompson, Horace McCoy, John McPartland, old noir movie posters on the wall: *Force of Evil*, *Try and Get Me!*, *He Ran All the Way*. A single black IKEA couch dominated the main room, and three (or was it six?) vast charcoal-gray cats, surely siblings, dominated the couch. The only other place to sit, a water-damaged Eames chair, was occupied by a large stack of carefully folded towels. Angie picked them up, put them on the floor, sat, and waited for her host. She wondered what his bed was like. Certainly unmade, certainly soiled. A twin, a full, a queen? The pillows, denuded, drool-stained, deflated memory foam? Who was the last person he'd slept with here? A hooker? A teenager? An ex-con? Some scabby, straw-haired, halter-topped combination of the three, like Jodie Foster in *Taxi Driver*, measuring the duration of his privilege with a burning cigarette? Was there a picture of her in his billfold?

Angie sipped her tequila. It was smooth, smoky, reminded her vaguely of bandages. She heard the shower running. Well, good.

"Don't forget to shave!" she shouted.

Glenda reminded Angie that she liked the smell of soap on men.

But her dominant tequila persona, whom Angie decided to call Lanie, reminded her that soap did not wash away herpes simplex.

Carrollton emerged from the bathroom in a royal-blue bathrobe, a tiny square of toilet paper with a crimson dot in the center stuck to his chin. He handed Angie a forest-green but otherwise identical robe.

"You've found the towels, I see."

"Yeah."

"Want to shower?"

"Maybe later."

"After?"

"After what?"

"After *what*? What are we doing here?"

Angie didn't think she could explain about Glenda and Lanie, that she was essentially two people at the moment, two angry mothers throwing flint at each other across a pencil-thin DMZ.

She swigged her tequila, stood up unsteadily, and put the robe on over her clothes.

"What are you doing, Angie?"

"I'm drunk and filled with mixed emotions, Carrollton. I just simply cannot make a decision about life at this moment."

"Can I be direct?"

"Get to the point whichever way you want."

"More tequila?"

"No. Okay. A little."

He poured another double. He offered it to her, but when she reached for it, he pulled it slowly out of her range. Angie, her arm outstretched, groped for the drink. Carrollton led her into the bedroom, Angie snatching at the tequila like a carrot on the stick. In the middle of the unmade bed—a queen—was a copy of Whit Masterson's *Badge of Evil*. Carrollton placed the tumbler on the book. Glenda and Lanie stood at the edge of the bed and threw smithereens at each other. Glenda struck Lanie in the forehead with a sliver of obsidian and took her out; Angie climbed on the mattress and grabbed the drink. She lay back against a hard, pillowcase-less pillow, crossed her legs, and sipped.

"Well done," she said.

"Thank you."

Carrollton climbed onto the bed. He reached over and pulled on her sash. He opened her robe, exposing her black dress, dirty from the roadhouse parking lot. Lanie came to. Angie covered herself back up again. Carrollton sighed and fell back against his own pillow, a sage corduroy comfort cushion with arms.

"Jesus."

"I'm sorry," said Angie. "Try to put yourself in my position. In fact, hell, I'm *not* sorry."

"You're in bed with a nice guy who's ready to make you feel good. That's as vicarious as I can get, Angie. I know you've suffered, I know what today is, but can't you allow yourself to forget it all for a few hours? Isn't that why you're here now?"

"What?"

"What what?"

"Forget what?"

Angie peered into the tumbler of tequila. She tried to hold it still so the surface of the liquid held steady, glassy, and she could see her reflection. The person there, distorted by the meniscus climbing the walls of the tumbler, could not remember what it was she was supposed to be here to forget. She recalled a thick, endless Joseph Heller novel she had read years ago called *Something Happened*. She remembered nothing about the book but its title. She knew there was a reason it was coming back to her now, that fat, almost unfinishable paperback with an orange cover. Something happened.

"I think I'm going to vomit."

"Let's get you into the bathroom."

Carrollton efficiently shuttled Angie to the toilet and let her be. Three hours of commode worship followed. He brought her a blanket and pillow. Sometime in the late afternoon she emerged, sober, hungry, thirsty, Lanie and Glenda gone, reposado and mayonnaise-jar house tequila metabolized, her head like a microwaved gourd.

With the suddenness of a truck wreck, Angie remembered what she had been with Carrollton that day to forget.

"How many Advils would you like?"

"Sixteen. I'm sorry I didn't fuck you, Carrollton. Wait. Did I?"

"No. That's all right. I don't really blame you."

"Maybe someday."

Carrollton slapped the end of his robe sash against his thigh.

"Do you feel like I was trying to take advantage of you?"

"No, you were just being a man."

"I'm truly sorry for what happened to you."

"Nothing happened to me," said Angie. "It wasn't me that something happened to."

"All right."

"Let's go. Try not to go over any speed bumps."

"You're not going back to Dean Lee."

She was. There was, after all, nowhere else to go. She was estranged from her mother, now worse than ever. She had no close friends. Lolly was owed money still. Even if she did have somewhere to go, she couldn't leave without Nadine. And the truth was, she loved her husband.

That she had also forgotten to stop at Dotteridge to buy playing cards for Sophie to shuffle in heaven was just a little too much.

Carrollton dropped her at home. Night. Angie, the fatalist, began to attenuate. As far as she was concerned, the sun and moon were gone for good, the sky would forever be spinel-black. Her fingers itched for the hack of a sickle. Her side of the bed, a tempest of sheets and fear-sweat, the floor around it a sierra of trash and the pins of the grenades she armed in her head. She imagined placing a glass against a wall, listening for the escape hatches long ago lost among the jacks of slap-jack and little fistfuls of chocolate-colored pennies and other peelings of childhood. When, my God, oh when, would the mouth of evening open, when would the switches be thrown, when would traffic ravel with birdsong and the moon again rub its muzzle along the brushy tops of the sycamores? Through her bedroom window Angie counted satellites bisecting the backyard sky. Her madding interior stage-whispered like acetylene torches.

This was just the beginning.

# CHAPTER SIX

# A Sea of Chifforobes

TO HER KNOWLEDGE, DEAN Lee had only ever window-shopped other women, never going into a store, but now he began actively, if idly, philandering. He didn't brag about his activities, but he didn't necessarily hide them either, leaving matchbooks around with phone numbers written inside, coming home smelling like he'd been in a stranger's house, not coming home at all. Angie did nothing about it, almost welcoming the new household ways. She would never leave him, and there was nowhere to go in any case—her old garage apartment was rented out, there was no room at her mother's, who Angie was certain would not welcome them anyway. And Angie had not a dime to her name. She imagined staying with Carrollton, but thinking for even a few seconds of the details and logistics of *that* made her almost ill. She—they—needed Dean Lee. For one thing, it was the health insurance through his job at Nelson Kallendorf's bottling plant that provided the care Nadine increasingly needed.

It was also around this time that Dean Lee stopped reading. Angie was unsure if this was connected to Sophie or the philandering or some unknown factor, but it caused in her a steep and pressing grief. Not seeing her husband with a cheap Spanish paperback jammed in his back pocket or sunning on the dash of his pickup was a negation she felt she could hardly tolerate.

One night, Angie got her laptop and began researching "Important Spanish Literature" while sitting in front of Dean Lee's bookcase in the den. It was an hour before she found a promising author she was pretty sure he hadn't read: Vicente Huidobro, a Chilean avant-garde poet of the '20s and '30s. She bought an edition of his selected works online, and when it came, she wrapped it and gave it to her husband at dinner.

"I read Huidobro to Aintzane when I was a boy," he said, putting the book down, pushing away his empty bowl of chili, and opening a can of Pearl. "Can't say I cared much for his style."

"Are there any books you need? I'll get you whatever you want."

"Nope."

Angie was witnessing a cadaver of Dean Lee, at least as seen through a certain lens. A lifeless body she could no longer love as an intellect, as narrowly defined as it was. She went into the bathroom to cry and clench, and when she came back, the book was gone. Later she investigated his bookcase, the trash, the dumpster in the alley, but Vicente Huidobro was nowhere to be found. That night she dreamt Dean Lee had eaten it between two slices of sourdough bread with mustard and a wheel of tomato the size of a 45-rpm record—all in one bite, his mouth opening like the hinged jaws of a mako.

The last time they'd had sex had been two days before Sophie's death, memorable only because of an electrical storm which cut the power while Dean Lee was busy climaxing. She had zero desire to ever touch her husband intimately again; the thought of even brushing up against him in the corridors of the house gave her profound discomfort. The memory of his hands on her breasts, his tongue in her mouth, his penis inside her caused a kind of choking, vagal nausea to rush up her pipes.

During this period, Angie was largely without allies. She found therapists condescending, distant, and too expensive. She had no close friends, with the exception of Darcy Violette, the mother of one of Sophie's daycare mates. Darcy was a well-known collagist and fiber artist, and moreover could chatter endlessly about nothing, which comforted Angie, who, in general, had very little to say. Even the shadowy and unshorn Dean Lee, with his gun and beer, couldn't shut Darcy up. She would bring her big hatbox of collage imagery and glue sticks and Bristol board, and that—along with her millions of stories about her inadequate boyfriends, shitbox cars, and the inequities of the low end of the art world—was all she needed to entertain Angie, and sometimes even Nadine, who would silently, idly collage at the dining room table with her mother and Darcy, for many hours at a stretch.

As Nadine Grandet slowly fragmented and found herself more and more under the care of doctors and psychiatrists, her collages grew bizarre. One featured a chimera of animal bodies with heads of machines. Another was red and black cubes. Yet another only teeth, hundreds and hundreds of teeth, carefully snipped out of magazines and pasted down in a cascade. One of her last was simply a series of slits in the Bristol board into which she inserted images of pistols, large and small.

Darcy exclaimed over these collages and wanted to exhibit them somewhere; Angie waffled, not wanting to compromise Nadine's privacy; and Nadine didn't care one way or another. Finally, Angie relented, and Darcy, at her own expense, had ten of Nadine's collages varnished and framed, and shopped them around the coffeeshop galleries of Austin, eventually getting Flightpath Coffeehouse on Duval to exhibit them for two months. The prices Darcy assigned initially kept them from selling, but they got the attention of the *Austin Chronicle*, which wrote a story about Nadine and her art, and before long, every piece had sold, and Nadine had her own money, an old-fashioned passbook savings account with $3,300 in it. Nadine's success—and the money—left her unmoved. Angie's beautiful, damaged daughter was slowly supernovaing before her eyes, every brilliant neutrino of her tumbling irreversibly through space and time. There was no holding her together. No universal embrace arrested this kind of burst. Angie felt she was watching her daughter die.

One year after Sophie's death, during a visit from Darcy, a great hailstorm unshingled the roof of the house on Fawn Street. It also disintegrated Dean Lee's lawn chair, cracked several windows, and comically pockmarked the pickup. Nadine, who was radically medicated, was not bothered by the terrific racket, but Dean Lee spent the deluge crouched on his knees, rocking back and forth in the middle of the den floor with his hands over his ears, clench-screaming, *"Goddammit! Goddammit!"* When it was over, they went outside to behold branches and power lines and bits and pieces of the neighborhood half-buried in three inches of dirty, misshapen hailstones as big as racquetballs, which took a day to melt. Darcy couldn't leave immediately, so she stayed the night.

That evening, Angie and Darcy sat at the kitchen table and painted each other's nails. Darcy told Angie about a local artist she'd heard about.

"You have to go see. Trust me."

The next morning, after Darcy went home, Angie drove to the Collectors' Showroom, a large, tin-roofed warehouse on US 331 just south of McCandless that she'd driven past a thousand times and never gone into. Inside, there were dozens of booths containing curios, books, antiques, and art, but the proprietors were not present. If one wanted to purchase something, one had to go to an older woman who guarded a cash register by the entrance, give her the booth and item number, and wait for her to fetch it and ring it up.

The building smelled faintly of acetone. Angie wandered the catacomb of unmanned booths, pausing to examine a Tiffany brooch in a glass case, a highboy decorated with an exquisite intarsia of jungle animals, a row of worthless, ineptly produced Oz reprints, and an old pewter bell, two hundred pounds at least.

The odor of acetone grew stronger. Angie climbed a footstool and looked around. She appeared to be the only customer in the building. In a far corner of the gloamy place, a brighter light shone, but she couldn't see what was there because the sea of dressers and chifforobes blocked her view.

Angie climbed down and headed toward the corner. When she arrived, she found a woman sitting at a desk illuminated by the pale yellowish light of two matching antique floor lamps. She was painting something—Angie couldn't see what—on a small, desktop easel. Across the desk sat another woman, facing the painter, unmoving. They didn't seem to notice Angie, who stood just a few feet away, frozen, not wanting to interrupt. It appeared that the woman was painting on a dessert-size paper plate with a tiny brush. Before her sat dozens of little bottles with tall, white lids. Fingernail polish. To the artist's left was a roll of Bounty, a plastic palette, a can of industrial acetone, a small beaker of cloudy liquid, and a cracked glass jar holding charcoal pencils.

Ten minutes later the artist turned the easel around so the customer could see the paper-plate portrait. Angie got a good look. The multidimensional movement the artist had imparted into the painting was astonishing, with its glazed shadows, subtle impasto highlights, draughtsman-like detail, and harmonious if somewhat otherworldly palette.

"This is exquisite," said the model, a look of childlike awe on her pretty, top-lit face.

"Don't touch it for twenty-four hours," said the artist.

"What do I owe you?"

"One fifty."

"Credit okay?"

"Cash, sorry."

"Check?"

"Local?"

"Yes."

"Okay. Pay the lady up front."

The customer left, staring at the painting, nearly walking into a mahogany side table covered in dust.

Angie stepped out of the shadows, startling the artist. She looked to be about thirty-five. She wore an apron over a light, flower-print dress, its sleeves rolled up to her cable-like biceps. Her face was slack at the jawline but taut at the forehead and temples. In the low light, she looked like a Walker Evans photograph.

"Sorry," said Angie. "I didn't know you didn't know I was there. Do you have time to do another portrait?"

She nodded. Angie sat.

"I've only got a check, like the other woman," said Angie, wiggling her bottom on the metal folding chair, trying to find a comfortable position. "I live less than a mile from here."

"That'll be fine."

Angie sat perfectly still. An hour passed. She should be at home. She should already have gone to the grocery store. She should be with Nadine.

Finally, the artist turned the easel around. Angie was again dumbstruck. It was an exact likeness, except she was beautiful. She had never been beautiful before—at least she never thought she was.

"Do you have a card?" said Angie.

"No," she said, screwing lids on nail polish bottles.

"Do you know where I can get a circular frame?"

"Maybe try Jerry's Artarama in Austin."

"What's your name?"

"Shea Babb."

"I'm Angie Grandet. You're incredible."

"Thanks."

"I wonder if I could ask a favor of you."

"What."

"My daughter, she's seven and doesn't like to leave the house. Could I hire you to bring your supplies and come over and paint her portrait? She's not well and I think she'd really like it."

"I don't—"

"I could pay you extra. How about $300?"

"All right."

Shea Babb did not seem to be used to talking, or getting attention. She leaned back in her chair, the kind of body language that expressed fear or uncertainty. Dean Lee would have called it a tell.

"And one more thing. Can you paint from a photo?"

"Sure."

Angie produced a small photo-booth image of Sophie from her purse.

"This is my other daughter. She can't be here either."

Shea set to work. In an hour, she was finished.

"Don't touch either one for twenty-four hours. When would you like me to come to your house?"

"This Saturday, around noon?"

"Okay. Pay the lady up front, and leave your address and phone number with her."

On Saturday Shea Babb showed up on Fawn Street with two plastic toolboxes and a card table. Dean Lee was sitting in the yard in his new lawn chair, but Angie was watching for Shea and met her at the end of the driveway so that Dean Lee, with his stormy countenance and shoulder piece, wouldn't scare her off.

"Who's this?" he said, opening a Pearl.

"This is Shea Babb. She's an artist and she's going to paint Nadine today."

"Who's paying for that?"

"I am, Dean Lee."

Nadine's mounting medical bills had forced Angie to find a job. She had always wanted to work in a bookstore, and so had found full-time work at BookPeople in Austin, twenty-five minutes away. The pay was only minimum wage, but they were generous with overtime. She worked evenings and weekends, so Dean Lee took care of Nadine, and when they were both working, a neighbor girl, Bonnie, thirteen, would come and babysit for next to nothing. Over the months, Angie had saved a few dollars.

"Come in, Shea."

Nadine lay on the couch in front of the TV, under a blanket, holding a stuffed leopard. John Deere was curled up on top of her head. Both cat and child were asleep.

Shea whispered, "Do you want me to paint them just like that?"

"Okay," said Angie.

Shea unpacked and set up as quietly as possible. The perfume of acetone began to waft through the house. Shea did a rapid preliminary drawing in charcoal and began a thin underpainting. Then she started in with thicker passages, painting with a brush and palette knife. Angie watched. She realized she was holding her breath. It was going to be a living, signal portrait.

When she was almost finished, Dean Lee came in.

"What is that *smell?*" he said, waking up Nadine and startling John Deere. Nadine sat up and started to cry.

"Goddammit, Dean Lee," said Angie.

"What?"

"Nadine, can you go back to sleep, honey?"

"I can't finish. It won't be the same," said Shea, gesturing at the eyeless portrait.

"No!" said Nadine.

"Let's start again," said Angie, desperate. "Nadine, can you sit still for Shea, sweetie? She wants to paint you."

Nadine slowly climbed off the couch and ran off with her leopard.

"That's unusual," said Dean Lee, leaning over and pointing at Shea's unfinished portrait. "Is that a paper plate?"

"I'm sorry," said Angie. "Maybe another time. Can I keep what you did?"

"Yeah, though I don't know why you'd want it."

"I just do."

"I have to charge you the full amount."

"That's fine."

Shea began to pack her belongings.

Angie did not often feel like she might cry, but she felt that way now. She wanted to kill Dean Lee, even though he hadn't really done anything wrong. It wasn't the first time she'd wanted to kill him, to really make him hurt for everything he'd done and not done.

# PART II

CHAPTER SEVEN

# Meringue

IT WAS AT THE nadir of the Grandet marriage, four years later, that someone from Angie's past reappeared in her life.

Angie lately had been spending her valuable alone time out on the porch watching videos of people doing things with each other that her husband no longer wanted to do with her.

True pornography grossed her out; all that writhing corporeal overperfection made her feel bad about her own body—her inflating saddlebags, drooping belly, and sagging breasts—so she watched films of the lesser intimacies absent from their marriage. Hugging, spooning, holding hands. Couples asleep in the same bed. Kissing.

Angie lay on the old couch on the porch, her ancient laptop open on her sternum, the screen eight inches from her face, watching muted, full-screen videos of kisses—not the movie-star, soldiers-home-from-war, awkward-first-date kisses that are the products of romance and embrace, but breathless, close-up theater of coiling tongues and gnawed lips and jaws distended by need—*those* sorts of kisses—when she was startled by the clangor of the landline.

Angie usually ignored the phone—she did not like to talk to people, since she felt she had few social skills and always said something foolish or ill-informed or unintentionally rude, or else made hasty, regrettable promises. But today she was expecting to hear from one of Nadine's doctors, so she paused the video—a short clip of a young man and an older woman lying on a long kidskin couch in identical wife-beaters, chewing on each other in famished haste—and went into the house.

It was not a number Angie recognized. She picked it up anyway.

"Um, Angie?"

"Yes?"

"This is someone from long ago. Please don't hang up. Do you remember me? Harper DeBaecque, actually DeBaecque hyphen Miller. Sorry I didn't just write to you on Facebook or whatever, but I couldn't find your account. Can you talk for a minute?"

"Uh... who is this again?" said Angie, wishing fervently that she hadn't answered. This was exactly the kind of call her policy of ignoring the phone was meant to circumvent, and this unknown Harvard Dubuque was exactly the type of person she wanted to avoid by having precisely zero web presence.

"Harper DeBaecque?" said the woman, who sounded panicky, like she needed to finish the call before someone caught her in the middle of it.

"I'm sorry—"

"High school, junior year. Nick Freed?"

*Oh. Wait a minute.*

Harper. Angie remembered.

They had met at the end of the first quarter of eleventh grade. Harper was a little different—she loved the 1940s and wore the bold, matte makeup of the time, styled her long, wavy reddish-brown hair in complicated '40s dos, wore period dresses she made herself, and could even talk like the day's screen stars. Angie had admired her. Angie had wanted to be like her, but not to copy her, and had tried to find her own style—1950s, hardcore punk, preppie, *something*—but nothing really stuck. Harper seemed to live the '40s wholly, her mind and body vested with the decade. She knew its movies, its writers, its battles, its dramatis personae, its flavors and fashion.

When they weren't scheming for a motif Angie could inhabit, they talked a lot about boys, especially Nick Freed. The memory of him came back to Angie now like a shark in warm, shallow waters.

"Oh! Harper. How are you? It's nice to hear from you, after, what, a dozen years?"

"Sixteen," Harper said, her voice quavering. "Look. Angie. I know this is out of the blue. But do you remember we were behind the school that time, on that hill where all the druggies used to go to get stoned? It was a few days after New Year's and so cold even the stoners stayed away, and you were crying really hard about Nick, how he used to sit next to you in social studies but earlier that day had gotten up and moved to the back corner of the room, as far away as he could get, remember?"

"No," said Angie, although she did.

"Well, I helped you through that day. You slept over at my house, even though it was a school night, and you told me how much better I made you feel about Nick, and that if I ever had boy problems, I could come to you, and you promised you'd be there for me."

Angie did not remember this.

"It was a solemn promise," said Harper.

"Because you helped me."

"Yes."

"Uh…" said Angie, angry at herself in advance for not being able to refrain from asking: "What can I do?"

"Well," said Harper, who sounded like she might cry, "I caught my husband in bed with another woman."

"God, I'm sorry."

Angie regretted taking this call with even greater fervor than she had thirty seconds earlier.

"Not in bed. They were fucking each other on the dining room table. In my own house."

A memory flared of Jessica Lange and Jack Nicholson in a groping, starved embrace on a kitchen table in *The Postman Always Rings Twice*. The succulent violence of that scene had shocked and titillated Angie, and afterward she tried to have sex with Dean Lee on their coffee table, but it hurt his knees and her back and they gave up before they ever really got started. Later, Lolly confiscated that coffee table, and she was frankly happy to see it go.

"When—"

Harper unloaded a cry of oceanic depth. Angie waited.

"Harper?"

"About forty-five minutes ago."

"You—you caught your husband *forty-five minutes ago?*"

"Yeah."

The front door opened: Dean Lee.

"Angie?" he said, walking into the kitchen.

"Angie?" said Harper. "Are you married? Is your husband there? Or boyfriend? Who is that talking?"

"Who are you talking to?" said Dean Lee, walking out onto the porch.

Angie responded to neither Harper nor Dean Lee. "I'm at the

airport," said Harper. "My flight, American—I'm in Denver—lands in Austin at 5:10 your time. Will you pick me up?"

"Angie?" said Dean Lee.

"Harper, Jesus, I—this is weird, look, I—"

"I need you now, Angie. Remember? You promised."

"Who's Harper?"

"Dean Lee, just a minute."

"Angie?"

"God almighty, what are you watching?" said Dean Lee, picking up Angie's laptop, where it was paused on the kissing video. He unpaused it and watched. "Jesus Christ, that's almost like porn."

"Dean Lee, you meddlesome son of a bitch. Put that down."

"Angie?" said Harper. "I won't be in the way. Just a few days? Please?"

"Harper, I'll be at the airport."

"Oh, thank you. Thank you, Angie."

"Who's Harper?" said Dean Lee, holding the laptop, trying to bring motion back to the picture.

"High school friend in need."

"She gonna stay with us?"

"Yes. Put that down."

Angie could sense Dean Lee's next question: *What's she look like?* but he did not ask it.


Harper DeBaecque in fact proved to look much the same, even more so, if that was at all possible. Her hair was styled like Veronica Lake's, a long lavender gown flowed off her like water in an infinitely pool, a matching hat brought out her extraordinary lashes. Leopard clutch, lavender patent slingback heels, and, incredibly, a fox stole. She had been crying and her makeup was running. She was getting no little attention in the baggage claim area. No fewer than ten people had secretly—and some not so secretly—snapped photos of her.

"Harper, I don't know what to say," Angie said, hugging her old friend. Her body felt the same in her arms as it had a decade and a half before. "You are a vision."

"And you are an angel. I need to fix my face. I need my bag, though. It's old."

"Like that?"

Angie pointed to a magnificently bestickered calfskin vellum valise wedged between two giant, black hardshell suitcases moving past them on the carousel. Harper dove for it, plucked it out, and headed for the bathroom.

"Back in a sec," she called over her shoulder.

Angie watched her old friend balance perfectly on her precarious shoes. She returned in ten minutes, her face flawlessly contoured.

"How do you do that?"

"I am a kind of machine, Angie, but not in a good way. Can you take me somewhere that has caffeine and pork on the menu?"

At the Frisco, a waiter brought them ice waters and menus.

"I'll also need carbs and dairy," said Harper.

"You can have that here."

"Denver," said Harper. "Christ. I'm so glad to be out of that nosebleed hell, I almost feel normal. I feel like I've awakened from a nightmare."

"Not to ruin the good feeling," said Angie, stirring the ice cubes in her water with her fingertip, "but it was no nightmare, it was—is—real. Your husband is cheating on you."

"That feels a million miles away, and I don't care. All I care about is overcooked bacon, cold-water biscuits, and truck-stop 'coffee.' And Austin. And you, my good friend Angie. Tell me about you."

"Oh, no. You don't wanna know."

"Sure I do."

Angie sucked on her ice-cold finger.

"Really."

"Yeah."

"Well then, I'll tell you. My husband is cheating, regularly, like it's a job he goes to, one of my daughters is dead, the other is an emotional wreck. I'm broke, friendless, angry, and stuck in a marriage I'm afraid to leave because I don't want to be alone and don't want my daughter to have divorced parents, and besides, I need my husband's insurance for my daughter's health care. My teeth hurt and I can't afford to go to the dentist. I'm on bad terms with my mother because she hates my husband, me, and her granddaughter, and I think she blames all three of us for my other daughter's death, but I don't know because I haven't seen her in years and years. My husband can't decide if he's angrier at his daughter or himself or me for Sophie's death. Are our fifty minutes up? Do you take Blue Cross Blue Shield?"

Harper stared.

"Harper."

"Yes. Yes. I'm listening."

Angie realized she had never issued a summation of her state in life. It felt good. She was out of breath from talking so fast.

"I left something out, Harper. A detail that makes it worse, worse, worse."

Scarcely taking her eyes off her friend, Harper constructed a bacon, egg, and toast sandwich, shook out a puddle of Tabasco onto the plate, dipped a corner of her sandwich in the crimson sauce, and took a careful bite, somehow managing not to distress the perfection of her lipstick.

"Go on," she said, taking another Tabasco-y sandwich bite.

"I don't think you know what you're getting yourself into, coming to Austin to spend time with the Grandet family."

Harper was silent.

"We are disintegrating," said Angie. "We were a unit of four. Now we are three. Three fragmentation grenades, each of us with hands on the pins of the others. There is no answer for us but a loud, gory burst, an inevitable collision of despair."

"What are you not telling me?"

Angie thought hard about how to summarize the essential meeting of fact and circumstance. She drank down the last of her coffee, started in on her water. She crunched up an ice cube, and another.

"While I was asleep," said Angie, tracing a circle of condensation on the table with her straw wrapper, "my six-year-old daughter, Nadine, killed her four-year-old sister, Sophie, with her father's gun."

"*Angie.*"

"I am trying to keep what is left of us together. But we will fly apart, all of us, one day. And it will be my fault."

The waiter appeared, topped off the coffees, and asked if there was anything else they could use. He spoke to Harper, not to Angie.

"Another side of bacon and a slice of lemon meringue," said Harper, shooing the waiter away with a look.

And like that, the moment was gone.

"Harper, you look absolutely stunning. My husband is a hound dog. His tastes run to strippers and rat-rod models in general, but you're still going to have quite an effect on him. Are you wearing a corset or is your waist really that narrow?"

Angie sometimes saw something out of the corner of her eye, some-thing in motion, a wraith. It was closer to a feeling than a sighting, and she was see-feeling it now. She glanced to her left. Nothing.

"God, no. I've been corset-training for years. Twenty-two inches. I'm wearing a little underbust right now that I made myself. My insides are all bottlenecked. My liver is up between my lungs, I'm sure, and my heart is in my throat. Look, I don't want to cause problems with your husband, your family. Maybe I should stay in a hotel."

"No, stay with us. I want you to meet Nadine, too. When you first called, I was honestly dreading your visit. Not because it was you, but because it was a visitation from an unknown. But over the last few hours… well. How long can you stay?"

Angie truly thought she would like Harper to move in and stay forever. To be her sister, Nadine's aunt. Angie experienced a moment when she thought that Harper just might be the gravitational glue her fragmenting family needed.

"I don't know," said Harper, dividing her lemon meringue down the middle with a spoon and giving half to Angie on a napkin. "I don't want to go back at all. I left with what I was wearing, and I always have a suitcase packed—I just grabbed it, walked to the hardware store down the street, called a cab. All I could think about on the way to the airport was that woman on her back, her legs in the air, thigh-high rainbow socks, yellow patent-leather Mary Janes, and from that angle all I could see was the top of her pink wig with little-girl barrettes in it. No idea who she was, maybe a hooker. Who dresses like that? Couldn't tell how old she was, fifteen or fifty, I don't know. Ken has never cheated on me in the six years that we've been married, that I know of. Now this, so flagrant—I was supposed to be out all afternoon wine-tasting with a friend, but business interceded and my friend had to cancel, so she dropped me back off at home and surprise, there's Ken and that absurd sex doll with one hand in Ken's mouth and the other squeezing his nipple, both of them pumping away, my mother's dining room table rocking on its seventy-year-old legs. I wonder if it collapsed after I left—part of me hopes not, for the sake of my mother's memory, but part of me prays it splintered and crashed to the floor and broke both their bloody fucking necks and they're there right now, forever coupled, forever paralyzed, unable to summon help, doomed to scream until their voices give out, the true beast with two backs, starving on the dining room floor, gnawing on each other's faces for sustenance—"

"*Harper.*"

"Oh. Sorry. Was I talking out loud?"

"That was ferocious. You all right?"

"Yeah," said Harper, examining her teeth in the reflection of a butter knife. "I thought…"

"What?"

"Never mind. So your husband cheats on you, too?"

"Yeah. Cocktail waitresses and that sort. I don't really know how he finds them. He doesn't use the internet."

"Jesus, Angie. That's not okay."

"Nothing's okay, but it has to be."

Angie did not often think about her husband and his history. It was not okay, yet it did have to be. She would explain it all to Harper in good time, the new algebra that Sophie's death had forced upon their family. Angie had nearly failed her first test, on the day of the funeral.

"God, Harper, I just remembered something."

Harper looked at Angie like nothing could surprise her, though there was a trace of hostility in the hollows of her cheeks. Angie remembered that Harper had been that way in high school, too.

"I nearly slept with your old boyfriend. Carrollton DeGolyer."

Harper stared at Angie, hard, unblinking, for a long minute.

Angie looked down to cut off the burn of the stare, and told Harper the story of Sophie's funeral, Carrollton, Bain's Roadhouse, the tequila and cartwheels, the almost-sex, the nausea, going home.

"Well," said Harper, unreadable. "I liked Carrollton. Quite a bit. For quite a while there."

"I'm sorry."

"It's all right. You really didn't sleep with him?"

"I really didn't." Angie held her stare this time. Harper finally smiled.

"So," she said, in the manner of a TV interviewer intent on changing the subject. "Dean Lee, right?"

"Yeah."

"I'm going to shun him."

"No, just be civil and polite," said Angie, eating the meringue slice with her fingers. "Pretend you don't know anything about him. I'll tell you why: I want my Nadine to really love you. And if she sees you being kind to her father, who she loves and adores, then she'll love you. So pretend. For me."

"I'll do my best," said Harper, with a tension in her forehead that suggested she hadn't forgotten the Carrollton business. "Won't be easy, though. How old's Nadine?"

"Eleven. She's not stable."

"My lord, Angie, I just—"

"It's okay. Nadine just got out of a psychiatric hospital in Austin a few months ago. She's very delicate right now, medicated, angry, not sleeping well. I'm glad it's summer so at least we don't have to worry about school."

"What does she like?"

Angie smiled at Harper, leaned across the table, and gazed into her eyes.

"That's easy, Harper: makeup."

"Well, hell. We ought to have a lot to talk about."

"She also likes art. Collage and drawing."

"I'll take her to the co-op and get her some art supplies."

"Harper—"

"By the way, I intend to pay my way while I'm here—you will not spend a cent on me. I have plenty of money. All right?"

"That's good," said Angie, smiling at the waiter, communicating a need for more coffee. "Because I frankly just don't have it to spend."

"Then let me do some treating, starting with this meal."

"Thank you."

Angie wouldn't have been surprised if Dean Lee's eyes popped out of his head and his tongue lolled on his chest, a lust-stricken wolf suddenly in the demesne of a she-wolf, like in a Hanna-Barbera cartoon. In fact, Dean Lee did not look at Harper DeBaecque at all, but he did stick his finger in his collar and wipe his brow with the back of his hand.

"Uh, Harper," said Dean Lee, clearly affected. "Wanna Pearl? It's a beer, a Texas brand of br—"

"I know that. I grew up in Chamberlain, Dean Lee. And yes, I will take a Pearl, thank you."

"Chamberlain girls are so polite. You and Angie here, all please and thank you. One Pearl, coming right up. Well, two. I'll have one with you. Angie, a Pearl?"

"No thank you, Dean Lee." Angie did not mind this new side of Dean Lee, this cautious and slightly fearful side.

"And where's Nadine?"

"In her room," said Angie. "I'll go fetch her in a little bit."

Angie and Harper stood in the den while they waited for Dean Lee to return with the beer. In her heels, Harper stood nearly six feet, and the hat added another four inches. Angie studied her friend openly, smiling.

"I didn't appreciate you in high school, Harper. Nobody did. You had such style. There was nobody like you. There is nobody like you."

"I'm not sure if I'm a real person, Angie. I hide behind the identity of a decade. Do you understand what I'm telling you?"

"Yeah, but I don't believe you. I don't think you're just some cipher, some goose egg."

"It ain't that cold," said Dean Lee, coming in from the kitchen, looking upset. In Dean Lee's mind, there were few greater gustatory crimes than the service of a less-than-ice-cold beer. "There must be something wrong with the icebox thermostat."

"That's all right," said Harper, cracking open the beer and taking a long gulp.

"Harper, what is it you do?"

Angie watched Dean Lee studying their painting of gray kittens over the TV, trying not to look at Harper, but clearly dying to. There—he glanced at her shoes, then at her face, then back at the kittens, then down at his own beer for a few seconds, then at her chest for a tenth of a second. Enough.

"Patent attorney."

"Oh. Huh. You must be making boocoo dollars, huh."

"Yep."

Harper took another long pull on her beer, watching Dean Lee.

"I bet you could make even more as a, you know, model, but I bet you've been told that."

"Too old."

Dean Lee clearly took this as permission to glance at Harper, offer an opinion on her viability as a model. He quickly looked away, his face turning red as a cinder.

"Don't look it."

"Mm."

"So y'all were friends in high school? Real good friends?"

"Best friends," said Harper, finishing the beer. "But my family and I moved to another school district in eleventh grade. Can I have another beer?"

Dean Lee smiled. Angie knew what he was thinking: that he sure did appreciate a woman who could put away a beer that fast and demand another one; that he sure would like to watch the Longhorns play OU with this woman; that he would—

Dean Lee disappeared into the kitchen.

"He's a piece of work."

"Told ya."

Angie actually felt a little defensive of Dean Lee at the moment. He was behaving, knocked off his guard by Angie's old friend. A vague thrill crept up through her insides. Angie thought it might be hope.

"He keeps glancing at my mouth like it's a vagina," said Harper, smiling crookedly. She produced a lipstick from somewhere, expertly restored color to the corners, and vanished the tube, all in seconds.

"You do have a highly vaginal mouth, Harper."

"It's this kidney-colored lipstick."

"Mom?"

In the entrance to the hallway stood Nadine in her nightgown, her stuffed leopard in one arm, John Deere in the other. John Deere was one of those sorts of cats that could be held any which way and appear to be perfectly satisfied. When Lolly had taken him and hid him in his Stetson that time, John Deere had simply curled up and gone to sleep. Lolly forgot he was even there, and John Deere forgot about Lolly. John Deere was limp and insensible now to the dynamics in the room.

"Oh, hi sweetie! Honey, this is Harper. She's here visiting from Denver. She's going to stay with us for a while. Say hi, now."

"Hi."

"Hello, Nadine, how are you?"

"Fine."

"I hear you're a really good artist."

"Yeah."

"Will you show me your drawings sometime? Your collages?"

Angie loved Harper at that moment. She had remembered.

"Nadine, what you think of our Harper here," said Dean Lee, handing Harper a beer.

Nadine turned and ran out of the room with her felines.

"So Harper, what you doing here?" said Dean Lee.

"I caught my husband cheating. This is kind of an escape. Know what I mean?"

"I guess."

"Really? Ever cheated on your Angie?"

"Harper!"

"I'll plead the fifth here."

Dean Lee took a seat on his old, cow-leather couch, put his boots up on the coffee table, and dug around in the cushions till he found the remote.

"That's a yes."

"Don't really matter, Harper. Angie and me don't have sex no more. It ain't cheating unless there's something to cheat on, at least that's how

I see it. I gotta get it someplace. If she wanted to go out and screw some dude, I'd be fine with it. I mean, I'd kill him, but I'd be okay with it."

"I see."

A moment of quiet passed while the TV warmed up, and Angie had a sudden and very palpable fear that Harper was going to mention Carrollton, the near miss. Then, with a rainy fizz, the TV came on. Dean Lee clicked around until he found an Astros game. He turned the sound off and said: "We used to have great sex, me and Angie, screwing like angora rabbits on crystal for our first couple years together, then it all went south."

"That happens in every relationship, Dean Lee. What makes you so special?"

"Well," said Dean Lee, crossing his arms under his gun, "I guess Angie ain't told you everything, huh."

"Dean Lee, don't you misbehave in front of my friend, so help me God. And yes, she knows everything."

"She asked, Angie."

"All right," said Harper, her hands on her hips.

Angie noticed she was standing in exactly the spot Nadine had been when Dean Lee found her with his gun, where Angie had found both of them, at first not noticing Sophie lying on the floor like a broken doll.

"I'm sorry," said Harper, "but it's still cheating. You're in a marriage, a holy matrimony, where you swore before God that you would do no such thing. You can't go sticking your dick in every warm, wet hole that comes bobbing across your periscope."

The Astros were losing 19-2 to the Cards. Angie felt bad for Dean Lee. He loved his Astros.

"Harper, I'm sure you're a nice person, but I don't appreciate the lecture," said Dean Lee, his eyes closed, a smile playing on his face.

Angie knew that when her husband began to smile, he was fixing to get in a fistfight, or shoplift, or get arrested. "I've confessed to Angie every time I've done it, and she forgives me, or she says she does. In fact, and you may find this hard to believe, she seems to like to hear about my conquests."

Harper tilted her head and arched an eyebrow so high it nearly disappeared into her hairline.

"I do find that hard to believe. Angie?"

There was in fact a part of Angie that found Dean Lee's confessions of his exploits titillating and felt the vicarious fireworks of his sexual roguery deeply enough to satisfy an erotic vacancy of her own, at least for a while. But Angie was no fool—she did not confuse this satisfaction with forgiveness. Or did she? Had she forgiven Dean Lee? For the gun, Sophie, Nadine's troubles, her own? His escapades were not forgivable, but they were tolerable, to be dealt with for the sake of Nadine. On the other hand, she did realize that the man was a sex addict. She hadn't recognized this when they were monogamous, before the sky fell; Angie simply thought he loved her so deeply that he could never get enough. Pathologizing his behavior now allowed for a measure of tolerance in Angie. She was certain that he was a sex addict, and much of the balance of peace in what remained of their relationship depended on his being one. Curious about the nature of the addiction, Angie had watched a harrowing documentary called *Jeremy Plus One Thousand*, which followed an Oakland man on his daily, obsessive "hunts" for sex. Dean Lee wasn't nearly as bad as Jeremy, but he shared some traits with the man, the most disturbing of which was the same bird-dog look in the eyes. Jeremy also bore a resemblance to Dean Lee—they had similar teeth, a like gait, and the same nose. As far as she knew, Dean Lee did not harbor Jeremy's goal of sleeping with a thousand different women in a year, but probably would have sex with as many as he could catch. Which likely wasn't that many—Dean Lee was, at heart, lazy. The kind of hunter who falls asleep in the deer blind.

More than a month before the arrival of Harper DeBaecque, Dean Lee had just made his latest confession: he had gone to an auto show in Austin, the sort with rat rods and lowriders and psychobilly bands, and through the combined charms of his ostrich skin boots, exceptional tattoo, good looks, blued open-carry .357, and fearless, aggressive need for sex, managed to advert the attentions of the winner of the pinup-girl competition that day, one Doris Peignot, though it took him two days to get her into the San Jose Motel on South Congress, where they spent four solid days, Dean Lee calling home every so often saying he was in jail in Bexar County on a gambling charge and not to worry about him—he'd just let the sentence run itself out and be home in short order. Angie didn't buy it, she knew something was up, but she allowed the charade to play out. To his minor credit, Dean Lee had a guilty streak running through him like a vein of pyrite, and it activated whenever his transgression had run its course—in Doris's case, when she went back to her boyfriend, Canute, a champion axe-throwing lumberjack—and Dean Lee made his confession to Angie.

Angie had googled Doris, and Canute, and found nothing. A part of Angie wondered if Dean Lee was inventing his trysts, but she honestly didn't think he had that in him, and *why* would he do such a thing?

A few days after Doris, Angie attended an after-hours BookPeople party at the big boss Marian's house in French Place. It had been the first social thing she had done in years.

Angie was sitting on a couch with a coworker, Lance Esmerian, listening to Nina Simone and talking about the best steaks they'd ever had, when someone turned out all the lights and yelled, *"Midnight!*

*Kiss the one you're with!*" and Lance, without hesitating, leaned over and gave Angie a kiss—the likes of which she had not experienced since long before Dean Lee, going perhaps as far back as her boyfriend Corning, a world-class smoocher. Angie allowed the kiss to happen, neither returning the ardor nor resisting the urgency. Lance suggested that he was familiar with the architecture of Marian's vast house and knew of a chamber in its far reaches that was private, little used, and equipped with a bed of generous acreage. He stood, took Angie's hand, and gently pulled her to her feet. He put his arm around her shoulder.

"I like you a lot," he said.

"I'm married."

"I know about you. This way."

An orange, chalky gibbous moon provided the only light in the dark hallways. They reached the room. The door was locked.

"Ah, curses," said Lance, in a mellow way.

Any other guy, thought Angie, would've been pretty upset at his chances of getting laid thwarted by a locked door. She had liked Lance ever since he started at BookPeople a few months before, and was liking him more and more every minute.

"We could just get busy on the floor here," he said.

"I don't think I'm ready, Lance."

"That's cool. Let's sit and talk about steak some more."

A few minutes of discussion about what a shell steak was, and then silence. The party raged, far away, in another wing of the house.

"You can kiss me again if you want," said Angie, too loud for the quiet, dark hallway. "But I have to remain passive and not kiss you back. It's the only way I feel like I'm remaining faithful to my husband."

Angie knew on some level this was pungent bullshit, but she bought it herself, at least in the moment.

"I have an idea," said Lance, eyes wide in the low, orange light. "Why don't you lie down on the floor. Pretend like you're asleep. I'll kiss your mouth. You don't have to move or react at all. The most erotic moment of my life was at a sleepover in a tent with my neighbor when we were thirteen. She fell asleep and I kissed her. So we'll both be getting our deepest erotic needs met."

"If I'm asleep and can't stop you," said Angie, a sudden thrill jouncing down her spine, "why stop at kissing?"

"Yesss," said Lance, stroking his chin thoughtfully. "Why stop there?"

Angie raised up her arms and gave Lance a take-it-off-me look. He pulled her sweater off over her head, taking care not to muss her hair. He took his time rolling up the sweater and tucking it behind her head as a pillow as she lay back on the hardwood floor. Lance sang "Rock-A-Bye Baby" all the way through. Angie thought she might actually fall asleep. Lance kissed her gently on the forehead. Then he kissed her nose, cheeks, eyes, chin, apples, lips. He lay next to her, tilted her head to kiss her mouth more deeply, pressed his body into hers. Angie told herself she was asleep, profoundly asleep, helpless, cataleptic. Lance untucked her T-shirt and pulled it up over her bra. *I am not cheating on my husband.* Lance undid the side zipper of her black skirt, then took his time working it over her hips. He pushed her knees apart and buried his face between her legs, breathing hard through the fabric of her panties. *I am not cheating on my husband, though I could cheat on my husband many times and not equal the magnitude of his crimes against me.* Lance pushed her panties aside and tasted her. He reached under the small of her back and pulled her into him. She kept her breathing steady, she fought the tremble, she battled against the moan. The only physiological telltales were her Gatling heartbeat and the unstoppable cataract of lubricant.

She was approaching orgasm, an event, for Angie, always rich in ineluctable groans and shudders. She would either have to push him away or allow him to make her come—either way, the moment the illusion of sleep and passivity burst, she would have cheated. Lance brought her to the brink, and Angie was going to allow it, she was going to come, she was going to cheat, she wanted it desperately, it had been years, she suddenly thought she understood how Dean Lee claimed he felt when he said he needed sex, felt deprived when he couldn't get it from his wife—and then Lance stopped. The sound of a belt being unbuckled, the tearing of plasticized foil, a brief silence, then Lance was on her, his weight, his mouth on hers, his tongue under her tongue, his hands deep in the crooks of her knees, gathering them up by her ears, then his cock at the entrance *I am asleep I cannot help what is happening I am not enjoying myself* and Lance pushed himself in, hard, his full immeasurable length, and there it was, the *yelp*, the tiny irruption, the breach, the wink, the game was over, and Angie had cheated.

Lance didn't notice the instant of the cheat, of course, and Angie pretended to herself that it hadn't happened, and continued to feign sleep while Lance, less gentle, more frantic now, fucked Angie recklessly, pushing her across the floor, against the wall. Within minutes he came, saying Angie's name over and over. Angie began to cry. Lance held her, stroking her hair, not saying anything, until she stopped. They dressed. They walked back through the baby-aspirin hallways holding hands. She let go of his hand when they rejoined the party.

Angie avoided Lance at work. He left sweet notes in her purse that she did not respond to. He called her once at home and Dean Lee answered. Two weeks later, Lance resigned from BookPeople without notice. Angie would never see him again.

Angie never confessed to Dean Lee, and never would. He would have gone berserk, somehow gotten Lance's name out of her, then gone and killed him. Angie considered this, her husband's jealous streak. Dean Lee would kill Carrollton, too, if he knew about that day.

It was a kind of love, murderous jealousy.


"Admit it, Angie, tell Harper you like to hear about when I have sex with other women."

Angie was staring at the wall, at a point about eighteen inches from the floor, where the bullet, which had fragmented while passing through Sophie's body, had found final rest in the cheap drywall. The McCandless police had taken up a collection to pay GoreBGawn, an Austin outfit that scrubbed crime scenes, to clean up the blood and the parts of Sophie swept out of her body by the force of the bullet, but the spackle they had used to patch the holes was faintly darker and cloudier than that of the surrounding drywall. Angie had searched in vain for some pattern, some meaning, a pareidolia in the darker matter, but there was nothing there.

"I'll admit," said Angie, turning away from the wall and speaking as though she were disserting, "that from a purely sexual point of view, I occasionally like to hear about Dean Lee's conquests, but I only ever thought of it as if I was reading *Penthouse Forum* or the like, as titillation. It's just another kind of self-satisfaction. It's as meaningless as the wind."

No one said anything for a moment.

"You sound a little like your mother, Angie."

"What?"

"Nice to have you here, Harper," said Dean Lee, clicking off the hopeless Astros game. "I got a card game to be at."

And Dean Lee got up and left.

\*    \*    \*

Dean Lee had to drive nearly forty miles to get to Squire Actiondale's dealer's choice game in Georgetown. On the way, he thought hard about what he was doing, who he was, where he was headed, the lies he'd told, the truths he'd held back, the blood on his hands.

"Dean Lee Grandet," said Squire, grinning through his black glaucoma spectacles and shaking Dean Lee's hand. "You the first one here. Why, we got beans, meatloaf, chicken-sausage gumbo, collards, buncha pies, more coffee than Mr. Starbuck in Seattle, Washington. Help 'self to a plate, have a seat, and we'll get started in a few. And we got us a new cocktail waitress—she'll be along in short order."

The game slowly filled up. Posey Fremantle and her two Chihuahuas—Lord and Have Mercy—sat all together in the one seat, Craigie Vauxhaul III sat in the eight seat, Trace Boyle from Sweetwater didn't sit down at all, but went immediately to the couch in the living room and fell asleep. Lovey Inge from Dripping Springs bought $10,000 in black chips and sat to the right of Dean Lee, and Crabb DeVorst bought $100 in white chips and installed himself to Dean Lee's left. Dean Lee himself got six hundred in red and told himself he would wait for nothing but strong hands and win all of Lovey's money.

The front door opened quietly and a young woman dressed in what looked like a Halloween French maid costume stepped inside Squire Actiondale's ranch house.

"Hey y'all, sorry I'm late," she said in a panhandle twang, crouching and dropping her purse in the corner next to Squire's greasy shotgun, an instrument he carried when he walked you out to your car after the game. If you left winner, that is. Losers, Squire reasoned, had nothing to lose and so took their chances with hijackers crouched in the bushes.

"Folks," said Squire with not a little proprietary glee, "this is Gwen. She'll be fetching beers and food plates for y'all tonight. She's also a licensed massage therapist, backrubs, uh, what, Gwen?"

"Two dollars a minute," said Gwen, grinning around at the rancorous poker players.

Dean Lee glanced once at Gwen, and looked away. He was not going to be tempted, even though sexy costumes got his attention, and waitresses so attired were especially desirable. He thought of Angie, how she thought he was some mad cheater. Dean Lee had had exactly one affair since... well, ever. He was not certain why he made up stories about trysts with sexy women and related the details to Angie as if they'd actually happened, but it was his habit now, whenever he encountered an attractive woman, to make up a scenario in his head in extraordinary detail, and then tell his wife as though the affair had actually taken place. Dean Lee thought of the avocation as a kind of penance. Angie loathed him for it—in spite of the dimension of titillation she said she experienced—and if Dean Lee deserved anything, it was to be loathed. Lying expertly about extramarital sexcapades was a simple shortcut. He glanced at Gwen.

She would be easy to make up a story about.

Dean Lee was not dealt strong hands. Fourteen in a row without even a face card, let alone an ace. He waited. He developed his story about Gwen in his head. He wrote dialogue for them both, he imagined the sexual act, what they would do to each other, where it would take place, the scents and sounds. He was good at this. In another life, Dean Lee might have been an author or a teller of tales. Maybe he would tell Angie when he got home tonight. Maybe he would tell Harper and Angie together.

Or maybe he would say nothing, save it for a rainy day. Or never.

Eventually Angie would divorce him. Someday Nadine, if she

survived, would understand her daddy, and her displaced love would evaporate. There was no redemption in all this for Dean Lee. It would end, it would all end, for him, in another violent discharge.

Finally, a pair of fucking jacks.

# CHAPTER EIGHT

# Gender Null

THAT FIRST NIGHT HARPER slept on the couch on the screened-in porch. At about 4:15 a.m. she became aware of a presence at the door.

"Harper?"

"Nadine? Is that you?"

"I can't sleep."

"Come on out here with me."

Nadine remained standing by the entrance, hugging the door jamb.

"I usually lie out here when I can't sleep."

"Oh, I'm sorry, honey."

"That's okay," said Nadine. "You're pretty."

"So are you."

"No, I'm horrible, ugly."

Harper sat up on the couch and straightened the collar of her nightgown.

"Who says?"

"Me, everybody."

"Not me, I think you're foxy. Turn that light on. Go ahead, switch it on." Nadine stepped into the room, reached up, and pulled the chain on the bare bulb hanging from the ceiling.

"See? Look at your cheekbones and your long eyelashes. And your shapely lips, you have lips like Dorothy Lamour. Do you know who she was?"

"No."

"A famous beauty and movie star of the '30s and '40s. Do you have any lipstick?"

"I have dumb little kid play lipstick, it's all pink and it doesn't really stay on and it tastes like gum."

"I have the real thing. Want to try it?"

"It's the middle of the night."

"Who cares? It's the middle of the night at least once every single day."

"Mm. Okay."

"Let's go in the bathroom. Shh."

Harper stood, letting the blanket on her lap fall to the floor. She slid her feet into a pair of bunny slippers, opened her vellum suitcase and extracted a similar, smaller case, also of worn vellum.

"What's that?"

"My makeup case."

"Wow."

"C'mon."

She took Nadine's hand and they tiptoed through the black-dark house.

In the bathroom, Harper cleared an area on the vanity, and quietly clicked the latches on her makeup case. It bloomed open like an exotic desert flower, the upper petals fringed with powdery, micaceous greens and blues, the inner with feathery fawns and beiges, the guts with

BILL COTTER

throbbing reds and every shade of black, and deep in the valley were the tools and brushes of the art.

"You want to try some?"

"Yeah."

"Before we do that, let's arch your brows, give you a real Lauren Bacall look."

"Who's that?"

"Forties screen siren. Real hot mama. Ah, you have nice thick brows, good to work with. Why don't you sit up here on the sink."

"Are you living with us?"

"For a short time, honey." Harper rolled up the sleeves of her nightgown and pinned them with bobby pins. She washed her hands for a long time with soap and water.

"You don't really want to sleep on the couch on the porch, do you?" said Nadine. "It has springs that poke through and it smells like Crisco."

"I don't mind."

"You could have my room."

"Well, aren't you kind."

"I used to share it with my sister. She's dead. I killed her."

"I know, Nadine. It's all right."

Harper found an old hand towel in the closet and laid it out on the vanity. She spread out her tools—brushes and crimpers and clippers.

"I don't really sleep much, and I could take the porch," said Nadine.

"Then you would get the springs and Crisco."

"I don't care. I deserve it."

"Tilt your head this way, *just* a bit. What do you mean, *deserve*?"

"I don't know."

Harper dug around in her makeup case and came up with a handful of glimmering tubes.

"You haven't had an easy time of it, have you?"

"I don't know. I can't sleep."

"Your mother told me about the hospitals."

"Mom has a big mouth."

"Your mother loves you more than life itself. So does your father. They're just hurting, like you are. There, what do you think?"

Harper handed Nadine a mirror.

"Wow. Neato. Now what?"

"Now some foundation. Let's tie your hair back."

"Mom won't let me do makeup, except a little bit when she's watching. That's the one good thing about Meecker-Lang."

"What's that?"

"A mental hospital in Austin I was at a few times. I can do as much makeup as I want inside, and I do. I do goth."

"I admire the goth palette and the extraordinary skill it takes to apply," said Harper. "But it's easy to mess up, and in the wrong hands it just looks dumb. Don't you think?"

Nadine was quiet for a moment. Then she said:

"Yeah. I knew a girl it looked dumb on. She was mean and covered in scars from razor cuts she did herself. But I know a boy it looks great on. His name is Gil. We're friends. He's my best friend in the whole world, ever."

"Yeah?"

"Daddy didn't like him, though. He tried to put a stop to it."


At eleven years old, Nadine was really too young for the adolescent unit at Meecker-Lang, but they didn't have a children's unit, and she had most decidedly outgrown the other children's units in the greater

Austin area, having either been kicked out for behavioral issues or grown too old for their programs. Meecker-Lang was the only alternative available without having to travel out of the area, which Angie did not wish to do. So, even though Nadine was the youngest on the unit by fourteen months and barely a tween, there she was, being treated as an adolescent by the good doctors and staff of Meecker-Lang.

In a previous hospital stay, another patient had taught Nadine a trick with magazines.

Miles Voinovitch found freshly admitted Nadine Grandet in the TV room thumbing an old September issue of *Vogue* as thick as a Dallas phone book.

"Hey. You. What's your name? Never mind. Tear out a page of that and hand it over. Any page, even the cover. Just do it."

Nadine looked at Miles for a moment, then tore out a page with Kate Moss holding a Hermes bag in her teeth, staring at the camera as if daring the world to take it away from her.

"Now watch."

Miles held the edge of the sheet against the skin of his inner arm, drew it a certain way, and *ssnk*, a neat little paper cut bloomed a seam of blood.

"Done right, you can get a stitch or two. But you gave me a bad page, your fault. See ya round, new girl."

Miles walked off, a thread of blood trailing down his arm to his fingertips. Nadine never saw him again. She never forgot him, though.

Nadine figured out that the newest magazines were the best. Glossies. Pages from the back. Untouched edges. She got good.

Cutting is an addictive avocation, and it required intensive dialectical behavior therapy to break Nadine of the habit. Re-admission to Meecker-Lang rekindled the addictive behavior, and she began paper-cutting again, which landed her, repeatedly, in isolation and four-point restraint. She made enemies of the staff and was vindictively medicated. Her therapist, Dr. Singh, could not get through to Nadine, and told Nadine she thought that she was a bastille of self-loathing, a juggernaut of guilt, none of which her young patient would talk about.

Nadine had been at Meecker-Lang a week before her first appointment with Dr. Singh.

"Nadine, how have you been sleeping?" said Dr. Singh, adjusting herself in her chair and opening a notebook.

"What difference does it make?"

"I would just like to know."

Nadine looked closely at Dr. Singh. The woman had absolutely no style, and it made Nadine immediately, irrationally mad. There was no reason to go through life that way, colorless, your hair a shipwreck, shoes merely sensible, clothes dun from a thousand wash and dry cycles, runs in your stockings, no makeup, no jewels.

"No one cares."

"Who would you like to care?"

"There's no one to care how I sleep."

Nadine had half expected Dr. Singh to say *I care*, but she didn't, and Nadine knew from that moment on exactly who she was dealing with. She looked around the office. No books, no art on the walls, just a framed and glazed diploma with lettering so ornate she couldn't read it. Two landline telephones on a barren desk. A couch, but not the kind for lying on, the kind for family to sit on during family therapy. The office smelled like hot-dog water.

"Do you feel alone?"

"Utterly."

It was one of Nadine's favorite words, in both its adjectival and adverbial forms. But it was not misused: she was alone. She had no friends, either among doctors, staff, or patients. Her mother visited every day, her father a few times a week, but Nadine rejected even their companionship. She was angry at her mother for ineffable reasons. She was not angry with her father. She loved him and wanted more than anything for him to love her back. He was so distant though, so self-conscious on the juvenile unit, without his gun, anxious to leave, never staying more than fifteen minutes. He tried; Nadine could tell he was trying. Mom said guilt was eating him from the inside out like an ulcer. How could the same guilt be consuming them all?

"How do you feel about loneliness?"

The leather of the armchair in Dr. Singh's office reminded Nadine of her father's shoulder holster. She touched it with her thumb, felt the smooth, buttery nap of the hide.

"This chair reminds me of my dad."

"You love him."

"My dad is a great gambler, can curse in Spanish, can quick draw, knows all of Latin America's literature by heart. And he's handsome. I wish... oh, never mind. I think he hates me because I killed the daughter he really loved. And that is the fact of the world. My little stupid world. Nothing I can do about it."

Nadine had said too much.

"But you love him."

She did. It made no sense maybe, but she did.

"Yeah, so?" Nadine crossed her arms, the leather of the armchair suddenly noxious.

"Have you told him?"

"I don't know."

"Would you like me to invite him in someday so you can?"

"No!"

"Why?"

"He would never. Come to therapy. He doesn't even like to visit."

Nadine tried to imagine her father in therapy, talking to the doctor. Dr. Singh and her cloying, New England–educated condescension. Nadine imagined her father shooting Dr. Singh, and this made her laugh.

"What's funny?"

"I can't tell you."

"It is unusual, but not unheard of, for a child to love a parent who does not reciprocate the love. It is also not unfixable. Do you understand?"

Nadine was tired of being spoken to like she was three years old, or like she was an especially dim breed of dog. She glared at Dr. Singh.

"I don't want to talk about it anymore."

"I see."

"I hate it here."

"Have you tried making friends?"

"Everyone is so much older than me. I hate them. I shouldn't be here. This is no place for me."

"There is nowhere else for you, Nadine, not nearby. You'll have to make do." Dr. Singh must have told a couple of staff members to try to make friends with Nadine, because the day floats, Gordon and Ty, started being nice to her and asking questions about her life and hobbies and "touching base" with her all the time, seeing if she wanted to play games and a bunch of other bullshit. But Nadine wasn't falling for it—she told them to fuck off.

Then someone new was admitted. He was twelve. On his first day, he sat next to Nadine in the TV room. *Alien* was on.

"I love Jones the cat," the boy eventually said. "If I could have any cat in the world, it would be Jonesy from *Alien*."

Nadine didn't say anything. During the darker scenes, she could see the boy's reflection in the TV screen. He was dressed in black pants, a long-sleeved, button-down black shirt, his face made up in subtle black-and-white maquillage, his long, straight hair dyed black.

"Another great cat is Audrey Hepburn's cat, Cat, from *Breakfast at Tiffany's*. Did you see that?"

"No."

"I'd give my pinkie for a cigarette."

"Yeah."

Nadine had at least managed to avoid taking up smoking, in spite of ample opportunities. Now she would give her pinkie to learn.

"So," said the boy. "What's your favorite movie cat?"

"I don't know."

"Do you have a cat?"

"Yeah. His name is John Deere."

"Like the tractor?"

The boy expertly pantomimed peeling the glassine off a pack of cigarettes, opening it, plucking out the foil wrapper, tamping out a cigarette, putting it between his lips, and lighting it, shielding the "flame" from a nonexistent breeze. A deep drag and exhale. He even picked a bit of phantom tobacco from his tongue and flicked it on the ground. "Filterless, of course. Are you a farm girl or something?"

"No, I live in McCandless. It's a dumb small town."

"Small-town girl."

The boy "smoked" his cigarette.

"Oh, I like Otis from *Milo and Otis*."

"Otis is the dog," said the boy, exhaling with some drama. "Milo is the cat."

"Oh. Well, I was little."

"They treated the animals so badly. From now on you should repudiate that film."

"Really?"

Nadine did not know what "repudiate" meant, but she could guess.

"Totally."

"What's that brand you're smoking?"

Nadine had learned a lot about cigarettes in her many hospital stays. She could tell the difference between all the different sorts of Benson & Hedges cigarettes just from the color of the boxes.

"Why, how good of you to ask," said the boy, pretending to examine his pack of cigarettes up close, as though nearsighted. "These are Player's Navy Cut."

The boy finished smoking his imaginary cigarette, ground it out on his thumbnail, and flicked the butt into a little trash can under the TV.

"I just thought of who my favorite movie cat is."

"Better be good," said the boy. "I know 'em all."

"The Cowardly Lion. *Wizard of Oz*."

"Oh, well done, you're amazing. What's your name?"

"Nadine."

"Shake Gil's hand, Nadine."

Nadine shook hands with Gil.

Jonesy was about to meet his end.

"Goodbye, Jones!" they said.

"What are you doing here?" said Gil.

"I don't know," said Nadine. "There's nowhere else."

"I know what you mean. What's your DSM-IV?"

"I have a bunch of diagnoses. They can't seem to decide. I killed my little sister."

"Ah."

"She was harmless."

"Oh."

"I was only six. I don't remember it very well. I don't even remember if I did it on purpose. All I know is I don't sleep. And when I do I have these terrors that I don't remember when I wake up. I just wake up all sweaty and shaky and twisted up in the sheets and not sure where I'm at. My parents feel responsible for my actions, especially my daddy, so they don't like me much. What are you doing here?"

Gil smiled, crossed his legs, wove his fingers together, and cracked his knuckles.

"I want to cut off my privates."

Nadine was not immediately sure what he meant by "privates." Her ankle was falling asleep. She stretched her legs to buy a moment of contemplation.

"Why?"

"Well. I want to be sexless. I wanted to be a cipher human, without a reproductive role, without hormones. Gender null."

Gil stretched, yawned.

"Do you think you will?" said Nadine, after picturing the process. She was not even totally sure what male privates looked like, except from the marble statues in the Michelangelo art books of her mother's. "Cut them off?"

"Yes, if I can't get somebody to do it for me. My parents are no help. They just hide the sharps and stick me in places like this and hope for the best."

"How long have you felt this way?" Nadine suddenly felt like an idiot. It was something stupid Dr. Singh would say.

"Since I was five. Seven years now. It feels more urgent every day. I haven't reached puberty yet and it's right around the corner and I'm afraid my feelings will change when I do, so I'm really anxious to do this. But I'm afraid I'll bleed to death if I do it myself. I just feel so stuck."

Never in her young life had Nadine felt the urge to reach out and hold someone's hand in compassion, but she did so instinctively now. Gil allowed her.

"No PC, no PC," said Milton, one of the day staff, a short, skinny hipster covered with arm and shin tattoos illustrating gristle and gear chains.

"What's your name?"

"Why, what's yours?" said Gil, with an attitude that promised Milton trouble down the road.

"I asked you first."

"Go away," said Gil. "I'm talking to my friend."

"Want me to separate you two for the length of your stay? 'Cause I can do that. Would you like that? Right now?"

"No, we won't touch, Milton, sorry," said Nadine.

"Good. Name?"

"It's your job to know my fucking name, pal," said Gil. "Go ask one of your many superiors."

Milton left.

"Uh-oh," said Nadine. "That guy's an asshole. I'm worried he's gonna make trouble for you."

"I don't care."

"Who's your doctor?"

"Somebody called MacIreland," said Gil. "I haven't seen him yet. Who's yours?"

"Singh. She's a bitch. She'll never let me out. I kind of don't blame her though. I never get any better. Can't you get an operation? A real operation?"

Gil seemed to think about this. Nadine wondered if Gil wasn't sure he could trust her. Then Gil stood up, and with some effort dragged his chair closer to Nadine's. He sat back down, cross-legged, shook his hair out of his face.

"I have to have my parents' permission," he said. "They won't give it. They're religious. You know the Reverend Orpus Tulalip?"

"No."

"Let me tell you about him. I did a report on him for school, so I've got all the facts in my head. 'Kay, ready?"

Nadine nodded, a little nervous. She had not been this physically close to another human being in a long time. Neither of her parents sat next to her when they visited, though she sensed, sometimes, that her daddy wanted to snatch her into his arms and barrel through the double-locked doors to freedom.

Gil took a deep breath. Nadine could feel warmth radiating from his body in the over-air-conditioned ward.

"Okay. Orpus 'Shouty' Tulalip is a preacher. He came from a long line of man-child evangelists in Arkansas. In the '60s, when he was just eight years old, he started preaching his hellfire and brimstone sermons in revival tents and chautauquas along the Texarkana-Houston corridor. By the time he was twelve, he had his own church and congregation out in Conroe, you know, that demon's armpit near Houston?"

"My aunt Suzanne lives there, my daddy's sister. I've never been though, never even met her."

"Well, when the reverend turned fourteen, he got married to his thirteen-year-old cousin, Vickie Day Zimmer. When Orpus turned fifteen, he found his first mistress, this lady named Donna Boyle, thirty-two years old and the wife of a plumber at the old airport in Houston. It was like Sonny and Ruth in *The Last Picture Show*, except Orpus was gross and insensitive, and Donna's plumber husband wasn't gay."

There was a beat-up paperback of *The Last Picture Show* in the bookcase at home, but Nadine had never felt like she was old enough to read it. She would when she got home, if she ever did get home.

"The next year," continued Gil, eyes bright, "when he was sixteen, Orpus had his first book published. It was called *Sinners A-Suckle at the Teat of Mephistopheles*. He was a millionaire by nineteen, and a few years later, when he turned twenty-four, he got his first telecast on KRIV in Houston. A couple years later he opened his first megachurch, the Holy Warrior Fellowship, in Richmond-Rosenberg, and a couple years after *that* he chalked up his one hundredth mistress, a rare-book cataloguer at the Fondren Library at the University of Houston—this ugly lady named Bertie Nance who used to steal rare books for Orpus's library. He was only thirty-one when someone finally tried to kill him—some cuckold shot at him in a mini-mall parking lot with a big, nickel-plated Colt Python, but all four bullets sailed in and out of Tulalip without so much as winging a vital. He was a hundred-millionaire by age thirty-four, and on his thirty-eighth birthday he finally got arrested for wire fraud, but beat the case, and got even famouser and richer. At age forty-three, he was committed to a detox center for Vicodin addiction following a botched vasectomy, and was out and clean in six months. He was well on his way to making his five hundredth million. His tenth book, *Bowels of Lava, Safes of Krugerrands*, was self-published in 2004, and when he turned fifty, he consummated with his five hundredth mistress, a *Playboy* Playmate of the Year who had lied about her age and was really sixteen. When he turned fifty-four, Vickie Day Zimmer-Tulalip, the cousin he married, had had enough, and divorced him. There had been no prenup—thirteen- and fourteen-year-olds don't think about stuff like that, I guess, so she got an awful lot of money. That was the beginning of the end. More investigations, including statutory rape. Jail for that. Testicular cancer. Eight-digit fines for dis dat dudder. A withering supply of mistresses. Sudden and thorough baldness. Meniere's disease. A thirty-five-year-old woman claiming to be his daughter and suing him for cash. *Her* eighteen-year-old son suing his mother for the money she got from Orpus. But Orpus is still preaching, still rich. And there you have it! What do you think of my dissertation?"

"Wow," said Nadine, not wanting to tell Gil she had shot her sister with her daddy's Colt Python. "You know your Orpus. I bet you got a good grade."

"It was an oral presentation, and I got a C-minus-minus. I'm still mad about it."

"A C-minus-minus? Well, that's bullshit."

Nadine was indignant. She'd had teachers like that.

"Thank you, Miss Nadine. Wait, there's more. So. My parents belong to Orpus's congregation, and he doesn't permit anything like changing or nullifying your gender. Unthinkable to him. He has a book called *B.L.G.*, which stands for *Boy Loves Girl*, and it's all about how there are exactly two genders and exactly one sexuality. How anyone else is a perversion of the Lord's intention, is infectious, and should be 'recontextualized.' He even outlines how he proposes to do it, with these 'humane' camps, way up in the Dakotas someplace, to 'depervify' gay and trans people, funded with either taxpayer dollars or with his own private fortune."

Gil grinned, lit another fake cigarette, slouched down in his chair, put a boot up on Nadine's armrest, and "smoked."

"I don't know what to say," said Nadine, shifting in her chair, feeling like she might cry. She stared at this boy Gil, wishing desperately she could help him, knowing she could not. Her hands felt numb, without strength. "And your parents listen to this guy? And give him money?"

"My parents don't get it. They don't get anything. They are sheep."

Nadine had a sudden urge to run, to take Gil with her, to scoop him up like a teddy bear, throw him over her shoulder, bust through the doors and out into the green world.

"Maybe there's a foundation that can help you?"

"There are plenty, but I still need my parents' permission. That's why I'm going to have to do this myself."

"I wish I had some money. Money helps with stuff like getting around parents."

She imagined finding a FedEx box stuffed full of hundred-dollar bills in the bathroom.

"You and me both."

"Wait a minute," said Nadine, remembering. "I *do* have money. I have like $3,300. I used to be an artist—long story. You can have it. All of it."

Nadine wondered if that money was still there. She hadn't thought about it in years.

Gil was about to say something when Milton came back with a clipboard and an attitude.

"Okay, Gil Moorehead, New Guy, you're officially on my Shit List," he said, waggling the clipboard in Gil's face. "People on my Shit List can easily make it to my Seclusion Room List. People on my Seclusion Room List can easily jump to my Five-Point Restraint List. And it's just one little step from my FPRL to my SJAPSL. You don't want to know what that is. Got it? *Gil?*"

"What's your name again?" said Gil, sprawling even more luxuriantly, becoming one with the chair. He produced a comb and slowly parted his voluptuous black hair, perfectly down the middle, keeping his eyes on the day staffer the whole time.

"Milton."

"Well, Milton, you have officially made my Douchebag List. Those on my Douchebag List stay there forever. Other people on my Douchebag List are Mel Gibson, Phil Spector, Gilles de Rais, Hetty Green, Joseph McCarthy, Tamerlane, O.J. Simpson, and Ted Nugent. My list has 1,140 douchebags. You're way down at the bottom, which means you're not even good at being a douchebag. What do you think about that?"

"Do you want to jump to my Seclusion Room List right fucking now, pal? Huh? Do you?"

"No!" said Nadine. "Milton, no, he doesn't. We're just playing around here, right, Gil?"

"Sure, just playing around," said Gil.

"No seclusion rooms," said Nadine. "Milton, can you find out what the movie is tonight?"

Milton looked hard at Nadine and Gil, then stalked off.

"Whoa," said Nadine. "Gil, you gotta watch that guy. He'll tie you down for real. He's done it to me, for sixty-five straight hours once."

"Holy hell, really?"

"Really."

"I'll fuck him up for that."

"No, don't do anything, there's nothing you can do in here. Nothing. You just have to deal. You've been in other hospitals, right?"

"Lots."

"They're not like this place. Here, they punish, for control, not for treatment. Toe the line, Gil Moorehead."

"All right. What's the SJAPSL, do you think?"

"Straitjacket and Prolixin Suppository List."

For once, Gil Moorehead had nothing to say.


Harper adjusted the lamp in the bathroom so that it illuminated Nadine's face. Despite the hour—it was 4:45 a.m.—Nadine was bright-eyed, excited about what was to come. And nothing made her happier than thinking about her friend Gil. And makeup.

"Gil reminds me of how I imagine Oscar Wilde might have been as a young person," said Harper. "Nadine, do you like green or blue for eye shadow?"

"Green."

"Green it is. In the 1940s, women wore eye shadow only in the evenings, for parties and events. Well, it's certainly evening now. The light's not great in this bathroom. I wish I could do goth for you. Hell, maybe you could teach me."

"Okay."

"Did Gil teach you?"


"That is one thing I like about this horrible place," said Gil, standing up in front of the TV and doing three rapid jumping jacks.

"What?"

"They let me have my clothes and makeup," he said, sitting down, clearly exhausted from his exertion. "Not every place does. I've been at Institute for Living, Menninger, McLean, and a half dozen other little places around the country, and only a couple allowed me to be myself. The only thing they won't let me have is nail polish remover because it's poison. I guess I can dig that. Hey, can I make a confession?"

"You've made a lot, what's one more?"

"You're witty for a... um... how old are you?"

"Eleven."

"I want to do your nails," said Gil, rubbing his hands together till they squeaked.

"What color?"

"Take a wild, crazy stab in the dark with a Bowie knife."

"Black?"

"Bring the woman a stuffed tapir!"

"Okay."

"Actually, you have a point," said Gil, suddenly feeling his shirt pockets for his "cigarettes."

"Yeah?"

"There are many shades of black. I'm going to use an especially bottomless variety called Intergalactic. Made by this now-defunct company that had a whole palette of colors based on Beastie Boys songs. I'm almost out, and there won't be any more when it's gone, but I can't think of anyone it would look better on than you. Sit still."

Nadine sat, her right hand on the edge of the chair.

"When I was seven," said Nadine, "my mother hired an artist to paint me. Her name was Shea Babb. She worked in nail polish on little paper plates. She came over to the house with all her painting stuff. I was asleep and didn't know I was being painted. She was just about finished, had done everything but my eyes, when my daddy burst into the room and woke me up. I ran off like a baby. I was sicker then than now. Shea Babb never finished. The painting's really weird and spooky but kind of neat."

"Awesome. You must treasure it."

"Yeah."

Nadine wondered briefly where it was. Probably in her mother's bureau drawer with all the other junk like that, photos and greeting cards and kid-made Christmas ornaments.

"You know…"

"What?"

Gil shook the bottle of Intergalactic, unscrewed the cap with the brush, and painted a perfect black circle on the arm of the chair.

"Why stop at fingernails?"

"What?"

"Want me to make you up?"

Nadine curled up tighter in her chair, smiling. "Oh, I don't know…"

"C'mon, you'd look awesome. I'm really good."

A group let out; the room began to fill. Most of the patients were female and a good bit older than Nadine and Gil. If the statistics were to be believed, five out of eight were there for eating disorders. Visual evidence seemed to bear this up.

"Well… okay."

"Right on."

"Can I have red lips instead of black?"

"Of course. *Vive la différence!*"

Halfway through the making-up, Milton came by.

"What did I tell you two about no PC, for christfuckingsake?"

"*I* am not touching her, Milton, you peasant, the *tools* are touching her, the brushes only, don't you understand the distinction? Not once have I laid a finger on Nadine."

"Stop."

"No. I'm in the middle of this, I can't stop now."

Milton grabbed the lipstick brush out of Gil's hand and snapped it in half, smearing his palm with a rich, waxy cinnabar.

156

"Motherfuck. Gil, go to your room. Nadine, clean your face. You look like a preadolescent clown in a cheap horror flick."

Nadine recoiled at the comment but was secretly delighted.

The next day they tried again.

"This time I'm going to direct you, Nadine. You can do it. I'll have you looking like Siouxsie in no time."

Milton kept an eye on them.

"No offense, but explain to me the urge to do that to yourself." said Milton. "To do that to your face, to clownify yourself? I don't get it."

"Explain to me," said Gil, "the urge to pay a small fortune to permanently ink your body with silly effigies and meaningless symbols that will slowly disperse into a black-green murk that by the time you are seventy-five will look like a body-wide hematoma. What is that urge, Milton? Whose urge is worse? Yours or mine? I will say that all I have to do is wash my face. But all that will fix yours is cremation. Or a flesh-eating disease."

"You're a smart little shit, aren't you?"

"IQ 176 and rising."

"That's not what I meant."

"Now, Nadine," said Gil, ignoring Milton so thoroughly that he seemed to shrink. "Carefully put the white eyeliner on the lower lid— it'll make your eyes look bigger. And your eyes are already huge, you'll look beautifully freaky."

"Jesus," said Milton, who clearly did not appreciate being ignored.

"Milton, can't you fuck off?" said Gil. "You're like a turkey vulture."

Milton finally fucked off.

"My IQ's not really 176," said Gil. "But Milton's too stupid to figure that out."

"I don't know what mine is," said Nadine, examining herself in the reflection of the nurses' station window. "I won't let Dr. Singh do the test. I don't even want to know."

Dr. Singh took the new facial display as a sign of emotional deterioration and Nadine's friendship with Gil as a danger.

"Gil Moorehead is a highly disturbed individual, Nadine." Dr. Singh kept rubbing her forehead and the bridge of her nose, as if the actions would wipe away the makeup on her patient's face.

"He's a beautiful person and he's my friend."

Nadine refrained from telling Dr. Singh that she was going to help him in any way she could.

"I don't think you should spend time with him."

"Why?"

"Has he made advances?"

All this word brought to mind was her daddy getting cash out of ATMs off of credit cards.

"What?"

"Has he made… moves? Touched you?"

Why was everyone so preoccupied with touching? Nadine was seized by an urge to rub her nose all over Dr. Singh's face.

"Are you kidding? You obviously don't know the first thing about him, do you?"

"Would you answer my question."

"No!"

"'No,' you won't answer my question, or 'no,' he hasn't—"

"No, he hasn't touched me. Jesus!"

Dr. Singh's regular office was being remodeled, so she was holding her sessions in a converted storage room. It was without windows or ventilation. A hole had been knocked through a wall to gain access to a small bathroom, and a flimsy door had been put in place. Even with the door firmly shut, every sound uttered in the bathroom escaped into the makeshift office, so Nadine avoided going in there, even when she needed to. Occasionally a patron of the bathroom would exit through Dr. Singh's office, sometimes during Nadine's sessions. Eventually Dr. Singh installed a deadbolt. Much of the small, converted storage room was taken up by Dr. Singh's new chair, an immense black ergonomic space-age booster seat with a complex system of gears and levers and pneumatic bladders. Whenever she felt the need, Dr. Singh would unconsciously inflate or deflate a bladder on her chair. She deflated one now, with attendant whoopee-cushion flatulence.

"I can't help but feel, Nadine, that you are hiding behind this new makeup."

"You would be right."

"I would be? Why are you hiding? What from?"

"You. Me. The world. My crime."

"I see."

"You know how on Halloween you're in costume and you've got a mask on and you're bolder, more daring, you're not afraid of doing stuff?"

"I've never dressed up for Halloween."

A rare personal disclosure from Dr. Singh, who wouldn't even reveal her age to Nadine, whether she was married, had kids, had siblings.

"But I know what you mean," said the doctor. "You feel bolder?"

"Yeah."

"That's good, I suppose."

"I think I just realized something."

Now that she had Gil to talk to, there was somehow less risk in disclosing her feelings and thoughts to Dr. Singh.

"Yes?"

"I think... when I found that gun of my dad's when I was six... it was like I was wearing a costume. A gunslinger costume, or a stickup man costume. It was like a mask. For my hands. I became a stickup man. I stuck up my little sister, but the mask exploded in my hands, and the game was over and her life was over and my life was over."

"This is an important realization, Nadine. But your life is not over."

"God, Dr. Singh."

"Yes?"

Nadine stared at her doctor for a long moment, maybe sixty true, real, ticking seconds. Then Nadine laughed, hard, a bark.

"What is funny?"

"You know there's a scene in *One Flew Over the Cuckoo's Nest* where all the acutes are in group therapy with Nurse Ratched, and—I don't remember it exactly—one of the patients says out of the blue, 'Oh God' or something, and Nurse Ratched turns toward him and says, 'Yes?' like she was God? You just did that."

"I see."

Clearly Dr. Singh did not care for this observation: her nostrils flared a millimeter or two.

"Something else."

Nadine, when she was six, had needed two hands to hold her father's gun. She wondered now if she was strong enough to hold it, to fire it, with one hand.

"Yes?"

"You know my daddy still has his gun, the one I killed Sophie with? He wears it every day in his shoulder holster? Can't live without it?"

"I see."

"It's his mask."

Dr. Singh did not respond in any way, not even a nostril-flare. Nadine thought of the word "mask" in the context of her doctor's face.

"Don't separate me and Gil. He's my friend."

"Nadine, he's not the kind of friend someone with your state of mind should have."

"How would you know, since you know nothing about him? Or me?"

"I know enough."

Dr. Singh adjusted a chair lever, a signal that the session was coming to an end. A few more minutes. The sessions were always either endlessly long or breathlessly short.

"What are you going to do?" Nadine thought she might cry.

"It is time to start talking about discharge," said Dr. Singh. "You've been here twelve weeks."

All she had wanted, before Gil came, was to leave this place. To go home. To be away from the likes of Milton, Nurse Conchli, Nurse Bahl, Dr. Singh, the monstrous Dr. Gundersohn, who was old enough to have actually performed lobotomies on people. Nadine had tried to sign herself out, but it never worked—some great edifice of psychiatric bureaucracy she did not understand always blocked her way. But now, Gil. Her friend. Who she thought about before she went to sleep, who she went to when she woke. Who she sat with throughout the long days on the usually silent, occasionally rowdy, sometimes violent unit, talking to, laughing with, watching TV alongside, doing makeup, doing nothing. He was the only person she had ever known whom she could sit with and say nothing, and it was all right. And now she was going to be separated from him. She was being sent home. It was a capital sentence. She would never see him again. Nadine was sure of this.

"I'm not ready to go."

"You are. You've been doing well."

"I'm depressed."

"You want to stay because of Gil."

"No I don't. I want to kill myself."

"You haven't mentioned this before."

Dr. Singh looked uncomfortable. No, she looked pissed. She hated it when sessions went over the time limit and had said as much to Nadine. Three thousand seconds was all you fucking got in sessions with Dr. Singh. Make the most of them.

Nadine decided in that moment, with just a few seconds left, that she would make a dramatic but harmless gesture later that day. She would tell Gil. Yes, magazine paper. There was a new *Harper's Bazaar* in the break room, uncracked. A good, solid slit, not too deep, across the crook of her arm, something that would land her in solitary for a day or two, no more, but enough to extend her stay at Meecker-Lang, delay discharge for a while. What was there to go home to, anyway? Her mother was a depressed, meager wreck, her father an enraged, stoppered vacuum, she had no friends, there was no real money, nothing to do. She wasn't actually depressed enough to try suicide, and real cutting had lost its appeal.

"I don't tell you everything."

"Our time is up."

When Nadine arrived back on the unit, she went into the lounge where Gil was usually curled in a chair in the corner by the fake pineapple tree, either grooming or reading. Today he was not there. He was not in the TV room. He was not in the mini kitchen. He was not in his room. He was not in either of the isolation rooms. His therapy was in the morning; it was already past two in the afternoon.

Nadine knocked on the window of the nurses' station. Nurse Bahl slid the glass aside.

"Yes, Nadine?"

"Where's Gil?"

Nurse Bahl was busy grinding something up with a mortar and pestle. A tiny smutch of white powder frosted the tip of her nose.

"He was transferred."

"Where?"

"I'm sorry but I'm not at liberty to disclose."

"Why?" *Panic.*

"Because I'm not at liberty to disclose, that's why."

She slid the glass closed.

Nadine walked up and down the halls.

"Hey," she said, addressing a patient she had never spoken to before, a teenage manic depressive missing an arm. "Do you know where they transferred Gil?"

"Who?"

"The goth kid?"

"No idea."

She approached two girls playing Othello and eating those orange peanut-butter crackers.

"Do you know where they transferred that goth kid?"

"He your boyfriend or something?"

"No."

"They came and took him away about thirty minutes ago," said the older girl, who had bandages on both forearms and orange dust on her fingertips.

"Who? Who did?"

The girl shrugged.

"Some dudes. Your boyfriend didn't go quietly."

"Dudes? From here?"

"Can you, like, go away now?" said the other girl. Nadine went into her room. On her pillow was a scrap of paper. It read:

*Dear Nadine:*

*They're transferring me downstairs. They're doing it to separate us. My cell is 512-952-9688. Call me when we're both out. I wish I had thought to get your number. I love you. Your friend, Gil Moorehead, Esq.*


There were pay phones on the units, but no one was allowed to make inter-unit calls. Cell phones were verboten. Nadine read the note again. And again. She ran to the nurses' station and knocked on the glass.

"Now what?" said Nurse Bahl. The powder smutch was still there.

"I want to sign myself out."

"Too late."

"What?"

"You're being prepared for discharge. Day after tomorrow."

"Why doesn't anyone bother to tell me these things?"

"You're eleven, that's why. Now go wash your face."

"Go wash *your* face," said Nadine, tapping the tip of her own nose.

Nadine called her mother.

"They just told me, Nadine. I didn't know you didn't know. I cannot wait to have you home. Your father will be so relieved. And John Deere will be beside himself."

"Can I have a present? A coming-home present?"

"Well... of course, honey. What would you like?"

"My own phone."

"Oh, I don't know about that. Your father—"

"To hell with Daddy! Screw Daddy! You always bring him into it when you can't make a decision for yourself. I want *you* to do this for me. I want you to give me a present, from *you*. I'm old enough, I need one in case of emergencies, you know. Every kid my age has one. I saw some kid's seven-year-old *little brother* with his own phone. I'll pay for it—I have money, remember?"

"How about when you're twelve? That's only eight months away."

Nadine started to cry. Big, earthen sobs.

"Mom, I never ask for anything. Get me a phone. *Please.* I don't need apps or games or anything. Just a phone, the cheapest, dumbest phone they make. A phone phone. *Please.*"

Silence on the line. Nadine could hear *SpongeBob SquarePants* on in the background. Sophie had loved SpongeBob as much as she loved her own daddy.

"Okay, honey. Okay."

"Really?"

"Sure."

"Thank you."

Afraid her mother would change her mind if she saw her in goth makeup, Nadine scrubbed herself clean on the day of her discharge. Angie met her in the hospital lobby. Neither Nadine nor Angie were avid, full-body huggers—they tended to hold their hands way out like yardarms and drape them over the shoulders of their huggees, but this time they fell into each other's embrace, a sailor's knot of a hug. They were positively spliced.

"I missed you, honey. Your father is sorry he couldn't be here. He's at—"

"—work. It's okay, I know. Um..."

"I'm way ahead of you."

Angie reached into her purse and came out with a small white box.

"It's an iPhone," said Angie. "It does all kinds of neat stuff, supposedly. It has a camera. It's all ready to go. You want to know your phone number?"

"Yeah!"

"Ready to memorize? It's 512-472-6338. You can call and text people and send email. I know you don't have email, but it's easy to set up, and you're old enough now."

"I am. Thank you, Mom. Oh my god, this is so freakin' cool. Was it expensive?"

"Well… put it this way. To use it costs ten dollars a month extra on my phone plan is all. But the phone itself was a little, dear. If you really are serious about paying for it, we can talk about that. Or you can do stuff around the house."

"Okay."

Nadine didn't mention her $3,300 again. Maybe it was gone, maybe her daddy gambled it away. She planned in her head to scrub the entire house, top to bottom. She would Swiffer the ceiling, dust the picture frames, clean the drains. Hell, she'd repaint the living room, scrape the sycamore leaves out of the gutters with her bare hands. She would be a one-girl Merry Maid cleaning crew.

"Can I ask you something?" said Angie.

"Yeah. I know what you're going to ask. I did make a friend in the hospital. That's who I have to talk to."

"I see. What's her name?"

Nadine climbed into her mother's old Celica and put on her seatbelt. Out of habit, she opened the glove compartment to see if there were any Life Savers or Mentos. There were none. But there was an envelope with her name on it.

"That came for you, Nadine."

She opened it. A bank ATM card, in her name. Maybe her money was still there.

"Call the number on the sticker and set it up, then peel the sticker off. So what's her name, what's her story?"

"His name is Gil."

"Ah." Angie reached into her purse and found half a roll of fruit pastilles and handed them to her daughter. "How old?"

"Twelve. He's amazing, Mom. He's the best friend I've ever had. I want you to meet him, I want him to come over, I want him to live with us, I want to take care of him, he's so troubled, I worry about him a lot, he's so smart and funny, he knows everything, he's into goth but he's not scary at all, he's beautiful, he knows all about movies and mathematics and has read Dante and all the Jeeves books, his parents don't understand him, he's spent his life in hospitals like me, he's the only person that's ever liked me, Mom, but not in that way, I don't know why he does but he does, I can't believe it, I think you'd love him, he's not confused, he knows exactly what he wants in life but can't have it because they say he's too young to speak for himself and his parents just stick their heads in the sand and throw him in hospitals, oh I can't explain it, you wouldn't understand either, and now time is running out for him and I'm worried that he's going to hurt himself, and anyway, I needed this phone to stay in contact with Gil so that nothing ever happens to him—"

"Honey, honey, take a breath, you'll choke on your candy. Tell me, is Gil your boyfriend?"

"No, Mom! You don't understand! He's my friend, my best and only friend, closer than some dumb boyfriend could ever be!"

Nadine knew what was coming next. In that moment, her mother reminded Nadine of Dr. Singh, and she didn't like it at all.

"You don't—"

"Why are you adults all the same? No, we don't *do* anything! Gil is so far above *anything* like that. We talk. He shows me how to do goth makeup. Which I'm really good at, by the way, and when I get home, I'm going to get some."

"Oh, wonderful."

"Mom—"

Angie said nothing.

"Dad cannot know about Gil."

"Why?"

"He just can't. He wouldn't approve. They're opposites. Don't tell him? It's okay if he finds out about the phone, but not about Gil."

"It feels like you're wringing a lot of promises out of me."

"I just got discharged from a three-month inpatient hospital stay. I get promises."

"All right," said Angie, pulling into the parking lot of Dan's Hamburgers. "Shall we experiment with our phones over cheeseburgers and Dr Peppers?"

"Yeah!"

Angie and her daughter called and texted each other from opposite sides of a booth at Dan's. Like most tweens, Nadine proved digitally adept at texting, and fired off long observations about Dan's patrons as her mother struggled to keep up with what she noticed.

—Mom did you see redhead man eat hamburgr in 3 bites? He didnt even chew!!!

—What about breastfeeding mom. I'm against it. In public.

—isnt that baby too old too? its like 4!!!

—LMAO!!

—*What*

—Laugh My Ass Off

—Mom! and what about teenage girls with skatebords laughing too loud. they look tough. they would beat me up. I knew girls like that in hospitals.

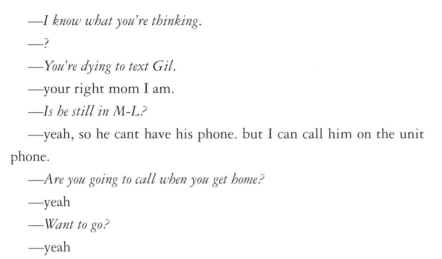

*—I know what you're thinking.*

*—?*

*—You're dying to text Gil.*

—your right mom I am.

*—Is he still in M-L?*

—yeah, so he cant have his phone. but I can call him on the unit phone.

*—Are you going to call when you get home?*

—yeah

*—Want to go?*

—yeah

At home Nadine went to her room, closed the door, jumped on her bed, and dialed Gil's unit.

"Hello?"

"Gil Moorehead, please?"

"Who?"

"The goth kid."

"Just a minute."

Nadine kicked off her sneakers and peeled her socks off with her toes. She pulled the bedspread over her like a quesadilla. She waited. Nadine knew the longer it took for Gil to come to the phone, the less likely he'd come at all.

Then, a voice.

"Hello, who's calling?"

"Um, Nadine Grandet?"

"This is Barbra Zander, staff. Gil can only take calls from family members. Sorry, Nadine."

She waited. She played with her phone, downloaded iTunes and Words with Friends, took pictures of her hands, studied herself in the selfie mode of the camera. She activated her new ATM bank card, downloaded a Chase bank app, and discovered that she did indeed have $3,323.28 in a passbook savings account in her own name. She set up a Hotmail account, downloaded Facebook and eBay. She got set up on PayPal. Nadine thought she might be able to control the world, at least her immediate world, with its radiating shells of spinning matter and bodies and virtual dollars, with nothing but a telephone and a bank card. Nadine felt like Wonder Woman, Queen Elizabeth, and Oprah all rolled up into one skinny tween.

Then she called Meecker-Lang again.

"Hello?"

"Gil Moorehead, please? This is his sister, Jane."

A long moment. Then:

"Hello?"

"Hello, this is Jane Moorehead? I'd like to speak to my brother, Gil?"

"This is Barbra. Nice try, Nadine. If you call here again, I will have Milton punish Gil."

Nadine called his phone, but the mailbox was full. She texted him.

—I cant reach you on the unit. I think you can see my number but if you cant its 512 GRANDET. call when you can. I hope you get out soon. Ill text you every day. I miss you.

Weeks passed. Nadine indeed texted Gil every day, without a response. She called his phone half a dozen times a day, his mailbox always full, but did not dare call the unit again. The idea of Milton and a bunch of big, strong floats and day staff with nothing to lose forcing

170

Gil into a straitjacket naked and placing big, greasy antipsychotic suppositories in his body made Nadine tremble with fear. There was no way to visit without arranging it beforehand. Nadine nearly talked her mother into driving over to the unit and letting her peek in the windows of the ground floor, but she balked at the last minute.

Meanwhile, Dean Lee, her daddy, the house ghost, had not discovered the existence of the phone. Or Gil.

Two months after her discharge, Nadine, Angie, and Dean Lee were eating dinner at the little table in the kitchen when a strange sound came into evidence: the voice of a young girl singing, "Porque te vas. Porque te vas. Porque te vas."

"What in the world is that?" said Dean Lee, sitting up straight, the first time he had seemed animated in the weeks she'd been home.

Angie realized what it was first.

"I think that's you, honey," she said, addressing her daughter.

Nadine jumped up from the table and ran off.

"What the hell was that?"

"Her phone, Dean Lee. I bought her a phone. She's getting a text."

"You've gotta be kidding me."

Dean Lee dropped his knife and fork onto his plate, pushed himself away from the table, and stood. When Dean Lee stood like that, he gave the impression of an abandoned, foot-lit lighthouse suddenly come to life, a million-candlepower beam shooting from his eyes.

"No, I'm not kidding," said Angie, looking up at her husband. "She's old enough, she needs one. I want to be able to stay in touch with her."

"So who's texting her?"

"A little friend from the hospital. Harmless."

"A boy?"

"Give her her privacy."

"Nadine!"

"Dean Lee, leave her alone."

"Nadine!"


Harper listened carefully, did not interrupt except for direction. She showed little emotion, fearing Nadine would abandon her narrative if she sensed any judgment. But inside, Harper was anxious, worried, knowing this story, even if it had not happened yet, would not end well.

"What do you think of this lipstick scheme?" said Harper, uncapping a tube that looked as big and heavy as a machine-gun bullet made of gold.

"Kind of reminds me of the edges of some of my grandmother Adeline's old books. Dusty and cool, hundreds of years old. And it looks kinda like blood, real blood. It's awesome. I wish Gil could see it."

"Want to try it?"

"Yeah."

"Okay, so do your lower lip first, then upper, draw it on, then put it on the lower lip in upward strokes, the upper lip in downward strokes, like this. See?"

Harper did her own lips in a matter of seconds, like a magician. It was like watching Bob Ross paint a sunset with a knife.

"Yeah."

"You try. Yes, that's right. Excellent. You know, back in the old, old days, girls used to do their lipstick with jellybeans. Lick them, then do their lips."

"Wow. It feels cool on my lips."

"It's a good-quality, handmade lipstick, one of a kind. It's called Parzival. Made by a friend of mine, Ramon. He's a genius. He makes my corsets, too."

"Gil is a genius. Gil is the only genius I know."

Harper shaped the tip of the tube of Parzival with her fingers, then touched up Nadine's efforts.

"There are not many real geniuses in the world," Harper said. "Maybe six or seven. Gil sounds like he might be one of them. Will you tell me what happened to him?"


Nadine climbed into bed with her phone and pulled the covers over her head.


—*Nadine!!! I'm out!!! Text me!!!*

—Gil I miss you so much where are you

—*Home in Abilene with my parents*

—so far away

—*All your texts I read them a hundred times thank you*

—your mailbox was full I called

—*I know, I emptied it, better not call, texting is better, my parents are always listening, they can hear a phone on vibrate a thousand yards away*

—okay. how will I ever see you again

—*Somehow we will*

—Gil are you okay

—*Yeah*

—do you want to cut still


A pause. Movement in the kitchen. Her daddy's voice, low and hard.


—*yeah*

—I dont want you to die

*—I read about a technique on the internet. You put a rubber band around your penis and testicles very tightly and leave it there. Slowly the circulation gets cut off. Eventually you can just slice everything off and there's very little pain or blood. You have to go to the emergency room afterward so they can do something so you can pee for the rest of your life, but that's it.*

A sound from deep in the house, like someone moving furniture, some heavy thing that had never been moved, a bookcase, scuttered by force across the floorboards, leaving trails of fresh-scarred wood.

—I worry

*—I'll be okay.*

—I dont want you to be by yourself in case something goes wrong. how will you get yourself to the emergency room?

*—I'll figure something out.*

—its dangerous.

*—I've already started. The rubber bands have been on for 20 hours.*

—OMG! can you take a bus here? I want to be with you. do you have any money?

*—No. It's a problem.*

—I have money, remember? Lets do paypal. I have it on my phone. So once you get to town, heres my idea. take a taxicab to mccandless general hospital. go to the ladys room by the emergency room. Ill meet you in there. Then youll be right where you need to be.

*—You're bloody brilliant you know that?*

—I know.

*—I'll text you back in a minute.*

"Nadine?"

Her mother. Nadine jammed her phone between her mattresses. *Why didn't she mute it, goddammit?*

"Yeah?"

"Can I come in?"

"No."

"Was that Gil?"

Nadine said nothing. She had to pee.

"Is he all right?"

"Yeah, he's fine."

"I'd really like to come in."

"Maybe later."

The need to pee was picking up speed along with the tension in the house.

"Nadine?"

Daddy.

"Yeah?"

"Who you talking to?"

"Nobody." It was the truth at least.

"You're too young to be talking to boys, you heard me?"

"I'm not *talking*, I'm *texting*, duh."

There was no lock on Nadine's door. Her daddy did not often come in uninvited. In fact, Nadine could count on one hand the times he had, and all of those had been to rescue her from some crisis involving bloodshed or threat therefrom. She stared at the knob, a fake crystal affair of old, cast resin, faintly yellowed with age, a deep fissure filled with dirt running through it, wobbly, loose, largely ineffective—a grand yank would kill it. She watched.

"Nadine."

"What!"

The pee situation was growing critical. How fast it came on some-times. She hadn't even had anything to drink today, except a Gatorade about five hours ago.

"Who is he?"

"Nobody!"

Nadine stared. The pale yellow of the resin doorknob seemed to glow. It did not move, but she could tell that her father's hand was on it, in the same way she knew if a house was occupied; she could just feel it. She knew. She waited. She would pee the bed, how bad could that be? Warm, maybe. When Sophie had peed her bed, she was always happy.

"Porque te vas."

Nadine reached between her mattresses and retrieved her phone.

"Nadine!" said Dean Lee. The doorknob shifted.

—*I got my ticket, Nadine are you there?*

—*Here! When!*

—*Tomorrow. I get in at 2:15. I figure I'll be at the hospital at 2:30. You'll be there?*

—its only about a two mile walk. Ill be there.

—*Im scared.*

The knob turned for real this time.

"Daddy!"

—*I know what I'm doing. I have a kit I put together. It won't hurt, but I'm taking some pain pills beforehand I stole from Mom. It'll all be over quick. You're not squeamish?*

"Daddy, do not come in!"
The knob stopped.

—Gil Im just worried that this is so, you know, permanent.
—*That's the point.*

"Nadine, this is for the best, now."
"Daddy!"

—do you want me to do it
—*Do what?*
—the subtraction. That's what I'm calling it.

It had been a word used on her sister's headstone. Sophie had been subtracted from the world.

—*You would do that for me?*
—yeah

"I'm coming in, Nadine."
"No, not yet! Daddy!"

—*I don't know what to say.*
—say yeah.

Nadine let go, unclenched. A delectable warmth.

—*Yeah.*
—good. wish you could move here. I wish—

The pale yellow turning glint of the knob. The warmth between her legs.

—*I'll be there in the hospital for a little while afterward probably.*
—Ill get mom to bring me to visit you everyday
—*Nadine I have to go to sleep. I'll see you in the emergency room women's bathroom tomorrow at 2:30. For the big day!*
—I love you.
—*I love you.*

The door began to open.
*"Stop!"*

Nadine quickly deleted the text thread, memorized Gil's phone number, then deleted that, too. She tossed her phone on her bedside table. The door swung open. Dean Lee strode across the room, took her phone, and examined it.

"Who are you texting with, Nadine? Who are you talking to? What's that smell?"

"Nobody, Daddy, nobody! Nothing!"

"Come on, now. I will not allow a boyfriend at your age. Period."

He took her phone away.

Nadine lay in her wet, cooling sheets.

Ready.

The next day, at 1:30 p.m., Nadine set out for McCandless General Hospital. On the way, she saw monk parrots roosting in a skylight on a soccer field and took it as a good sign. At 2:15 she entered the women's bathroom in the emergency room, sat in a stall, and waited.

At about 2:30 she saw a pair of black Chuck Taylors walk by under the door.

"Gil?" she whispered.

"Nadine!"

Gil ducked into the stall with Nadine, carrying an old-fashioned Dopp kit. They hugged. Gil looked faint, blanched even under the makeup.

"Are you all right?"

"I'm in some pain. A lot. It really hurts. It's supposed to be numb, but it's not."

"Did you take the pain pills?"

"Yeah, a bunch. I feel funny. I took them with a flat Sprite on the bus and one kinda got caught in my throat. I can still taste the bitter."

"We'll get this over fast. Take your pants down and sit on the seat."

Gil did as he was told. Nadine was not going to think about this. She was going to act. She had killed someone dead. She had spilled more of her own blood than she cared to remember. She could subtract a little unwanted flesh in her sleep.

Nadine opened the Dopp kit and removed a straight razor, a Solingen edge with a mother-of-pearl handle. She opened it, drew it across her thumbnail to test for keenness, kneeled between her friend's legs.

"My dad stropped it before I left, I saw him. He hides it in a shoe in his closet. Like I don't know where everything is in that house. It's as sharp as it can get, like a Japanese sword."

"Should I remove the rubber bands?"

"No, just cut in front of them, one quick slice, nice and easy. There's going to be blood, but hopefully not a lot. Once you're done, just flush it away and wash your hands and then run out there and get the emergency room peeps, okay? We'll tell 'em I did it so you don't get in any trouble."

Nadine held onto his penis and testicles, placed the razor by the first rubber band, a thick green band, the kind that holds broccoli in bunches. Nadine was about to push into the flesh when someone knocked on the door to the stall.

"What's going on in there?"

Then that person pushed the stall door open. Nadine had neglected to lock it.

"Oh my god!"

A nurse. She clapped a hand over her mouth, stepped back, and ran out.

"Nadine, hurry!"

Nadine, in a rush to finish the job, cut herself across the meat of her palm, and accidentally dropped the razor in the toilet.

"Ahh!"

"Are you okay?" said Gil, reaching into the water for the razor.

"Gil, I'm sorry! I screwed up!"

"It's okay my dear," he said, angling the dripping razor against his privates. "No harm done, we'll get you stitched up in no time, let me just take care of this…"

A massive security guard rushed in with pistol drawn, pointed first at Nadine, then at Gil, back to Nadine. Gil dropped the razor. Nadine raised her hands, her right palm open like the gill of a bluefish.

It was not the first time she had badly cut her hand. It was not the first time she had ruined a life.

# CHAPTER NINE

# You Better Stop
# the Things That You Do

HARPER STOPPED WHAT SHE was doing. She gently took Nadine's right wrist in one hand. The long scar on her palm, tracked on either side by the regular, pale keloids of suture holes, looked like a strange registration on a map.

"I'm sorry to tell you all that," said Nadine. "It's a terrible story, all the worse because it was a total failure. I got arrested. For attempted assault. And I got grounded. I'm still grounded, I think. I don't really know."

"Gil?"

"I haven't heard from him. I have no idea where he is. I can't call, my daddy still has my phone."

"Nadine. I can't help but think it's for the best that he didn't hurt himself, that you didn't hurt him."

"Yeah. Maybe. But there's no other way for him to get what he needs. He tried to explain how strong the urge was, but he said he couldn't. Once, when he was a little kid, he went camping with his family. He wandered off. He was lost for three days in the woods by himself. All he remembers is mosquito bites and hunger, but mostly thirst. He says that the urge to cut off his privates is like that thirst he felt when he was lost in the woods. It was only quenched by the Powerade he had after a family found him. Now, only subtraction can quench his thirst to be gender null. He says if he can't be that way, he doesn't want to live. He doesn't want to be a boy, or a sexual being, or anything. I'm worried now, since he can't have what he wants, that he—"

Nadine was quiet for a moment. Her throat was sore, raw, from talking. She never talked, except to Dr. Singh. And Gil, but those days were over now. She was sure of it. In the reflection of the bathroom mirror, Nadine watched Harper holding her wrist with one hand, her other palming Nadine's scarred hand. Nadine was reminded of a moment on a train, years before. The only train she'd ever taken, an Amtrak to Dallas with her mother to visit a cousin who was dying of a strange cancer growing in her jaw. The train slowed to pass through a small town. A boy was flying a box kite and waving at the train. The shadow of the kite crossed the boy's face, then slid over a patch of marigolds, then seemed to settle, frozen, on the side of an old galvanized tin shed whose doors were wide open. In the shed were hundreds of crutches, old wooden crutches, ambered by use and age and sweat, and newer aluminum crutches with dirty off-white balls of rubber at the tips. Some were split, others splintered, some looked like great swords, clotted with talc and scarred by battle and mishap. Others looked unused, as though they could be returned for refunds or store credit. The crutches were all leaning away from the bright sunlight the open door ushered in. The shadow of the box kite suddenly shifted, slipped to the grassy ground, and disappeared into the shed. It was at this instant that Nadine noticed not the scene outside, the crutches and the kite-shadow and the waving boy, but her mother's reflection in the train window. Angie was gazing at Nadine as though she were thinking about saying goodbye to her daughter forever. She turned away from the window to look at her mother, to see the goodbye on her face, but there was nothing there but a vacated chrysalis, a shell or exoskeletal effigy of her mother, staring at the fabric of the seat in front of her.

When was Harper going to say goodbye to Nadine? It would be sooner or later.

"Let's go visit him," said Harper.

"Huh?"

"Let's find out where Gil is," she said, snapping her beauty case shut.

"How?"

"I'll think of something. Now, you can't go to sleep with all that makeup on, so we should probably just stay up. It's about 6:20. What time do your parents wake up?"

"Daddy about 7:15, for work, and Mom about 8."

"Are there any breakfast places open?"

"There's a Nighthawk in town, open all the time."

"Hungry?"

"I'm always hungry. Meds."

"I'll call a cab. You leave a note for your parents. By the way, you look absolutely stunning."

"Really?"

"You bet."

"There aren't many Mooreheads in Abilene, but I bet these are them—2106 Spring Branch Road," said Harper, tapping on her phone while chewing a whole slice of bacon. "Let's try them first, what say?"

"Okay." Nadine folded a piece of Nighthawk bacon in half and wolfed it down. The salty fat, combined with the possibility that Harper might be able to find Gil—and that she cared enough to try—brought her close to tears. Nadine *never* cried.

"You find out how long it takes to get there. I'll call the car rental place."

"How do I do that?"

"Type in 'Austin Abilene driving.'"

"That's it?"

"Yes, darling."

Within an hour they were on the road to Abilene in a Mercedes W211. A three-and-a-half-hour drive, according to MapQuest, that Harper was determined to make in three.

"Now, Gil probably won't be there, so our job will be to charm his parents into telling us where he is. Obviously, we cannot tell them you are the infamous Nadine Grandet, who was going to bob their son's profile, so you will be my daughter, Liz."

"Do you really have a daughter named Liz?"

Harper was quiet for a moment.

"No," she said. "Not anymore."

They drove. Central Texas slid by in flat streaks of viridian and burnt sienna and Payne's gray, a painterly wasteland.

"So," said Harper eventually.

"What is our business?"

"I have an idea."

"Lay it on me."

When they finally got to Abilene, they pulled into a filling station bathroom to wash off Nadine's makeup, and so Harper could touch up her own.

They rang the bell at 2106 Spring Branch Road. A weary-looking man in his mid-thirties answered the door. His reddish hair was receding rapidly, his blue dress shirt laid untucked against his soft body. He held two TV remotes in one hand, a squat glass with an amber liquid in the other. He said nothing.

"Hi, Harper DeBaecque, my daughter, Liz. Gil invited us over today?"

"What?"

"Gil Moorehead? Oh dear, have we got the wrong address?"

"Uh, no. Yes. Er, Gil's not here. I'm sorry, I didn't know he was expecting anyone."

"Gil and I met at McLean," said Nadine. "I live in Dallas. We had plans today?"

"He never mentioned you. Liz, you said?"

Nadine nodded, her best look of innocent deception on her face. Nadine had seen the look on her daddy's face when he bluffed at cards.

"Why don't you come in," said the man, appraising Harper like a sex trafficker. "My wife's not home."

"When will Gil be back?" said Harper.

"I'm sorry to say he was admitted to another hospital, and there's no telling when he'll be home. You know how those places are," said Mr. Moorehead, now unreadable.

"Can we go visit him?" said Nadine.

Mr. Moorehead gave her a long, alien look, then said, "I'd rather give Gil his privacy. I hope you understand."

Nadine looked up at him. She peered around the room and saw a bookcase against a wall. She didn't see *B.L.G.*, but knew it must be in there somewhere. She tried to picture this man reading it, absorbing its words, imagining his own child being wrapped in a blanket, ceremented in silver duct tape, loaded onto a train, shipped off to North Dakota to a camp because he didn't want to be a *boy*, didn't want to be a *girl*.

Nadine pictured this man putting the book down, drinking the last of his bourbon or whatever that was, and writing a check for a hundred dollars or more to Reverend Orpus Tulalip. She pictured him sealing the check in an envelope and walking to the mailbox. She pictured him coming back into his house, going down the hall to check on his son, only to find that he had run away, leaving a note: *I have found a way out.*

"We understand," said Harper immediately. "May I give you our phone number, so that Gil can call Liz if he likes? I know he'd like to talk to her. They were good friends in Belmont."

"Well, okay, sure."

"May I use the bathroom?" said Nadine. Mr. Moorehead looked exasperated, as though he were finally allowed to get out of a dentist's chair after a painful procedure, only to be told that they were just going to take care of that last little bitty cavity before it got too bad.

"Down the hall, right."

In the hall, tacked up to a closed door on the left was a wrinkled piece of lined notebook paper with a poem in green crayon scrawled on it in a childish hand.

*LET US HAVE HIM NO*

> *I will not leave here*
> *It is my room*
> *The hall of my books and records*
> *Where the directory of my incremental decay resides*
> *Where I overstuff and underfeed*
> *It is where doctors advise I cry*
> *But I cannot*
> *It is where friends advise I shape up*

*But I cannot*

*The springs in my Anglepoise are shot*

*It droops over my desk like a victim*

*Frostwork crazes the panes*

*Neon tetras shiver in a tank*

*Fists sledge at the jamb*

*Be advised, sir, that if you don't open up*

*We will be obliged to break this door down*

Nadine tried the door, but it was locked. She turned around, ducked into the bathroom, flushed the toilet, waited a moment, ran the water in the sink, and headed back to the living room.

Mr. Moorehead stood up.

"My wife will be home soon."

It sounded like a warning. Nadine and Harper stood and headed for the door.

"You'd better not come back here," he said.

"What now?" said Nadine when they got back in the car.

"I'll program my phone so it has a special ring. What's Gil's favorite song?"

"'I Put a Spell on You,' the version by Screamin' Jay Hawkins."

"I have an idea," said Harper, tapping rapidly into her phone.

"Yeah?"

"You've heard of all the mental hospitals, right?"

Nadine was starting to worry what her parents were doing, thinking. It upset her to think they might be mad at Harper for sneaking off with their only remaining daughter. It was important that they like Harper, that Harper didn't mess things up. There was some promise in her advent, creeping in by degrees.

"A lot of them, yeah."

"Why don't you just start calling them all?"

"You have to have the numbers to the individual units, and those numbers you can't get from 411."

"But you can get them from the hospitals themselves, right?"

"Yeah."

"So start calling."

"McLean has like a million units. They'd get suspicious after a while."

Nadine was arguing because it was her nature to do so. She actually thought Harper had a pretty damn good idea.

"They probably only have a couple adolescent units."

"He's not always on adolescent units 'cause he's so weird."

"Here's my phone."

After two hours with no luck, Nadine ran out of hospitals to call.

They had seen an awful lot of Abilene driving in aimless circles. They had passed the same cop twice. It would not do to get pulled over.

"I couldn't get through to some wards," said Nadine, trying not to look at the cop, who they were now encountering for the third time. "I'll keep trying. And you know, he could be on the psych ward of a general hospital."

"In that case it would be local, right?" said Harper. "Abilene? Try that."

She did, with no luck. She tried the psychiatric wards of general hospitals in surrounding towns, also no luck. At least she was getting good at phone-googling.

"I guess we should head back to Austin."

"I don't think I'll ever see him again."

"You will. I know it."

"How do you know?"

Harper pulled onto a minor highway. She turned on the radio.

"Because I want it, and I usually get what I want. So. What did we do today?"

Sarah Vaughan came on. "Broken Hearted Melody."

"Huh?"

"We went shopping," she said, turning the song up.

"Shopping. Okay."

When Angie got home from work Nadine was sitting with her legs crossed on the table in the kitchen, her hair in pin curls.

"Wow!" said Angie. "And who is this young beauty on my kitchen-table throne?"

"You should've seen her makeup earlier," said Harper. "We finally washed it off. How was work?"

"Easy. Books are easy. You just need to read a lot and know most of the alphabet. Is that your Mercedes out there?"

"Rental."

"What about your work?" said Angie, digging through a kitchen drawer and coming up with an ice pick with a cracked wooden handle. "International patent attorneys can't just up and leave their jobs. Can they?"

"Sure we can. We burn a few bridges, poison a few rivers, but hell, why not? I'll make a few calls, probably have to go back to the office in Denver once or twice, fire the paralegals and secretaries—"

"Oh, Harper. Are you... staying?"

"For a bit."

Angie opened the freezer door and began chipping away at a massif of ice, which occupied nearly half the compartment.

"And I don't care about work," said Harper. "I couldn't be happier. Whatcha doing?"

"I was at work today and remembered that there's a pint of dulce de leche buried somewhere in this berg. I want it."

"I want some," said Harper and Nadine at the same time.

"Gotta dig it out before Dean Lee gets home."

"Nadine," said Harper, licking her fingers and moistening her young charge's pin curls, "you're going to look like Betty Grable in an hour."

"Who?"

"She was a World War II pinup girl. She was on every barracks wall in the entire U.S. Armed Forces during the war. Get my laptop, I'll show you pictures."

A knock came at the door.

"I recognize that," said Angie wearily, dropping the ice pick and pushing the freezer door shut with her forehead. She briefly explained the fact and existence of Lolly Prager to Harper, then went to get the door.

"Lolly—Harper DeBaecque, friend from high school, here in town for a visit."

"How do," said Lolly, shaking hands. "You the spitting image of Veronica Lake, you know that, Miss Harper?"

Lolly could say things like that without offending, without creepiness or double entendre, and Harper blushed right through her makeup.

"Didn't see ol' Dean Lee's truck outside," said Lolly, picking up the ice pick as though valuating it for seizure. "Mind if I wait for him?"

"What's he owe?"

"His total obligation is $10,425. So. Four hundred and twenty-six dollars will keep him out the oven today."

"What's that mean?" Harper whispered to Nadine.

"Hello, Nadine, how're you, sweetie? Y'all look like y'all backstage at a David O. Selznick picture." Lolly put the ice pick down.

"Fine, Lolly. Miss Harper is making me look like Betty Grady. And Daddy took my new phone. I bet that's worth $426, if you can find it."

"Why don't you let the adults talk, hon," said Angie.

Nadine didn't move.

"Will you take a Colorado check?" said Harper.

"Harper, no."

"I'm afraid mine is a cash 'n' carry operation, Miss Harper."

"C'mon, Nadine," said Harper. "Let's you and me run down to the ATM. We'll roll the windows down, the air'll be good for your curls."

"Harper, no," said Angie again. "It's Dean Lee's problem."

"What's the oven?" said Harper. Lolly looked at Angie, then at Harper, then at Nadine.

"Well, I, uh, it's just—"

"It's the hospital," said Nadine, uncrossing her legs and climbing down from the table. "It means Lolly will send somebody to beat Daddy up."

"Oh, no, not true now," said Lolly and Angie at once, though it was.

"Yes, it is, Lolly. Don't lie."

Dean Lee came in.

"Lolly, what the hell! Embarrassing me like this in front of the lady. Goddammit, how much?"

"Four hundred and twenty-six dollars, bare minimum," said Lolly, not looking at Dean Lee. "That'll keep you in one piece for twenty-four hours. Then we play again."

"When?"

"Now. Now, Dean Lee, now. Goddammit. *Now.*"

"Ain't got it."

"Gimme the piece then. Where is it?"

"My cold, dead fingers."

"You know I got Ron DeGroot in the pickup with me. Right out-side, nappin' in the bed. He's dreamin' about you, Dean Lee. And he's got his jumper cables."

"Oh for chrissake."

Nadine's daddy did not look in the least concerned. Her daddy might be a bad gambler, but he could take care of himself in a fistfight, even if the other guy had jumper cables. She was proud of Daddy right this minute, even if he had made things difficult taking her phone away.

"*Yes* for chrissake," said Lolly, looking all at once uncharacteristically fierce. Nadine knew his reputation, and it was suddenly clear to her just how well deserved it must be. Just like that, she was afraid for her daddy, the untouchable Dean Lee Grandet.

"Oh my god," said Angie. "Lolly—"

"Nadine," said Harper, "c'mon, we're going to the ATM right now. Let's go."

"Hurry, please, Miss Harper," said Lolly. "Ron DeGroot is a light sleeper and moreover an impatient individual, upon whom dissuasive rhetoric has little effect."

On the way to the Chase drive-thru, Nadine said, "Lolly introduced Mom and Dad."

"Really?" said Harper. "Did he really bring a man in the bed of his truck to beat your dad up?"

"I think so. He's never done it before that I know about, but Lolly looks really serious today. Dad has had this debt since their wedding night, and just can't pay it, because of the interest. And because he's a terrible gambler. Lolly sometimes takes things out of our house to pay the debt down, though he hasn't done that in a while either. He's my godfather."

"You're kidding."

"It has to do with toxoplasmosis."

"Maybe you'll explain that to me sometime. He seems like a nice man."

"He runs chicken fights, poker games, a sports book, bareknuckle fights, a craps game, a drag race, a strip joint, and a three-ex bookstore. He can fold a dollar bill into an armadillo shape."

Harper stayed with the Grandets for two weeks, then rented a house a couple doors down and across the street, so close they could hear one another's phones ringing on quiet nights.

Nadine and Angie flew with Harper to Denver to help clean her belongings out of the house one weekend when her husband, Ken, was away. Gidget—as Harper had dubbed the other woman—had apparently moved in, as numerous metallic-looking wigs and thigh-high patterned socks were in evidence in the bureau drawers. Harper took the opportunity to desecrate the articles in creative ways, much to Nadine and Angie's delight. Harper had so many vintage clothes they filled thirteen closet-boxes and eleven regular boxes, and so many high-heel shoes that even after taking two-thirds of them to St. Ignatius Thrift, the remainder still filled three medium-sized boxes. Two Gringos and a Semi assured Harper they could be in McCandless in less than twenty-four hours with her stuff intact, and in fact they were. Graf and Kev, the gringos, unloaded the whole truck in less than thirty minutes, gratefully accepted a hundred-dollar tip, and disappeared down Fawn Street at dusk in a storm of fireflies. Nadine was allowed to stay up late helping Harper unpack over at her new place.

It was past eleven when Harper's phone rang with a tone she didn't recognize. But Nadine did.

"'I Put a Spell on You!'"

"You better go ahead and answer it."

"Can I go in the bathroom?"

"You can go in my room and shut the door."

Nadine closed Harper's bedroom door behind her. She flopped down on her bed, covered herself with a crocheted University of Texas blanket, plugged one ear with a finger, and whispered into the phone.

"Gil?"

"This is Juliette Moorehead. May I speak to Mrs., um, DeBaecque."

"She's, ah, asleep. Can I take a message?"

"You're Liz? Gilbert's friend?"

"Gilbert?"

"Yes."

Nadine had forgotten for a moment that she had been Liz DeBaecque, Harper's daughter, for an afternoon on the edge of West Texas.

"You're really Nadine Grandet, though," said Juliette Moorehead.

"Um, no..."

"It's okay. I... listen, uh, Gilbert, he... I'm calling to tell you and your, ah, mom, that Gilbert didn't... he didn't... Gilbert couldn't..."

Juliette took a breath.

"Gilbert is gone."

"Where?" said Nadine. That was the word that came out of her mouth.

"He passed."

Nadine remembered something then. Something that Gil told her, a quote from a writer who he loved. The writer had said something like this. *Words that come from the heart are never spoken, they get caught in the throat and can only be read in ones's eyes.* There was no one in the room to read the words in Nadine's eyes. There was no mirror even. There was nothing, no witness. When Nadine fired her daddy's gun at her little sister Sophie and subtracted her tiny slapjack life from the history of the world five years before—the opening of the great parenthesis of Nadine's existence—she had not known it would all be over, that the parenthesis would close, in this room, where her words caught in her throat like the slender, transparent bones of a fish.

"I'm sorry," said Juliette Moorehead.

"——"

"He…"

"——"

"Gil took his life."

"——"

"I'm sorry to have to tell you over the phone."

"——"

"Nadine?"

"———"

"Honey, he's gone. To a better place. I have to get off the phone now, Nadine Grandet. Goodbye."


The way Angie remembered it was as a silent evening suddenly punctured by a low, distant moan growing louder until it burst through the front door of the house and then the door to their bedroom and landed on the bed between her and her husband, and Angie was stroking her daughter's hair and saying, "What's the matter, honey?" while Nadine lay face down, shivering, moaning, clutching her shoulders, then suddenly arching and spinning onto her back, her hair streaking her face, screaming soundlessly at the ceiling and clawing at her throat, digging her nails into her flesh, drawing beads of blood, Dean Lee scooting in to protect her from what he didn't understand, Angie clutching her daughter in her arms, as if trying to keep a cat hit by a car from slipping away, when Nadine became still, quiet, calm, covered in sweat, heart beating rapidly… and then she curled up and went to sleep. Angie looked up to see Harper standing at the door to their bedroom; she had followed Nadine there.

The room was still for a long while.

In the morning, Nadine told Angie and Harper and her daddy about Gil.

"Gone," she said, resting her head on the kitchen table.

"I'm sorry, honey," said Dean Lee. He sat next to her, head bent in supplication. Nadine did not blame him for anything. She knew, she could see, he was suffering.

Harper said nothing.

"I don't want to be around anymore."

"Don't say that, baby, please," said Dean Lee.

"I don't. Daddy, give me your gun."

"Oh, Nadine."

"I have nothing."

"You have your momma and your daddy," said Harper. "And me."

"I want Gil."

"Are you serious, Nadine?" said Angie. "Do I need to protect you from yourself?"

"Yes, you do."

"Do you want to go to Meecker-Lang?"

"Yes."

"All right. Let's pack you a bag."


Angie advised the admitting doctor that she felt her daughter was at risk of taking her own life as the result of the suicide of a close friend.

It wasn't until much later that Angie found out her daughter spent nearly forty hours in four-point restraints upon admission because of her mother's opinion, nearly a week in solitary confinement, and her entire five-month stay heavily medicated, including Prolixin delivered twice daily by anal suppository. She did emerge alive, however, and that, Meecker-Lang would argue, had been the goal. The staff at M-L was highly cautious about who Nadine spent time with this time, evidently feeling some responsibility for her befriending such a high-risk individual as Gil Moorehead the first time around. They were careful to separate her from boys especially, and any piquant temperaments in particular. It was a lonesome stretch for Nadine.

Dr. Singh's office had finally been renovated. She had decorated the walls with prints from Jean-Michel Basquiat's oeuvre. To Nadine, it looked like a bunch of kindergarten crap, and it annoyed her to be surrounded by it. She felt she could do better, and it made her want to draw.

"How is your SI today, Nadine?"

"Pretty low, I guess. I don't feel like I wanna die today."

"I'm very glad to hear that. What has changed?"

"I'm ready to get out."

There were two places to sit in Dr. Singh's office: a chair and a couch. The couch smelled overwhelmingly of Febreze, an aromatic that transferred to her clothes and made her reek until she could launder them. The chair was, for some reason, jacked up on four red bricks, so her feet didn't reach the ground when she sat. The arrangement made her feel like a child. She hated this office.

"I'm not sure you're ready for that."

"I want to get back to Mom and Daddy and Harper. I've been here for months."

"Who is Harper?"

"A friend. I've told you about her. You just don't remember. You don't pay attention all the time, Dr. Singh. I catch you looking at your clock a lot."

"I remember. Your mother's stylish friend?"

"*My* friend."

"Is she a good influence?"

"Why are you so worried about good influences?"

"I was right about Gil, wasn't I?"

Nadine swung her feet under the chair. If Gil had been here, he would've said something witty and damning that would've shut Singh up.

"Don't go there, Dr. Singh," said Nadine with as much menace as she could summon, which was quite a bit.

"All right."

"When are you going to let me out?"

"All in good time."

It felt like there was a lime trapped under her sternum. Nadine put both hands to her solar plexus, pressed hard, took a deep breath, and held it as long as she could. Then she said: "Why can't you give me an answer? Tomorrow, a week, a month, never? Why not?"

"Because I don't know, that's why."

"Then *say* that. Don't say, '*All in good time.*'"

Dr. Singh's cell phone rang. That was against the rules. Phones, both patients' and doctors', were supposed to be off during sessions.

"You can be very rude," said Dr. Singh.

"Me? Your phone just went off. And you want rude? I hate your art, I hate it. I want to rip it off the walls. It's garbage, it makes me furious!"

Nadine felt her rear end sliding off the chair, she felt her feet reaching for the floor; she was going to stride across the room, peel a poster off the wall, wad it up, stomp it into a pancake. But she stopped herself.

"Basquiat was a very important artist."

"He sucks."

"I'm sorry you don't like it."

"It's disruptive. You should take it down. I bet I'm not the only one it makes mad."

By saying that, she practically guaranteed Singh would fill, by tomorrow, the two blank spots on the wall with more miserable Basquiat daubs.

"What would I put up in its place?"

"I don't know. Gil and I like Lisa Yuskavage."

"Really."

"Yeah."

"I don't know how her art would go over in here."

"You know her?"

Dr. Singh had a habit of remaining perfectly silent and still, a Renaissance half-smile on her face, fingers interlaced on her notebook in her threadbare lap, a micro-expression of self-satisfaction evident at her widow's peak, all of which worked in concert to communicate a bitchrocket know-it-all-ness that made Nadine madder than anything her doctor could actually say, and it was always a relief when Dr. Singh finally ended her arrogant trances by opening her mouth and uttering something that made Nadine feel small.

"This surprises you."

"I like to think she is mine and Gil's. Alone."

"That no one else knows about her?"

Nadine experimented briefly with a penetrating Singh-like silence. Singh probably just thought Nadine hadn't heard or didn't understand.

"That no one else knows about her? She's quite famous."

Nadine felt naked. She felt like a girl in a Yuskavage painting, distorted, objectified. But more, she felt violated, deceived, snared, robbed from. She hated that Singh knew about Lisa Yuskavage. Gil had told her all about Lisa, and had even done some extraordinary drawings from memory of her work. Then Nadine had looked them up on her phone after she was discharged and had been in shock and in love. Lisa was hers and Gil's alone.

"Do you think of Gil as still being alive?"

"I don't know. No."

"You referred to him in the present tense."

"I—I can't think of him as gone."

"Do you communicate with him?"

"I'm not crazy. You're always trying to catch me doing or saying something nuts so you can keep me in this place longer or try some new med on me or give me more of some med I'm already on or throw down some other kind of psychiatric punishment. You don't have any interest in helping me. You're listening to me only because I killed my sister, because I'm *interesting*. You like having me around because I'm exotic and weird, but not quite exotic and weird enough, so you place weirdness on me. You hope and pray that I think I'm communicating with the dead, that I'm constantly in danger of committing suicide, that I may kill again. None of that is true. All that's true is that I hate your stupid art, I don't like you, I don't respect you, I want a new doctor, and I want out of this fucking hospital."

Nadine did not get a new doctor, but she was discharged three weeks later. She was twelve years old.

During her daughter's stay, Angie received a letter from Juliette

Moorehead. Or, more precisely, she received an envelope from Juliette
Moorehead. Inside was a thousand dollars in fifties, and a single yellow
Post-it Note, the adhesive strip on verso covered with bits of dust and
dirt. Written in a tiny, childlike hand in blue ink, covering both sides
of the Post-it was:

*EQUINOX.*

*Hands open,*
*like drogue parachutes,*
*we palm November,*
*the reptile month,*
*the brain-stem month.*
*Now an evening rusts,*
*and we wait*
*for the shatter of traffic to die out,*
*our embraces*
*lie muzzled in a corner,*
*and our harrowings,*
*accelerated by darkness,*
*accumulate on the ceiling,*
*watching us*
*bite through pens*
*in our sleep.*

*We wake to a flare*
*beneath the breastbone,*
*a ping in the marrow,*
*a gut dislocation,*

*the fragrant fragile landslide*
*of December,*
*the hair-trigger month,*
*when potatoes*
*and secobarbital marry,*
*and we stamp our final postcards.*
—G. M.

Dear Nadine:
I'm showing signs.
It's too late.
I know you tried.
You're my only friend.
I love you.
Goodbye.

Angie, following a moment when she considered eating the Post-it, taped the envelope with the poem and the suicide note and the money to the underside of her bottom bureau drawer.

# CHAPTER TEN

# The Barrens

ANGIE'S MOTHER, ADELINE BIGELOW, had never forgiven her daughter for eloping to Las Vegas with Dean Lee Grandet. She sent no gift, no card, made no phone call, and in fact vanished like a mist from every aspect of Angie's new life. Even the birth of Nadine went unacknowledged. Through almost seven years of living in neighboring towns, Angie and her mother never once ran into each other in a grocery store, the dry cleaners, the old book swap on Main Street. Angie thought she once saw her mother's old green Valiant driving in the wrong direction down a one-way on the east side of town, but when Angie followed and finally got close enough to see, the dents in the car proved to be in the wrong places, and some hipster kid with a fedora and Buddy Holly glasses was behind the wheel. Another time, Angie thought she saw her mother in the ice cream aisle at an H-E-B in Lockhart, but it wasn't her. It wasn't even a woman, Angie discovered when the man turned around, clearly aware someone was staring at him as he chose his half-gallon of Bridal Cake ice cream. He was just some old Hill Country hippie with a spectacularly wavy and luxuriant silver coiffure.

But, of course, Adeline Bigelow did turn up at Sophie's funeral. She appeared, then disappeared, greeting no one, offering no condolences. It gave Angie hope, or at least what passed for hope on that hopeless, helpless day. If Angie's consolation for a daughter gored and disintegrated—by a bullet that weighed even less than Sophie's life savings of nine quarters—was going to be a sighting of Angie's own mother, then she would not complain.

It would be seven more years before she saw her mother again.

Angie was on the first floor of BookPeople, down on her knees shelving books in the graphic novels section, when she became aware of a presence. She looked up.

"Mom?"

"Hello, Angie."

"I don't know what to say. How… how did you know I worked here? No—let me go back: how are you?"

"I'm a very resourceful old bird. And I'm fine. Better than fine, even."

It was Angie's first good, close look at her mother in nearly fourteen years. And Adeline looked fourteen years older. Angie calculated quickly—her mother was almost sixty now. Vibrant still, beautiful always, but a lifetime of superior rancor did function as a kind of Oil of Olay. Angie wondered what her mother thought about her—did she think she looked thirty-eight? Or forty-eight?

"Do you—"

"I need *The Book of Margery Kempe*."

"We have that—this way."

"Good girl, I knew you'd know it."

As Angie led her mother around the corner, she could feel Adeline's eyes assessing her from behind. *Wider. Lower. Saggier. Pokier. Jigglier.*

*And what has happened to the shine in your hair? From Breck Girl to Black Forest witch.*

"Do you have time to sit for coffee?" said Angie, taking the paperback off the shelf and handing it to her mother. "I haven't seen you since the, um, your granddaughter's funeral."

Angie was reminded, non-sequitur, of a Louise Brooks quotation: "If I bore you, it'll be with a knife."

"And before that, since who knows."

Adeline smiled serenely.

"Lead the way."

"Triple espresso, Juana," said Angie, ordering at the coffeeshop in the back of the store. "And an iced mocha for me. Let's sit, Mom. What do you want with Margery Kempe?"

"I just want the modern version of the text. For a friend."

Adeline Bigelow was quiet for a moment. Looking down, she absently traced the illuminated cover of the paperback with a fingertip. She tilted her head to one side, looked up at her daughter from under what Angie realized were *violet* false eyelashes. Angie stared at her.

"Angie, coffees!" called Juana.

When Angie returned to the table, she gave her mother a hard look.

"What's going on?"

"Nothing."

"You mentioned a friend, then got all weird. And you're wearing purple falsies."

"I most certainly did n—"

"Did. Who is this friend?"

"Just a friend."

Angie worked at a store whose one-time general manager had murdered her lover's husband, then came to work the next day. If Angie wanted to have a little public fight with her freshly rediscovered mother, no one at BookPeople would give a shit.

"Explain yourself, goddammit," said Angie. "One sighting of you in a decade and a half, like a fucking black-tailed godwit."

"I see you have added some color and vigor to your discourse markers. Barney's influence?"

"Dean Lee."

"You used to be so eloquent."

Again, Adeline tilted her head and began tracing Margery's head with her fingertip. Her daughter grabbed her mother's wrist.

"Mom! What!"

Adeline gently withdrew from her daughter's grasp and took a sip of her espresso.

"It just so happens that I met a nice boy."

Angie at first pictured some freckled redhead with a fishing pole in a Norman Rockwell painting, but then realized what her mother was actually saying.

"Really. Who? Is it serious? How long? What's he do? Is he retired? What's his—"

"Slow down, Angie. I'll tell you everything."

A strange sensation came over Angie, a kind of partition falling between her mind and her body. Its effect was one of enlightenment—an expansion of perspective where she could see, or, more accurately, feel, a larger truth that had been hidden. Therapists had told Angie that it was possible to love someone and dislike them at the same time. Angie's larger truth, rising over her like the starry dome of the night sky, was that she both disliked and *hated* her mother.

"His name is Foster Luckenbach," Adeline said. "He is a librarian. Head of rare books for a private library here in Austin, the Golub

Repository. I had never heard of it until Foster approached me after their restorer took ill. The Golub collects pre-revolutionary French legal manuscripts and early printed books, and it's the largest collector of such documents outside of France. He's a deeply learned man, and a true gentleman, the only one I've ever met besides your father."

"Well, Mom, it sounds like you're in love."

"There is a possibility of that, yes."

Her mother was sometimes so infuriatingly empirical that Angie wanted to slap her hard enough to make her hair dance.

"Are you or aren't you in love?" said Angie, evenly. "Mom?"

"It's only been a few weeks. A few dates."

"Slept with him?"

Adeline tried to remain passive, but a smile shone through, moonlight through shutters.

"Good for you," said Angie. Adeline Bigelow blushed a pleasant damask rose.

"How old is he?"

Adeline Bigelow blushed a deep cherry cerise.

"Thirty-nine."

"What?"

"You heard me. I'm twenty years his senior. Who cares? Want to see a picture?"

Adeline took out her phone and scrolled through her photos until she found one of a man who resembled James Agee in his youth. He was standing beside an old Mustang convertible, lighting two cigarettes at once. A hand, the hand of a woman, was reaching toward him from outside the frame of the photo. It was not the picture, but rather that her mother had a cell phone, and seemed to understand how it worked, that surprised Angie.

"Shit, Mom, well done."

"He's not quite the man your father was in bed, but he's very skilled and attentive, and there's room for improvement."

"I don't want to hear it," said Angie, clamping her hands over her ears.

"You brought it up. He does this trick with his—"

"Stop!"

"Who knew librarians were so dirty?"

"So, when do I get to meet him?"

Her mother took out her phone and quickly sent a text. *A text?*

"In about ninety seconds."

"What?"

"He's upstairs looking at art books. Well, he was. Now he's on his way downstairs to meet you."

Angie looked to her left. Possibly the most attractive human male she had ever laid eyes on was entering the coffeeshop, dressed in a slightly rumpled gray suit, hair out of order but demanding one run one's hands through it, sighing. He was carrying under one arm a reprint of the *Codex Seraphinianus.*

"Foster, I'd like you to meet my daughter, Angie. Angie, Foster."

"This is an extraordinary book. Why have I never heard of it?" said Foster, sitting down, shaking Angie's hand, and opening his book all at once. "Do you know it, Angie?"

"The writing is meaningless," said Angie, watching her mother watch her. "I think Serafini wanted to give the 'reader' the feeling a child who is too young to read has when presented with a book—that combined sensation of wonder and helplessness. He succeeds."

Adeline leaned over and gave Foster a kiss.

"I like your daughter," he said, smiling. Angie could feel herself blushing, a twinkling of the nerve endings in her face. "We must all get together for dinner. Justine's? Tonight?"

"This is a poker night for Dean Lee," said Angie, quickly. "I don't know if I'll be able to get a sitter for Nadine."

"Why, let's bring her along," said Foster. "I'd love to meet her."

"She's only thirteen."

"We'll make an early night of it," said Adeline. This surprised Angie. It sounded almost as if her mother wanted Nadine to come along. "She's not exactly… healthy."

"I know someone who might be able to sit," said Foster. "Someone at the repository where I work, a librarian, Meghan Thurible. She's twenty-four, brilliant and of overarching responsibility, loves children, needs the money. Shall I call her?"

"Oh, do call her," said Adeline.

Angie did not like to leave Nadine with sitters, except Bonnie, the young neighbor girl. Angie had only done so a few times, and then only out of necessity, scarcely ever to go out and have fun. But Nadine was quite heavily medicated, still, and generally out of it, and Angie thought it would be okay this once. "I don't live in town," she said. "Out in McCandless. But all right."

That evening, Nadine was in bed, deep under the covers, when Meghan came by.

"Nadine, would you say hello to Meghan? Nadine? Please?"

Nadine did not respond. Angie led Meghan to the kitchen.

"Emergency numbers on the fridge, here are Nadine's meds, instructions here. She probably won't get out of bed."

"Mrs. Grandet, is she all right?"

"She had…" Angie started to explain. "A shock."

"I see."

"She is not well, but it's nothing you have to worry about."

"Anything I can do?"

"Just keep an eye on her, ask her if she needs anything, be kind to her, let her know you're here, keep reminding her that her mother will be home around eleven. All right?"

Justine's was crowded, loud. It was a restaurant that never seemed quite at home in Austin, or rather like it had been there since the dawn of cuisine, and Austin had grown up around it.

Foster Luckenbach told stories of harrowing acquisitions of famous rare manuscripts, the personalities of the collectors who parted with them, the booksellers who brokered the deals, the restorers who brought the manuscripts back to life. He spoke in rich, unbroken narratives, in the manner of the most veracious storyteller, and Angie and Adeline were rapt, their *bifteks au poivre et frites* cooling before they could cut into them. Angie noted how Foster would look at her mother and smile, how she could stand it for only an instant before blushing, then looking away. But Angie would not look away.

She left the restaurant feeling like she'd been on a date. Foster and Adeline became something of an item. Morgan, Foster's wife of eleven years, amicably divorced her husband after suddenly discovering a latent taste for butch women. But the two continued to live in the same house on Eilers Street with Morgan's girlfriend Frankie, making for a harmonious trio that experimented every morning with a vintage espresso machine and ate lumberjack breakfasts together and in the evenings mixed experimental cocktails from a tattered, century-old copy of *Cocktail Boothby's American Bartender*, playing Caruso 78s on a windup Victrola; a trio of which two thirds were not exactly ready to welcome an interloper, a straight (almost) sexagenarian who drank only Spanish reds, whose powerful Hill Country accent she strove desperately to mask but which still bubbled up in twangy shibboleths, who couldn't sit outside without drenching herself in Deep Woods Off!, whose only conversational gambits were bibliographic or ornithologic, except when she tried to talk about the erotic, assays that would quickly get shut down by Morgan, who of course did not want to hear about her ex-husband's bedroom adventures with another woman.

Lately, Angie was often invited to these get togethers. The couple quickly grew to adore Angie, but Adeline was clearly not much liked by Frankie and Morgan—all Adeline's attempts at wit fell flat, the emphases always on the wrong words, and she sounded like she was almost going out of her way to offend. Morgan even joked that Angie seemed like she might be a better match for ol' Foster than crusty, witless Adeline.

But Angie did notice that her mother had softened. Adeline had grown less raptorlike and vindictive. She was simply awkward and tragic now.

One evening, a few weeks after Justine's, Angie dropped by the Foster/Morgan/Frankie compound. Foster was in the backyard, bent over a clay chiminea, stuffing it with old issues of *National Geographic*. Sparks flew out of the top and disappeared into the boughs of a stately magnolia. Dusk was moments away. A Maxfield Parrish sunset had blown up the western sky and shut everybody up for a solid five minutes. Morgan and Frankie were lying next to each other on chaise longues on the deck, their elbows touching. Each was sipping a cocktail called a Sabina Sling, a concoction of scotch, lime juice, egg white, ginger ale, and simple syrup, garnished with a cherry and slice of orange. Adeline was chewing on her typical cheap Tempranillo, Angie and Foster drinking reposado margaritas with salt.

Foster sat down. He took Adeline's hand, but looked at Angie and smiled.

"So when's the wedding?" said Frankie.

"Ha!" said Adeline. Foster said nothing.

"Whoa, sensitive topic, much?" said Morgan.

"I think they're not sure who we're talking about," said Frankie, making everyone even more uncomfortable.

"Who wants more booze?" said Foster, quickly standing up and heading for the kitchen.

"Did you see that?" said Morgan.

"What?" asked Angie, though she knew exactly what.

"You can't handle the truth!" Frankie shouted in perfect Jack Nicholson.

"Stop it, Frankie," said Morgan.

"Okay, okay."

"I have to use the little girls' room," said Adeline, getting to her feet slowly. She'd had a lot of wine.

"Head to the back, to the right—"

"I know where it is."

Morgan, Frankie, and Angie sat in the growing dark for a full minute, listening to Foster bustle about the kitchen.

"What's he doing in there?"

"Avoiding us, duh," said Morgan.

"We're onto him."

"What're y'all talking about?"

"C'mon, Angie," said Morgan. "My ex-husband likes you. More than he likes his sixty-year-old girlfriend. A lot more. Isn't that obvious?"

It was obvious, but Angie wasn't going to let them know that.

"He told you that?"

"No, but he doesn't have to."

"It's pretty crystal," said Frankie. "The way he looks at you, laughs at everything that comes out of your mouth, listens to what you have to say, touches Adeline's arm or shoulder whenever he gets a chance, refreshes your drinks first, chooses his words carefully, tries to sound extra smart, extra funny, extra witty, extra extra. He's throwing perfect spirals every time around you. And he always shaves before you come by—a dead giveaway that he's into you. A clean, close shave, with three disposable razors. He doesn't shave every time he sees Adeline, that's for sure."

"He didn't even shave for me when we were dating," said Morgan. "And he liked me quite a bit."

"I'm married, doesn't he know that?"

"Maybe your mother told him something about the state of your marriage. Maybe your mother told all of us something about it."

"Jesus Christ."

"Sorry."

"It's all right," Angie said. "But look, Adeline knows nothing about my marriage. My husband is far from perfect, but I love him, and more importantly, my daughter, my remaining daughter, loves him. And none of this means I'm looking for another man."

Angie realized she'd had quite a few margaritas.

"Foster might not know what you're looking for," said Frankie.

"Is he courting me?"

"I don't think so," said Morgan. "I don't think he thinks he is. He's not very self-aware. He's a rare-book librarian, remember, and all he really cares about is the beauty of a *lettre bâtarde*. But I guess the question is, are you available, married or not?"

"I could never steal a man away from my mother, you guys. Under no circumstances, and not for the reasons you might expect."

There was a little vinegar in her delivery. It was getting easier to piss off Angie Grandet as the years rolled by.

Yet there was a fragment of Angie that could not help but imagine how much it might hurt Adeline to steal her boyfriend. Angie had not forgotten her satori at BookPeople, when she understood that she both hated and disliked her mother. There was no competing love/hate dialectic.

"Do you like Foster?"

She did like him. There was an intellectual attraction, for certain: he was incandescently bright, understood Latin, Greek, French, Middle French, Old French, German, Italian, Russian, Japanese, and Elvish. He was a 2494-FIDE-rated chess player. And he had never played a hand of poker. There was an attraction of character: she liked the way he dressed, in rumpled British bespoke gray suits, sometimes with suspenders. She liked his watch, a 1940 Rolex Precision. She liked the way he smelled, a scent, she learned from her mother, called l'Eau du Navigateur, reminiscent of leather and cinnamon. But most distressingly, there was an undeniable physical attraction, one that sometimes caused her actual discomfort—slight headache, shallow breathing, and an inner-thigh cramping from keeping her legs closed in an effort to stanch the vaginal perfumes she was sure would betray her state of arousal when in his company.

"He seems like a nice man," she said.

"Oh come on, Angie!"

"Angie and Foster, sittin' in a tree—"

Foster and Adeline came back out at the same time, and everybody shut up.

"What are you kids talking about?" said Adeline. She always made a point of highlighting their difference in age, as though pointing a Klieg light would mitigate the truth of it.

"Juuuust the lovely evening," said Frankie.

"How great you two are as a couple," said Morgan.

Foster leaned over and gave Adeline a chaste kiss on the lips. Adeline took his head in both hands and returned the buss with thunder and lightning.

"Woooo!"

Foster returned fire, and Angie, Frankie, and Morgan watched in a combination of fascination, discomfort, and appall as Adeline and Foster made out in the dark, drunk, hands searching like TSA agents, seeming to forget momentarily that they were not alone, until Frankie's "*ahem*" stopped their exertions cold.

"Sorry, sorry," said Foster. "That was getting out of hand, wasn't it."

"I thought we were going to have to pay to stay for the rest of that show," said Morgan, who seemed the least offended. "I need to go," said Angie, standing. "Got to get home to Nadine and Meghan."

"I'll drop by BookPeople," said Foster, a note of anxiety in his voice. "I need something."

"Bye, y'all."


Angie went to work every day, waiting for Foster to drop by to get the thing that he needed. Two weeks later, he did.

Angie was on her knees on the first floor alphabetizing the R section of fiction when she felt a warm hand on her shoulder. Some force, greater than electricity, maybe more akin to a gravitational wave, thrummed through her whole body, making her feel limp and cashed. She looked up. It was, of course, Foster Luckenbach.

"Angie. Got a minute?"

They got iced coffees and sat down outside. It was the hottest day of the decade so far.

"Your mother and I..."

"Yes?"

"We have plans to get married."

"That's fantastic, Foster!"

"Yes, yes, I know, but..."

"What?"

"You know I have feelings for you. From the first moment. There, I've said it."

The heat of the day, even in the shade, engulfed the outdoor patio like fog on the stage of a hair-metal rock show.

"I didn't know. Well. Maybe."

"Ah. Well. There you have it. What do you think?"

There was no way she was going to tell the truth. Why, she did not know. Now would be the time. Angie sucked on her iced coffee and looked up at Foster.

"Why are you telling me now?"

"I—my reasons are... well, I've not just had feelings for you, Angie. I think you are utter perfection. In every way. I want you. God, I cannot believe I'm saying this. When I'm with your mother I think of you, and if you would come with me, be with me, I would leave your mother, right now. For good."

Foster held out his hand. She looked at him. She had only seen a look of that magnitude of sexual desperation in a man's eyes once before. When she was first dating her old boyfriend Bracchus and they were waiting for his labs to come in so they could do it without a rubber, Bracchus had had that look in his eyes, a small-pupiled, malarial, lachrymose aspect that betrayed a wolverine lust combined with a teenage impatience.

She took his hand. It was cool from the condensation on his iced coffee.

How many affairs had her husband had? She'd had one, and she wasn't sure she even counted that. What if she just spent one night with Foster? What could it hurt? It would be fun. And what if she fell in love with Foster? Shit. No. It was an easy no.

"No."

Angie took her hand back. Under the picnic table, she put her cool, damp palm on her knee. A thrill swept through her body.

"Yes. That's the obvious answer," said Foster, slumping over.

"I like you. I just can't do it to my mother, Foster."

The truth was, she couldn't do it to her husband, to her child. It was at this moment Angie realized that she truly loved Dean Lee, and no matter what he'd done or hadn't done, she did not want to hurt him. To hurt him would be to hurt Nadine.

"I admire you, Angie. Listen, we're going to get married soon, when your mother retires. I haven't formally asked her yet, that's why she hasn't told you. But she will."

"All right."

"I'm sorry about my behavior. I simply couldn't help myself. I had to know if you felt the same way."

"Feel better?"

Foster was quiet for a moment. He looked down at the picnic table, where long ago someone had stenciled a chess board, incorrectly rotated ninety degrees, so the black squares were at the bottom right of either side. He moved an acorn like a bishop along the black squares.

"We are a delicate experiment, humankind, Angie, drifting toward vanishment, and languor will eventually fell us."

Angie was not sure she understood.

"We are the authors of our own appetites," Foster continued. "And with loaded pens we cobble together the edges of our torn stomachs. Do you understand what I'm telling you?"

"No, Foster."

"Cut-paper tongues spit certainties out of kicked-out transoms; we, all of us, buy every word. And evening creeps in by increments, disfigured by mercury vapor lamps and the ghosts of the punctured soldiers our mothers carry on their hips. Autumn, hard as uranium glass, bothers the knockout roses along a fence line while the cold sun rises, and we run for the shade of the dunes."

"I'm not following, Foster. But I am following. In a way. Go on."

"Let the past be laced up and tied off, airless, delible, unavailable to reason, a kidnap rolled up in carpet and thrown down a well."

Foster threw his acorn with some vigor into the parking lot.

"My heart is broken."


During the few weeks Foster Luckenbach was pining after Angie, Adeline had grown unexpectedly fond of Nadine. Adeline invited her over one afternoon to look at the books in the house, to see how and where her own mother and grandmother had grown up. Nadine got ever closer to her grandmother's heart, and against all odds, Adeline fell toward Nadine. Angie was there for that first intersection, a hug over a game of Scrabble on the floor of Adeline's house among stacks of antiquarian books. Nadine had just played *wizen* on a triple word score and gone ahead of her grandmother on the scoresheet, and as quick as a cobra Adeline leaned across the board and embraced Nadine and did not let go until she wriggled away, smiling for the first time in months. At first Angie was suspicious of this—she thought the camaraderie was another of Adeline's offenses started against Dean Lee, and that she was simply using Nadine, but after a few more visits, Angie changed her mind—her mother seemed truly growing to cherish her granddaughter.

But it was not to last.

Adeline died one afternoon in the depths of a Hill Country winter, at home, a few moments after Nadine and Angie had visited. A quick and massive stroke in her swinging chair on her front porch. Adeline didn't suffer the post-mortem indignity of not being discovered for hours. She had been gone less than ten minutes before a DHL deliverywoman found her.

At the funeral, Nadine refused to cry, refused to sit in the front pews with her mother and Daddy and Harper, refused to sing hymns, refused to eat barbecue brisket sandwiches or drink lemonade afterward. When it was all over, she went out in the parking lot and sat on the hood of Harper's Mercedes and waited.

The funeral was the first Angie had been to since Sophie's. Angie tried to keep her mind on good, happy memories of her mother, but all she could think about was Sophie: her daughter was buried in a plot two spots up and one spot over, a knight's move, from Adeline. Angie could see the pewter-toned granite of her daughter's headstone, and could even read the epitaph:

SOPHIE DIXIE GRANDET
December 12, 2000 — October 1, 2005

My God, My God,
You Have Subtracted Me
From the Green Earth,

Dismantled Me,
And Rebuilt Me,
Whole in Heaven,
Your Eternal One,
Light Imperishable.

Angie ripped her gaze away and forced herself to fix it upon the wound in the earth that was her mother's grave.

*I miss you I miss you I miss you I want my daughter.*

It was now mid-March. The bluebonnets had finished colonizing the farm-to-market roads leading in and out of McCandless, crowding the highways to and from Austin. But it felt to Angie like the lonesome stretch between Christmas and New Year's, when the failures of the year line themselves up like convicts in the psyche, when the unexpected yet inevitable come to pass; that cold, shallow valley of a week when one thinks hard about where the gun in the house is, what part of the body to point it at so that it works quickly but sends the proper message. Angie did not think much about suicide, but she thought she might like to shoot herself in the stomach with Dean Lee's revolver among the bluebonnets and the honeybees on the side of FM 331. Harper would take Nadine, Dean Lee would drift off like an unmoored satellite that had fallen out of orbit. He would never disappear but would drift further into a deep space he could survive but never understand.

It was at the end of that week that Angie bought a lottery ticket with laundry change.

# PART III

# CHAPTER ELEVEN

# The Palisade

THE DAY THE MONEY fell, Angie and Dean Lee Grandet compared their deposits on their phones. Dean Lee's was one cent larger than Angie's: \$103,056,079.84 versus \$103,056,079.83. They laughed, hugged, kissed, fell on the bed, and, if Nadine hadn't knocked on the door to their bedroom, they might, just might, have had sex for the first time in seven years.

Sex with each other, that is. Angie was fairly sure Dean Lee had been having plenty of sex—just not with her. And Angie had slept with Lance that one time, about which she still felt no little guilt. But that was nothing in light of Dean Lee's extramarital exertions. The effects of these were always present in their marriage: she could not be physically near Dean Lee without thinking of the other women he'd been with—who he'd been with most recently, what she looked like, *does she look like me?* But Angie had grown used to this. She did not hold it against him. His grief was the wielding of his hard cock against the world. And for a moment, in the bedroom, looking at each other's bank statements, the tidal bore of two hundred million dollars washed all that away, leaving her husband a tabula rasa upon which she could ink her dirtiest notions and sketch her naughtiest scenarios, her husband as he was not when they were first married, but well before, when they were first dating, when the sex was explosive and surprising, always a new kind of shudder taking hold of her by the pelvis. This was the man that a cataract of digital dollars exposed for a few moments.

"Mom?" A voice from the other side of the door.

"Don't answer it, goddammit," hissed Dean Lee.

"What is it, honey?" said Angie, breathless, unbuttoned.

"Goddammit."

"There's some man on the landline, wants to talk to Daddy?"

"Who?"

"I don't know."

"Oh, for chrissake," said Dean Lee, rolling off the bed, furiously threading his belt back through the loops.

Angie arranged herself, yanked on the bedspread to smooth it out, and invited her daughter into the bedroom.

"Hi baby," said Dean Lee, patting his daughter on the head on his way down the hall to get the phone.

"Hi Daddy."

Nadine sat on the corner of the bed, almost slipping off. Angie propped herself up on the other corner. Both mother and daughter wore their wavy black hair with long bangs and cut shoulder length these days, but Nadine's was tinted blue and silver, an effect once shockingly clinquant but long since faded. Nadine was almost supernaturally pale—she refused to go outside lately—and her father had taken away all the goth makeup. A little mascara, a thread of eyeliner, and a whisper of blush was all she could get away with. Nadine accused her mother of being lucky, of not needing the agency of MAC and Revlon, which was true—Angie had a high natural coloring that obviated makeup of any sort. Mother and daughter stared at each other.

"What?" said Nadine.

"What?" said Angie.

"Were you having sex?"

Nadine seemed bored on one level but genuinely curious on another. Freshly minted teenagers could pull this look off.

"What in the world do you know about sex?" said Angie, focusing sharply on her daughter. Angie herself was still buzzing from sudden and unexpected lust. She had wanted her husband badly only a few moments before. Angie did not want to be angry at her daughter's interruption, but she was.

"I know plenty," Nadine said, yawning aggressively, as though the subject were of such stale, passé tedium she could simply not be bothered.

"That's just what a mother likes to hear from her thirteen-year-old daughter."

"I mean I haven't—"

Nadine looked down at her bare feet. She tried to weave her toes together.

"Thank god," said her mother.

"I just—"

"Didn't your daddy take away all the Anaïs Nin books you 'borrowed' from Harper?"

"Not all. I still have *Delta of Venus* hidden behind the air conditioner filter in my room. Don't tell."

"Then you know that in general it is customary for people to have sex without their clothes on," said Angie, getting down on her knees and taking her daughter's feet in her hands. "And as you can plainly see, your father and I were fully dressed. Thus, we were not having sex. And we are now through talking about sex, forever, or at least until you are old enough."

"I'm a teenager. Mom. Is the divorce off?"

"I don't know, honey."

Angie didn't know. It was still on, officially, papers to be signed in July. But now. There was no way to see any kind of redemption in a monster pile of cash. Or was there? Even Dean Lee seemed reluctant to go through with it. Were they that shallow? And what about the business of a few moments ago? Dean Lee had been positively *rutty*, a raspy wheeze in his throat as he tore at his belt, her blouse. In the glaze of his eyes Angie had seen a future that did not look so bad, one laid out with corridors of cash and sex. "That's not a no."

"That's right, it's not."

"Then you're talking about it."

"Well, we're going to talk about it."

Nadine shifted herself so that her perch on the corner of the bed was less precarious. She pushed her bangs out of her eyes.

"What does it depend on?"

Angie stood up. She walked over to the mirror above the bureau and began to examine her left eye, which had begun to show signs of conjunctivitis.

"It depends upon your father's behavior over the next few months, that's what."

"You mean gambling?"

"Yes. No. He can spend his money however he wants."

Angie was not sure she meant that.

"And other ladies," said Nadine.

"And—yes. Other ladies."

Dean Lee's last "lady," whom he said he met after the lottery news but long before the money came in, was an exotic dancer named Phoebe Gottlieb who worked weekends at the Rose Petal, a strip joint out by Austin Bergstrom International. She had fallen hard for Dean Lee, or so he said—Dean Lee was still in the habit of sharing the details of his conquests with Angie—when he had proven pleasantly regular at tucking fives instead of ones in her ruffled garters on Friday nights after his shift at the bottling plant, and, one night, at three minutes before closing, when he tucked a twenty underneath the fake bunched silk and left his hand under there along with it. She climbed down off the stage and asked him if he could remember a ten-digit phone number by heart.

"Course," Dean Lee had said. He then closed his eyes, and did his best, but could only remember six numbers, and was moreover unsure of their order. But he didn't admit this.

"Better call me sooner than later," Phoebe said, "because I'm moving to Dime Box before long and will be unavailable for fun and who knows what else."

Phoebe winked. Dean Lee, annoyed at not having been able to commit her number to memory, too embarrassed to ask again, but also disabled by a fierce erection, suggested they go to a motel right now.

"The Grapevine Piedmont," said Dean Lee. "On US 32. Got cable."

"I'd prefer the Driskill."

"In Austin? I was thinking 'motel,' with an *m*. Driskill starts with an *h*."

"I like the Driskill's stylings. And their margaritas."

"I can make you a margarita."

A compromise sent them to the Best Western Plus, where Phoebe administered sensational erotic motifs all night long and made Dean Lee fall in love with her. At 8:15 in the morning he called Angie, praying for voicemail, not getting it.

"Dean Lee," said Angie. "Are you going to make me guess where you are?"

"Sorry babe, I, uh…"

"Whoever you're fucking, don't fucking tell her about the fucking money."

Angie hung up.

Phoebe put off her move to Dime Box so she could date Dean Lee Grandet, or so he said. She lived in a small shack on a commune, the Cinelle Isle Body Politick outside Bastrop. Dean Lee visited every day, telling Angie he was either playing poker or working overtime or something, anything. He finally confessed. It didn't matter. But she wasn't angry. Something about the pains Dean Lee had taken to tell the story of Phoebe Gottlieb had struck her as fantasy. Divorce was in the air anyway, Phoebe or not. It had always been in the air, ever since Sophie. But never had it come close to materializing—for Nadine's sake.

But now. The goddamn money.

In spite of it all, things were changing.

"Are we moving?"

Nadine stood next to her mother at the mirror, examining her nostrils for symmetry. Nadine had told her mother that she had noticed that fashion models in magazines had perfectly matching nostrils.

"Do you want to move?"

"Daddy does. That's all he talks about, getting the fuck—"

"Nadine."

Angie wondered briefly if other mothers tolerated the tongue and talk of sex from their thirteen-year-olds, or if she allowed Nadine special dispensation because of all her daughter had been through.

When Angie herself had been seven, she had uttered, most timidly, the mild oath "goddamn" in the presence of her father, the almighty Caspar Bigelow, and had gotten her mouth washed out with Lurro, a household surfactant that left an aftertaste for six weeks. If Angie tried to wash Nadine's mouth out with Lurro, she'd bite off the tips of her fingers.

Angie persisted: "You didn't answer my question."

"What!"

"Do you—"

"I don't care. It doesn't matter where I live. I'll be a zero nothing depressive borderline murderess no matter if I live in a dumb refrigerator box in McCandless or a mansion in Austin."

"I will absolutely not tolerate you speaking about yourself in that manner. You heard me?"

"Fine. Mom, people are asking me for money. What do I tell them?"

"What people?"

"I don't know. Kids, other people. Grownups."

"Like who?"

"Mr. MacEwan, the assistant theater director at school? He said the stage lighting has hot spots and needs rewiring. It'll cost $20,000. He said he saw on the news how much we got and that the wiring will cost about one ten-thousandth of that. And he said they could name the stage after us. And Irina's mom's ex-boyfriend Igor put sugar in the gas tank of her Camry, and so the engine needs rebuilding now, and that costs $3,400. And Mrs. Harris-Camperdown, the bus driver, asked me to sit up front with her yesterday so she could explain bail bonds to me, and manslaughter, and how her son Chariton was in the wrong place at the wrong time with that Korean barbecue shooting, and that I'd get back the sixty-five grand someday. Plus, every kid at school wants a hundred-dollar bill, except Billy Fatzinger, who wants a thousand-dollar bill for his banknote collection."

This was how it started. Angie had been reading books and online articles about lottery winners, almost all of whom squander their winnings and are reduced to a state of penury even greater than before their windfall—very few actually hang on to their winnings, invest carefully, save, spend soberly. And it all started with rampant, well-meaning generosity, like fixing the hot spots in the theater director's lighting or rebuilding sugar-damaged Toyotas or passing out hundreds of C-notes to eighth graders. A hundred million is a lot of money, and Angie could easily stand to break off half of it, even most of it, for altruistic purposes, and live off the remainder, never wanting for anything again. But somehow that seemed precarious. At the moment, Angie wanted it all, untouched, cherry. That money was a wall, a spiked palisade, between her past and her future.

"Do you want to give your friends money, Nadine?"

"I don't know, no, not really, they're all so..."

"Proprietary?"

"What?"

"Acting like they deserve it?"

"Yeah."

"Well, shit," said Dean Lee, coming back into the bedroom, looking around for his shoulder holster. "That was Chase Turnbough."

"Who is he—or she—and how much did he-she want?" said Angie.

"Nadine, run along, sweetie," said Dean Lee, sliding on his holster.

Nadine ceased flaring her nostrils in the mirror and left. She pulled the door shut behind her.

"Now hold on, Angie. It's my goddamn money and I can do what I want with it, and I don't even have to mention what I'm doing. So just keep your judgments to yourself or I won't even tell you."

"Okay. Fine. So who—?"

"Chase runs a card game, a little bigger than the usual. It's in Claude."

"Oh for god's sake. And where the hell is *Claude*?"

"Panhandle. It's an honor to even be invited to this game. And hell, what's *your* money doing?"

"It just came thirty minutes ago, so nothing yet."

"Well, what are you gonna do with it?" said Dean Lee. "Give it all to Planned Parenthood and Amnesty International and the Southern Poverty Law Center? Do you have pink eye?"

"I don't know, I don't know, and probably."

Angie looked at her husband. The sexual charge of half an hour ago had evaporated. It was difficult to believe it had even existed. She glanced at the bed. An Xtra King, as un-intimate as a bed could get, so much room that they could each lie on their respective sides, panto-mime snow angels, and never so much as brush fingertips. They slept in the bed together only when Nadine was home—that's to say not in a hospital—for the sake of appearances. When Nadine was inpatient, Dean Lee slept on his sticky leather sofa in the den.

"Well, then don't get near me. I don't need pink eye, not now," said Dean Lee, as if there were other times in his life when he could have used pink eye. "I have to go to the bank."

Dean Lee seemed to suddenly remember the intimate moment with his wife earlier and danced over to the mirror to examine his eyes.

"Angie, once and for all, are we calling off this goddamn divorce or not?"

"That all depends on you, Dean Lee."

"I'm not the only mess in this goddamn marriage. I'm not the only loser in this goddamn family."

"You're the only helpless recidivist. You're the only sex addict. Now I have to go to the bank, too. You're gonna have to stay here with Nadine till I get back."

"Don't call me a recidivist. And I'm no sex addict. I'm a goddamn red-blooded American male goddammit, and Nadine's thirteen and can take care of herself. I have to get to the bank before five. It's important. Need to get cash for Chase Turnbough's game."

"They have waitresses there?"

The only way Angie could really put up with Dean Lee's philandering was by attaching a pathology to it, thinking of him as a helpless addict, a slave to his desires, positively beholden to the uncontrollable throb in his Bermuda shorts. That he denied having an addiction, or even a problem, went even further in support of her theory. But none of it really mattered, anymore, anyway, since she hadn't been interested in sex with her husband since their daughter Sophie's death, thirty minutes before notwithstanding. The extinguishing of that little life had drawn thick blackout curtains around so much.

Two hundred million dollars were long bony fingers, though, drawing those blackouts aside, letting in a little light. Angie squinted in spite of herself.

"Well, I gotta get to the bank too, Dean Lee. Be patient. Tomorrow, if you want, you can go and buy a Maserati and hire a *Penthouse* pet to drive you out to Vegas at 160 miles an hour to play poker heads-up with Doyle Brunson. But today I'm taking the pickup to the bank and you're staying home to watch the child."

"Can we get a sitter?"

Angie opened the bedroom door to discover her daughter standing there. "Nadine, what are you doing?"

"Listening? I don't need a babysitter."

The only time they had experimented with leaving Nadine without a sitter had been three years before, before the Gil Moorehead business, when she had been free of hospitals for several months and seemed as stable as she ever had been in her young life. It was late on a stormy Thursday afternoon, supercells had spawned tornadoes north and west of the city, Dean Lee was at the bottling plant getting upbraided by his boss Nelson Kallendorf for running a card game on the lunch break, and Angie wanted to go to the Alamo Drafthouse on South Lamar to see *A Clockwork Orange*. The streets were largely deserted on the drive to the theater, even though it was near rush hour, everyone having gone home at noon on account of the tornado warnings. The barren city reminded Angie of a documentary she'd seen about the 1975 evacuation of Phnom Penh in which a forgotten child is seen crawling around in some trash in an alley between two abandoned buildings. Angie thought of her own child, alone in the house. When she got to the theater, there was not a soul in evidence, not even a ticket puncher. She walked right in without paying, sat down, and watched the movie. Angie loved the Korova Milk Bar, the sexy girls in the mall, the houseguest's sweater. She was shocked by the violence in the abandoned theater and could not believe how long the thug-cops held Alex's head underwater.

While Angie was at the theater, Nadine had been at home watching bits of the same film on her mother's laptop in grainy ten-minute YouTube chunks. The scene where Alex slices Dim's hand particularly affected her: it was something about the horror on Dim's face, coupled with the helplessness of being cut while waist-deep in water. Dean Lee paid roughly the same minute attention to the knives in the house that he did to his gun, and they were always surgically sharp, down to the last paring knife. Nadine found a Henckels boning edge in the maple knife block on the kitchen counter, shaved a few of the fine hairs off her forearm to test it, drew a bath, climbed in wearing a white dress, then, without hesitation, opened up her own hand in much the same way Alex had cut Dim's. Dean Lee got home from work and milled around the house for an hour before realizing how eerily silent it all was. He decided to investigate. There, in the tub, he found his daughter, semi-conscious, in the pink water. The wound required twenty-eight stitches to cobble. A year later she would cut her other hand with a straight razor in a hospital bathroom. Two cuts. Her stigmata.

"Nadine," said Angie, her hands on her hips. "Go, now, to Harper's. Your father and I have something to discuss."

Nadine smiled. It might have been the first time she'd smiled since Sophie died. Angie noticed. Dean Lee noticed. Nadine shut the bedroom door quietly. Her parents listened for the front door to close. When the latch had clicked, Dean Lee approached his wife. He hugged her close to him.

"I don't care about pink eye," he said.

Angie allowed her husband to fall into her. After a moment, she embraced him back.


Shortly after the money came through, the Grandets bought a house in Austin overlooking the lake, splitting the cost between them. Nadine called it a McMansion, and neither of her parents cared or argued with her. All that mattered was that it wasn't the house on Fawn Street. It was the first and only house they looked at, and their realtor, Miss Deborah May Treoar, seemed annoyed by this. The Grandets simply wanted to move, and they wanted to move *now*. It was maybe the only thing they had wanted, wholesale, as a family, ever, and they acquired the property with lightning efficiency. They threw away virtually everything they owned except for Dean Lee's beloved leather couch, a few boxes of keepsakes, and the big bureau, which had been Adeline's.

For weeks, Nadine and Angie shopped, filling the new house with furniture, drapes, silverware, art, rugs, lighting, and gadgetry. When they weren't out shopping, they were at home shopping on the internet. Nothing could compare to the pressing sweetness of those days for Angie, the ascendant hours spent with her fragile daughter coupled with utter checkbook freedom, all in a relative Dean Lee vacuum—he was almost always away in Dallas or Houston. Or *Claude*. Playing cards. It wasn't something Angie liked to think about.

The house occupied a cul-de-sac shaded with ancient sycamores, luscious magnolias, and live oaks whose boughs seemed to stretch for miles like cloud-to-cloud bolts of lightning. The ground cover was ivy, ivy, ivy, bisected by a long, winding gravel drive. The house had eight bedrooms and ten and a half baths on three floors. The first floor was almost entirely open, the northern third being dominated by a hypermodern kitchen with a big gas stove that looked like a figment of a Julia Child fever dream. The second floor was mostly bedrooms, and the third floor was again largely open, with a dance floor, rec area, gym, and open lounge. One whole wall was glass and looked down on the lake from several hundred feet. The house featured a genuine wine cellar, cut deep into the Texas limestone. It had a 1,200-bottle capacity and was naturally cool and dry. Actually, the house was not a McMansion at all, having been designed and built in 2001 by the infamous architect McBrady Poisson, who was now doing life without parole in Huntsville for murdering his wife Gala in 2007 for cheating on him with their stockbroker. Since the crime had not occurred *in* the house, Angie felt she could live with the peripheral taint. She also felt it made for a good story. She loved her house and believed she could make it her home. She *would* make it her home—hers and her husband's and Nadine's.

Mother and daughter went back to the house on Fawn Street to fetch a few things they'd forgotten. In the front yard, under the magnolia, sat the latest exemplar of Dean Lee's aluminum folding chairs, open and waiting for him, around it a horseshoe of bare dirt where his boots scraped the ground, where his beer cans sweated, where his bowls of pretzels would lie. Nadine collapsed the chair and put it in the trunk of her mother's car. In the backyard, against the fence separating the property from the Bjornboes', was an old rusty axe with a long wooden handle. Dean Lee had not wanted it to go to the new owners and had given orders for it to be brought to the new house.

"Anything else?" said Nadine, picking the axe up and holding it over her head like a serial killer.

"Yeah."

Angie and Nadine entered the old house through the back door. They stood in their old kitchen for a moment. Angie was so overcome with emotion that she thought she would burst out crying. At the same time, she felt as if she were watching herself in someone else's dream.

She took out a screwdriver from her purse and removed a switch plate in the kitchen that Nadine had painted when she was five. Then she unscrewed one in the hall and another in the bathroom. Angie took her daughter's hand and led her into the living room. Openly, without mutual disguise, mother and daughter studied the spackled drywall in front of which Sophie had slapped her last jack.

The house on Fawn Street was now suitably stripped of memory and witness, and the Grandet women took their leave.

# CHAPTER TWELVE

# The Money

IT WAS THE MONTH of May, in 2012, when a sweet blindness befell each of the Grandets. Dean Lee found redemption in hiding behind the staggering rampart of cash and the faux-leather gunwales of poker tables. Angie thought she might be able to donate her way out of the hatch she had been trapped in. And Nadine was beginning to believe that the monument of unassailable bank accounts, even if she did not have direct access, could, by their very existence, wither the great claws that clicked in the dark over her bed at night. The Grandets watched the world through pinholes in black hoods, through lenses smeared in Vaseline, and, for a while, all was good: life as a member of an obscenely well-to-do family in the city of Austin was supremely flexible, and not one of the Grandets minded, at first, the deferential ass-kissing the money unleashed. The ugly, disturbing world they inhabited in the early spring burst only a few weeks later into glimmer and flare; the Grandets were all pleasantly startled out of steep meditations on death and nothingness by the *thrunch* of a confetti cannon fired over their open, waiting coffins, and each sat up, wondering if they were, in fact, mistaken, and that heaven was a real place, and it looked much like the world they had come to know but had been stripped, sanded, and repainted to look like a merry-go-round, or a casino, or a kindergarten classroom.

The jugular moment for Dean Lee was not the nine-digit abstraction on his phone, but rather the call from Chase Turnbough. Now that he had the means, Dean Lee was on his way to becoming the greatest poker player the world had ever known. Chase's game was just the beginning. There was also Tob Aronian's game in Dallas and Ginger Fremantle's game in Houston. Who knew what else was out there. Dean Lee was invited to all of them. Not much luck yet, but he'd win everything. And soon he'd start his own game, here in Austin, and he'd invite all those assholes to try to win their money back. The stakes would be the highest known. The poker room—which would be on the third floor of the new house—would be the most luxurious, excelling even those in Monte Carlo and Hong Kong. The waitstaff would be the most fetching, the loveliest, the most variable and unattached. A little something for everyone.

For Nadine, freedom meant the fresh anonymity of a new school. No one knew who she was, what she had done. It would get out eventually, some little dick would google her family name—even though Nadine's identity was never revealed in the news reports—then pull the last block out of the Jenga, and it would all come rushing down. But for now, she was just another kid at school. Nobody bothered her, and most of the teachers didn't even remember her name. At home, Nadine had grown bored of googling "children who kill" and the infinity of cognate search terms. Instead, she began writing. Poems at first, all thin plagiaries of works from the grand literary pantheon of female suicides—Sylvia Plath, Anne Sexton, and Virginia Woolf. Then the skeleton of an autobiography, and finally, after reading Walker Percy's

*The Moviegoer*, a book. A novel set in the 1960s in a fictional town in the Texas Hill Country. Its heroes: two young, orphaned sisters who, in the attic of a vacant house, find an old tennis-ball can filled with gold coins. At first, the sisters fight over the coins, unable to agree on what to do with their sudden, private wealth. But on the brink of estrangement, they realize that in order to survive the harrowing conditions of the orphanage, they must stick together, and so decide to seek the confidence of the only adult they know: the owner of a small grocery store who had shown them minor kindnesses. The man and his wife immediately betray the sisters, steal their gold, and pay the orphanage manager to separate the sisters, sending the younger one to a foster home in Boston. Nadine wasn't sure how she was going to end the book, but she imagined the sisters would reunite as adult women, when the internet emerged and finding lost souls was no big deal. Nadine thought she would have the sisters spend the rest of their days together watching old movies and visiting wrath on their enemies. Nadine already had more than twenty-five thousand words of the book on her laptop. She wrote a thousand words a day because that's what Stephen King did. She was going to grow a new identity like a culture in agar. She would change her name. She would anneal the hard truths of her crimes against Sophie and Gil in her fiction. Nadine Grandet would write a book and be born again.

Angie studied the destitutions and privations of the world. She read about Orangi Town, the vast slum in Pakistan. She read about the modern slave trade. Sex traffickers in Eastern Europe. The poppy and coca scourges. The garbage choking out the sea. Overcome by the variety of unconquerable enormities, Angie switched scales: she read about and investigated individual people in need who she might be able to help. The stricken, the mishandled, the poor, the forgotten. Artists, sufferers of rare and horrific diseases, the disfigured, the falsely accused, people in unique and intractable straits. Angie tried to keep lists of these potential beneficiaries. She could not write fast enough. They piled up on one another, filling word-processing files like boxcars. They became uncountable, the people in need. Angie decided instead that she would assist the organizations already in place to help such people. Civil associations, charities, outreach programs, law firms, innocence projects. She reached out to the great philanthropists. It would just be a matter of choosing where to put her money, and how much. She lost a great deal of sleep over the matter, but it was an exquisite insomnia. When she had decided, when she had finally committed her money, Angie Grandet would get her teeth fixed.

And then she would have another child.

# CHAPTER THIRTEEN

# Venereae Sculptura

WHILE IN THE WAITING room of the office of Dr. Janyce Bluth-Indistege, PhD, Angie read an article about the Tamagotchi craze in a thirteen-year-old issue of *People*. Dean Lee stared at his boots. The couple had arrived for their appointment thirty minutes early.

Tamagotchi, Angie learned, was a portmanteau of two Japanese words, *tamago*, which means "egg," and *uotchi*, which means "watch." When Angie got to the part about the inventor winning an Ig Nobel prize for the toy, she realized that Dean Lee, seated next to her, his elbow touching hers, was reading something. A thick paperback. He was in the middle of it, maybe even further along. She tried to read the running titles at the head of the pages, but the print was too small.

The door to an office opened and the figure of Janyce, as she preferred to be addressed, appeared.

"Welcome, Grandets," she said. "Please darken your phones."

Dean Lee closed his book, and Angie glanced at the cover. *Los detectives salvajes* by Roberto Bolaño. Angie's heart leapt.

She and her husband followed Janyce Bluth-Indistege into her office. Dean Lee chose a chair in a corner and Angie sat on the couch.

"Well," said Janyce. "How do you both feel about being here?"

Angie looked around the office. Janyce fancied the comic grotesque, and her walls were filled with prints by Otto Dix, George Grosz, Max Beckmann, others. One wall was dominated by a floor-to-ceiling mahogany bookcase filled with old works on human sexuality. Giacomo Casanova's *Histoire de ma vie*, Richard von Krafft-Ebing's *Psychopathia Sexualis*, George Bataille's *Les larmes d'Éros*, Hans Bellmer's book on chimerical dolls, hundreds of others. Adeline would have scoffed at Janyce's stripe of bibliophily. On a marble pedestal in a corner was a polychrome faience sculpture of a stubby penis, about ten inches tall. A brass plaque was affixed to the plinth, too small to read. Angie was dying to get up and see what it said.

"I'm glad to be here, but nervous, too," said Angie, striving to say exactly what she thought and felt, and what she thought Janyce might want to hear. Dean Lee said nothing. She noticed his paperback, cover printed in sunset colors, the text block creased and rounded, sticking out of a pocket in his coveralls.

"You mentioned to me that it was because of a recent windfall that you entered couples counseling, hoping that you could patch a damaged marriage and stave off a pending divorce," said Janyce, sounding a bit like how Angie imagined Hans Bellmer's dolls might speak, childlike but sexually mechanized.

"You're probably wanting to know the size and nature of our windfall," said Dean Lee.

"No," said Janyce.

"We won the lottery," said Dean Lee. "More than $200 million."

"Now, you have a daughter?"

"Nadine," said Angie. "She's thirteen."

"Would you like to bring her in, too?"

"Not at this time," said Angie. "But maybe later."

"She's had problems," said Dean Lee.

"Oh?"

"Dean Lee, not now," said Angie.

"Why not? We're in therapy. Now's the time."

"I—"

"She killed her little sister," said Dean Lee.

"I see."

Angie looked around the room, at the distorted, contorted figures animating the walls of Janyce's little office. She looked at Janyce, who at that moment seemed like one of the idiosyncratic interbellum German women in the drawings—sly, crude, crooked, erotic smile, graveyard teeth, blue-black eyes, rollercoaster curves, hair a chocolate cataract, body a post-office box. Angie stared at the ceiling for relief. She had not wanted to talk about this, Sophie, the gun, Nadine. But that was what they were here for. This was a reunification, or an attempt at it.

"Janyce," said Dean Lee. "Can I call you Janyce?"

"Of course."

"Six is an age where you begin to take responsibility for your actions. Right? You know what you're doing. I knew what I was doing at six."

"Why don't you tell me a little more about what happened."

Angie told her. Dean Lee didn't interrupt.

"That's a very sad story. I'm sorry for your loss."

Her tone reminded Angie of the Sherilyn Fenn doppelgänger at Sophie's funeral.

"What happened, happened," said Angie. "We want to see if we can patch up what remains of the marriage, with the aid of this money. For the sake of Nadine, maybe even we can all learn to love one another again."

The last six words she uttered felt odd in her mouth. She didn't need to learn to love her husband again. She always had. It was Dean Lee who needed to learn to love her. No. To love himself. No. To *tolerate* himself.

"I see. Dean Lee, are you in accord?"

"Hell, I don't know."

"Do you want to learn to love your wife again? For the sake of the child? For the sake of Nadia?"

"Nadine," said Angie and Dean Lee together.

"Nadine. And for yourself?"

Dean Lee sat motionless. Then he nodded.

Angie watched her husband closely.

"All right then," said Janyce. "Let us get to work."

A wave of anxiety coursed through Angie like heat from a bonfire. She looked around for a clock. She spied a small, cheap digital on Janyce's brushed-steel desk, partially blocked by piles of overstuffed manila folders held together by rubber bands. Angie could see only a glowing red 3:. They had started at 3:30. There was something... *studied* about the disposition of the folders, as though Janyce had arranged them 1) to make herself look busier or more important than she really was, and 2) to block the *goddamn* clock.

"It is imperative that we get Nadine in here as soon as possible for a group session. We have a very fragmented family here, one that I believe can be reunited, but only if all the constituents are present. But let us now address what we can, and that is Angie and Dean Lee Grandet. How do you imagine your love, freshly regenerated, will look?"

"What?"

"Do you make love now?"

"That's a tough one, doc," said Dean Lee. Angie looked at the clock. Still 3:.

"All right," said Janyce. "The question is, do you want to? And I'm asking you both."

The light in the room changed. Angie recognized the warm, bruised glow that signaled a coming thunderstorm. She glanced at the clock. Ah, finally: 4:. No more than twenty minutes to go.

"I see we are not in a mood to communicate," said Janyce. "Therapy is difficult without it. Please let me try again. Do you enjoy making love now? I am not asking for details, but they are not verboten if you wish."

Janyce smiled in a horrific, lascivious way.

Angie estimated the time to be 4:04, sixteen minutes to go. Sixteen minutes to avoid answering the question. She knew the answer. She wanted her husband, as much now as she had when twenty-five-year-old Dean Lee Grandet had descended his porch, pulling on a T-shirt, to talk to Lolly Prager, the man she'd discussed Latin American literature with over the tractor-tire skeeter farm in the dark of Fawn Street, the one who once did strangely effortless things at odd angles in bed and sometimes shouted strophes from Quevedo when he climaxed. The Dean Lee she had loved, the one her mother had hated. *That* Dean Lee. She glanced at him now, the scruffy edge of his Bolaño paperback. She wanted him, even if he looked at this moment like he wanted to fold himself into two dimensions, slip into a pocket of spacetime, and disappear.

A distant thrum of thunder made the brass plaque on the ceramic penis shimmy. Janyce sat very still and quiet, waiting for the central air conditioning to kick on again.

"Angie?"

"I don't know." *I know.*

"Why don't you know?"

"I—"

"Let me ask you this," said Janyce. "What changes would Dean Lee need to effect in his life in order for you to begin having sexual relations with him again?"

A distinctly blue-tinged butterfly-flutter of lightning, followed two seconds later by a rounded-off shotgun blast of thunder. Everyone jumped. Janyce said, "What if, for instance, he—"

"Don't call me 'he,' please, I'm right here in the goddamn room." Dean Lee sounded exhausted. He loved thunderstorms, as long as it didn't hail, but he didn't seem to give one whit that there was a good one on the way.

"What if Dean Lee," said Janyce, exasperated for the first time, "stated here and now, with Janyce Bluth-Indistege, PhD, as witness, that he wanted to make love to you at the first available opportunity?"

*There couldn't be more than ten minutes left.*

"Angie? Dean Lee?" The rain started, accelerating to a roar in seconds. Janyce looked up. A large, old, tobacco-colored damp spot in the shape of Missouri stained an acoustic ceiling tile. Janyce stood, walked over to her desk, retrieved an industrial five-gallon bucket from beside it, placed it on the floor under the stain, and sat down again. Presently a steady drip began to fill the bucket. The drops landing in the bucket, about one every eight seconds, were inexplicably loud.

"Well?"

"Sure," said Dean Lee.

"Our time is up for today."

# CHAPTER FOURTEEN

# Breakfast in the Afternoon

PULLING OUT OF JANYCE'S office parking lot in Dean Lee's abominable new zebra-striped truck, rain sheeting down, Angie said: "Take me to Kerbey Lane, Dean Lee. I'm hungry."

"You got it."

Dean Lee pulled onto MoPac.

It was 3:30 in the afternoon and they both ordered breakfast. Unfortunately, they were assigned an extremely cute waitress, and Angie was sure she would have to put up with Dean Lee's oeillades and lame attempts at flirtation. But he seemed to be making an effort not to engage.

"Janyce is all right," said Angie, finally.

"She ruined my thunderstorm," said Dean Lee, scraping a fleck of something off his plastic menu. "And she's coyote ugly. But I guess couples' counselors should be."

"Why?"

"So the man doesn't get attracted to her and fuck everything up."

"You may have a point there."

They listened to the comforting din of the restaurant, the tail ends of thunderclaps to the east, the swamp coolers kicking in, the traffic on 35th Street. Angie fought the urge to ask him what he was reading. Her fear was that just noticing it, like Schrödinger's cat, would alter the outcome. She kept quiet; she kept her hope suppressed.

"Sweetie," said Dean Lee, breaking his last slice of bacon in two and handing half to his wife. "Lemme ask you something. Are we doing the right thing holding off on this goddamn divorce? Living together? Tryin' again?"

Angie picked up her butter knife and angled it so she could secretly study her husband in the reflection of the blade, a trick she had learned from Harper. She moved it to scan his face from chin to forehead. In the distorted, fuzzy mirror she detected something. There was no real word for what she saw, but it was close, she thought, to *need*.

"Yes," she said, popping the bacon in her mouth. "Let's give this money a chance to fix everything."

Dean Lee nodded. Angie waited for him to say something crude about fringe benefits, but he didn't, which was even more encouraging than if he'd smiled and made some shocking remark about getting busy in the back of his new pickup, that they had a hell of a lot of catching up to do.

The last rumble of thunder faded out in the distance. A cool quiet fell over the diner.

"Dean Lee, there's something else I wanted to bring up in the appointment today besides what we wound up talking about. I want to talk about it now."

Dean Lee made no obvious gesture that he'd heard what his wife had said.

"Well," said Angie, feeling like she could, with one word, ruin every gain made today. "It's poker. Gambling."

Dean Lee drank what was left in his coffee cup and looked around for the cute waitress.

"Poker's not gamblin'," he said finally. "Not the way I play."

Angie crossed her arms over her breasts and slunk down in the booth. She had erred. This was not the time. Too late now.

"I know I said you could play cards for the rest of your life, but look, I've changed my mind. You must stop playing. The sooner the better. Today. Now. This minute."

"Well, honey, now—"

"Don't you understand, Dean Lee? Back in the day, you couldn't even beat Lolly Prager and his circle of bourré halfwits. I know you're playing bigger now, but these guys, they're pros —"

"I'm a pro."

"No, Dean Lee, you're not. Not compared to them. They sit around and wait for you. I know they do. I bet they don't go home until you go home. Am I right? They dream about you at night. And they're going to take every penny you've got, unless you quit. You absolutely must quit. I know you love poker, but you simply can't play anymore. You have to come to terms with the fact that you're not good enough to play at the level you're playing and win. You heard me?"

"Everything delicious?" said the waitress, who had reappeared with a globe of coffee.

"Real delicious, thanks, darlin'," said Dean Lee, not looking at her. He was trying. Even Angie couldn't not look at the waitress, devastatingly attractive as she was. "Can you bring me some Tabasco?"

"Dean Lee?"

"What."

"Do you understand?"

"Yeah."

"So it's settled?"

"Yeah."

"No more poker?"

"Yeah."

"Say it."

"What if I put my money in some kind of a bond or trust where I cain't touch anything but the interest. And I can play with that. What about that? Deal?"

"Can I bring you folks anything else?" said the waitress, leaving the Tabasco and their bill on the table.

"No thanks, darlin', we're fine. This is for you, now. Keep the change." Dean Lee placed a hundred on her tip tray but did not look at her.

"I just don't think you'd stop," said Angie. "You're going to keep playing till it's gone. Then you're gonna keep *on* playing, and you'll find yourself in debt, not for ten grand like you were to Lolly for more than a decade, but five, ten million, and you'll come to *me* for it."

"That won't happen, Angie. Christ. I promise."

"I mean it, Dean Lee. Please quit."

"Stop it, Angie. Please. I'll quit soon."

"Soon?"

"I've still gotta play a couple more times. I'm obligated."

# CHAPTER FIFTEEN

# Silver Sulfide

THE FIRST THREE FLOORS of the parking garage on campus were full, but Angie finally found, on the fourth floor, a spot between an old Dodge Dart with an *Ass, Gas, or Grass* bumper sticker and a Jeep Wagoneer the size of a toolshed. Angie waited for the elevator. It was a four-block walk to the Perry Castañeda Library, where a young librarian, Xie Yuang, was going to help Angie research the best philanthropic way to shed herself of some of her money. Angie was leaning toward the big ocean-cleansing concerns. Her research had uncovered the bare and fundamental fact that there was nothing but suffering in the world. A hundred million was nothing. A hundred *billion* was nothing.

Angie was feeling defeated and limp when the elevator doors finally opened to reveal a red-haired woman wearing a yellow rain slicker.

"Oops, went too far," said the woman, pressing the button for the third floor. Angie boarded, pressed G. The doors closed. The elevator moved, jolted, moved, jolted, stopped.

No one budged.

The red-haired woman reached out and pressed a button.

Nothing happened.

Angie pressed the buttons for the first floor, then the second, then all the buttons. It was an old elevator, the kind with a little metal cabinet that housed a telephone. But the receiver had been ripped out maybe twenty years before. Both women began slapping at the control panel, then banging on the door and hollering. How could no one hear them?

They stopped banging and yelling, and all was quiet.

Angie at first had the rash feeling that the woman might try to assault her—behind the drape of her red hair a strange glimmer danced in her eyes—but instead the woman sat on the floor of the elevator and shared her bottled water and Goldfish crackers and the story of the death of her kitten. Angie put her arm around her, and they listened to the rumble of traffic on 29th Street and the creak of the old parking garage and the squawk of tires and the distant jets in their flight paths.

"Allison, by the way," said the red-haired woman.

"Angie."

"Do you have a cat?"

"Yeah. His name is John Deere. He's a little tuxedo cat. Getting older. He has a gray muzzle now."

And Angie told Allison the story of Lolly, of toxoplasmosis. Somehow the story of Sophie's death became unavoidable. Allison began to cry. Angie held her.

Angie realized all at once she did not want to be rescued from the stalled elevator. No one had ever cried for Sophie. Not Nadine, who was frozen, not even Dean Lee, who had cried once in his life, he claimed, and wouldn't tell his wife what for. For the first time in her life after Sophie, Angie felt a sweet sickness she did not at first recognize—not until after the man with the crowbar had pried the doors apart, after Allison had written her email on an AT&T envelope and handed it to Angie with a hug, after Angie had gotten home to the big new house and found Nadine asleep on the couch in the living room, after Angie had gone to bed, her husband out somewhere. In fact, it was only when she had awakened at 3:25 that morning, gone into the bathroom and searched the clothes she'd been wearing for a strand of Allison's hair, that she recognized the feeling was love. Not crush love, or sexual love, but the kind of love she imagined that truly spiritual people reserved for God. Allison had been a visitation, a yellow-slicker elevator saint.

Angie decided she would wait three days to write to Allison, and in those three days, Angie wondered why we sometimes go mad in the same instant and in the same choking breath that we taste love on our teeth, why they were one in this world—lunacy and devotional obses- sion—and what myopic demigod plaited them together, and when. After all, Angie had felt, along with the divine lust, an acceleration of something for which there seemed to be no other word than insanity: she had met a stranger in an elevator and had fallen, fallen.

On the third day, the email composed in her head, Angie went in search of the AT&T envelope. She tore the big new house into swatch ribbons looking for it. Finally, she was forced to go out to the alley, climb into a dumpster, and dig beneath a dozen bags of garbage to find the one at the bottom that was her family's, a bloated horror she carefully dissected until the envelope emerged. It was coated with coffee grounds and fermenting orange juice, but the email address was legible through the envelope's creases and amber stains. She wiped it clean on her jeans, tossed it onto the ground, and climbed out.

She went inside, opened her laptop, and wrote:

Dear Allison,
Elevator Woman here. I'm sorry I didn't write sooner—I misplaced your

email. Even though we were prisoners, I enjoyed our time together. I would like to see you again.

Yours,

Angie Grandet

Angie could not bring herself to hit send yet, and saved the letter as a draft. She brought an image of Allison to mind. Sitting cross-legged on the grimy floor of the elevator in a black velvet skirt and yellow rain slicker, her wavy red hair cut into bangs, her green eyes ever so slightly crossed, as though she were studying a word in a microprint dictionary, her long, aquiline nose, a faint galaxy of freckles stretching from apple to apple, her mouth a floral bloom in the low, flickering light.

Angie wished desperately that she had a photo of St. Allison.

*Send.*

Angie checked obsessively throughout the rest of the day, and woke every thirty minutes throughout the night, refreshing her email on her phone while Dean Lee, finally home from Amarillo ("Broke even," he had said, and turned on an Astros game), snored in bed next to her. Nothing. Nothing during the next day and night, and the following day, a Saturday.

On Sunday morning at 2:14 a.m. her phone chimed: an email. Angie sat up.

Mailer daemon: her email to Allison had gone to an unknown address. Why mailer daemon took its time sometimes was an internet mystery.

Angie jumped out of bed, turned on her phone flashlight and retrieved the envelope from a baggie in the drawer of her bedside table. No, she had the address right. Had Allison given her a fake email? Or was it an honest mistake? Angie felt despair coming on, and tears. She didn't know enough about Allison to google her.

Angie climbed out of bed. Dean Lee would not wake up unless a thunderstorm hit. She peeked into her daughter's room.

"Nadine, honey, why are you up?"

"I'm always up. Why are you up?"

"Do you want to go for a drive?"

"Now?"

"I need to get out."

"Can we stop for Sour Patch Kids?"

"Of course."

Angie and Nadine stopped at the twenty-four hour Walgreens for Sour Patch Kids, then headed to the campus parking garage. They boarded the elevator.

"Let's sit down."

Nadine must have been used to her mother behaving strangely and didn't hesitate to sit down on the filthy elevator floor next to her. They ate the candy. For thirty minutes, they sat in silence. No one used the elevator. They stood, stretched, and drove home. They sat in the car in the driveway and fell asleep. When Angie woke at dawn, Nadine was gone.

Later that morning Angie called a private investigator, but the man said he wouldn't be able to help; there wasn't enough to go on.

A week later, Angie visited the Collectors' Showroom on US 331. She made her way toward the warm light in the back, southwest corner, following the perfume of acetone. Shea Babb was alone, cleaning brushes.

"Mrs. Grandet?" said Shea, a slight look of alarm in her eyes. "Everything all right?"

"Can you do a drawing of someone for me?"

"Of course. Photo?"

"I'm going to describe her... her features. Can you work like that?"

"Like a police sketch?"

Angie arched at this, but she thought about it for a moment, and indeed that was exactly what it was.

"A police sketch. Yes."

"I'll try."

"Small, if you can. A miniature."

"For a locket?"

How could such a simple word bear such a steep charge? *Locket*.

"Yes."

"I'll do it on a kind of special prepared paper instead of a paper plate. In silverpoint. It'll get darker with age."

Shea taped a small rectangle of pinkish paper to a tabletop easel, sharpened a silver stylus on a scrap of superfine sandpaper.

"Now go," said Shea Babb.


Angie kept the tiny likeness with her at all times, in a Mylar sleeve, like a priceless Honus Wagner, tucked between the leaves of a small, hardcover address book. She took it out several times a day to adore—there was no other word for it. She would wake at night, slip out of bed, and hold it to her cheek in the bathroom mirror. She would remove the portrait from its sleeve and hold it between her hands, her breasts, her thighs.

Angie constructed elaborate fantasies in her head about what would happen when she met Allison again, how they would be. Everything that Harper couldn't be.

Over time, though, the fantasies began to lose their potency. Angie realized she no longer was interested in the real Allison—she was content with her portrait, this simulacrum in two dimensions, this imperfect effigy in sulfided silver. The relic of St. Allison.

Angie visited Kinko's on Medical Arts and made a color copy of her relic. Then she drove to Epic Dermis Tats to consult with the man responsible for Louise: Egulph.

"Yeah, I can do this. Take about five hours, cost you $800 plus. More if you want it someplace tricky, if you get my drift."

"My left forearm, here."

"Got someone ahead of you. 'Bout a two-hour wait."

"I'll come back."

Angie did not come back.

# CHAPTER SIXTEEN

# The Melted Crayons

"MOM, WHERE IS THAT picture of me, the one that lady painted on the paper plate?"

Nadine yelled her inquiry from her bedroom doorway into the general vastness of the house, because she did not know where her mother was, or even if she was home, and she didn't feel like tromping around the place looking for her.

Dean Lee was definitely not home—he was rarely there, instead spending his time flying back and forth to Houston, Dallas, Amarillo, and Las Vegas to play poker. He wouldn't know where the paper-plate portrait was anyway—Dean Lee, it seemed, didn't know where anything was in the new house. He was always squalling like a four-year-old when he couldn't find a Phillips head or the ice-cream scoop or his money clip, a custom-made twenty-two-karat-gold clamp designed with enough daylight to hold $10,000 in hundreds folded in half. Nadine felt a momentary flare of sadness as she imagined that her daddy might have come across the weird eyeless portrait of his only living daughter and thrown it away out of disgust or some even less effable emotion. Nadine hadn't seen the painting in years, since long before they moved.

Exactly one year had passed since the Grandet family had left the town of McCandless behind and moved into Charles Mansion, as Dean Lee had dubbed their new house, in honor of its murderous architect. Nadine stood in her doorway and listened for her mother. Nothing. That didn't mean she wasn't home. Both mother and daughter had grown tired of the hollering call-and-response communications system that had developed in the sprawling house, and sometimes, when either heard a summons from the other, they simply ignored it, too tired or too annoyed to take a breath deep enough to bellow out an acknowledgment.

And they couldn't just *telephone* each other—the house was architecturally situated in such a way that even within certain rooms there were cell phone dead zones that no known signal-boosting technology could overcome. Only in the three-car garage, the laundry room, and the third floor stretch by the wall of glass could one hope for a signal strong enough to execute a simple cell phone call. And even these areas were capricious. Sometimes nary a call could be made from anywhere in the house, and they were forced to climb up on the flat roof, where Dean Lee had set out his beloved folding chairs, and Angie had put up a big red beach umbrella, jammed in a trash can full of sand for stability, to protect her little family from the brutality of the Texas sun.

Two landlines, with extensions all over the house, were available for essential phone calling, but they failed utterly for in-house communication. Nadine's mother had talked about installing an intercom system, yet she said it seemed like the kind of thing that only really rich, lazy idiots did. She was really rich, true enough, and claimed she was slowly getting used to it, but she did not yet consider herself a lazy idiot. There was still plenty of time to become one, she told anyone who would listen, and installing an intercom system so she could tell her fourteen-year-old daughter to come downstairs for dinner was a quick route to the condition.

Nadine sensed her mother was indeed in the house, and finally decided to set out looking for her.

"Mom!"

Nadine walked up to the third floor, calling her mother's name, then climbed the outside spiral metal staircase that led to the rooftop. Her mother's fat book of grandmaster sudoku puzzles, corrugated by humidity and the forces of sunlight, was open face down on one of the lawn chairs under the umbrella. But Angie was nowhere to be seen. Even though Nadine was not comfortable with heights, she cautiously edged her way to the north perimeter of the rooftop and peered over the edge, down into the driveway. Neither her father's zebra-striped Ford F-350 pickup nor her mother's old Celica were in evidence.

Even as recently as a year or two ago, her parents would never have left Nadine alone in the house. Now the nine digits of cash in her parents' bank accounts somehow made it okay, even though Nadine felt she never saw any of it. Actually, Nadine's parents were both generous and willing to buy her what she wanted. She just didn't want anything. After Gil's death, her father relented and gave her back her iPhone. She still had it, as antiquated and useless as it was in the one-bar household. Anyway, there was no one to call or text. Nadine had missed quite a bit of school over the years, thanks to hospitalizations resulting from depression, anxiety, PTSD, general shame and guilt, or what have you, and had fallen behind by two grades. She was, by far, the oldest eighth grader at Carter Middle School.

Harper had rediscovered her old boyfriend, Carrollton DeGolyer. She spent most of her time with him and was not as available to Nadine as she used to be. It wasn't Carrollton's fault, or Harper's.

The real issue was the money and the move into Austin. Harper was a twenty-five-minute drive away now, and she had refused to accept the five million bucks Nadine's mother had offered her as a friendship gift. The offer of money had somehow insulted Harper in a way that neither Nadine nor Angie—especially Angie—really understood, and now the drive between Austin and McCandless was the least of the new barriers to Harper.

And so Nadine was alone. There was no one to call or text or Facebook with. Of all the things in the world, however, that Nadine was not fine with, being alone was not one of them. Aloneness was no problem. It was *lonesomeness* that hurt. She missed Gil with such ardent vigor and physical discomfort that she sometimes thought some terrible black acorn was growing into a terrible black oak right under her breastbone, cracking her, like the roots of an old tree will sometimes swell over the years and dislocate the sidewalks under which they grow. Nadine felt that way sometimes, like her very sternum was liable to crack from the force of a loss suffered out of her control.

Nadine screamed "*Mom!*" one last time, and when no response came, Nadine finally felt satisfied that she was alone in the house.

The capacious three-car garage was Charles Mansion's great repository of shameful crap. Flimsy, semi-crushed moving boxes of keepsakes and photographs and worthless nonsense from the McCandless house were stored there. Old furniture of her grandmother Adeline's that Angie couldn't part with, the painting of gray kittens, the rusty axe Dean Lee didn't want the new Fawn Street house owners—whoever they were—to have. Nadine's old collages, gross linens, Dean Lee's cheap, wrecked poker table and chairs, computers and adapters forced by time and competing technologies into obsolescence. One box was filled with Nadine's old stuffed animals, including the little floppy leopard she'd loved, the one which had been her companion and confidante in the fragile years immediately following Sophie's death.

Nadine felt it was a safe bet that the paper-plate painting was somewhere in the garage. She probably had at least an hour until her mother got home—Angie was no doubt at the library, either the Austin Public or the Perry Castañeda Library at UT. Her mother liked to research the fates of lottery winners and other recipients of great windfalls, and spent a lot of time conferring with librarians and spooling through microfilm. She was determined not to piss away her share of the lottery win and die buried in concrete, like some lottery winners she'd read about.

Nadine's daddy probably wouldn't be back until tomorrow or even the next day. Nadine could tell in an instant whether he had come home a winner or loser. If the former, he moped around, looking a bit like a sad, wet sheepdog, until someone asked him how he had done at the tables.

"Well," he might say, "I got lucky flushin', picked up a few dollars." Then he'd wait for someone to ask him how much. Nadine's mother never played that game, but Nadine had. She was not interested in money as an economical construct, but the idea of great sums of cash in a physical space—stacks of hundreds—fascinated her.

"How much, Daddy?" Nadine would ask.

"Well, I don't know, sweetness. I ain't counted it."

"But *about* how much?"

"I guess maybe too much to fit in my pockets. I'm thinkin' sixty thousand."

"Wow."

This was Nadine and her father's lingua franca, such as it was.

If Dean Lee came home a loser, however, he would wear a great, incisor-rich grin and stride about Charles Mansion drinking beer and avoiding his wife and daughter, pretending like he was looking for something. Nadine would follow him around, eventually cornering him in the living room or TV room.

"How much, Daddy?"

Then, nothing but teeth and twinkle, flash and filigree. "Why, I broke about even, sweetheart. Where's the goddamn Fantastic? My beer icebox is covered in fingerprints."

There were more *broke evens* than *well I don't knows*. Nadine never talked to her mother about Dean Lee's poker. Nadine didn't really want to know the poker truth, and she suspected her mother didn't want to know either.

In the kitchen, Nadine pulled a paring knife out of the ebony knife block on the marble-topped island, then walked through the house, wielding it against imaginary intruders, until she reached the west end, which abutted the garage. Opening the door to the garage was like checking on a roasting turkey: a wave of withering heat rolled over Nadine, making her squint. She took a step back, waited for her body to adjust, then entered the garage. The lights didn't work for some reason. She pushed the buttons on the wall that opened the garage doors, allowing some sunlight and a little ventilation in.

The stacks of boxes in one corner had softened from the annealing conditions inherent in garages, and the lower boxes were collapsing like bean-bag chairs under the weight of others piled on top. Nadine grabbed the highest box, a small, heavy cube with U-Haul ads all over it, and quickly dropped it on the floor in case there were spiders nesting behind it. One thing Nadine did not like was spiders, and the sort that made their homes in garages always seemed to be the meatiest and scariest. No spiders. Nadine carefully sliced through the clear tape sealing the box.

Letters. To and from people Nadine had heard mentioned once or twice in her life, if at all. Letters from third cousins, postcards from friends of Adeline's, a bunch of thick letters addressed to Angie ("Angela Bigelow") from someone named Tanye Theuerdank, penned in the loopy, carefree hand of a teenager. Mountains of old bank statements bundled in decaying rubber bands. Some letters had postmarks from the 1970s. Nadine felt dirty and shameful sifting through the correspondence, even though she didn't read any—except one, a postcard from one Thom Seudak to Adeline, that read: *Done with my book yet? More than a year, Adeline, jesus christ.* Someone had Sharpied the card with a big black X. Nadine held the postcard up to the sunlight. Four pinholes, one at each corner, revealed that the postcard had been thumbtacked up someplace long ago, for a long time.

Nadine had heard that her grandmother, though extremely skilled as a binder and book restorer, was a bit pokey, and sometimes had a two-year backlog, which eventually alienated all but her most patient clients. Nadine planned to google Thom Seudak later, see what his story was.

One box down, and Nadine was already slick with sweat. She picked up the paring knife and sliced through the tape on the next box.

Pans. She remembered them all. The sticky yellow-brown pot with a cracked lid her mother had used to make rice. The ever-greasy cast iron skillet her daddy used to fry rib eyes in—the only dish he liked to cook himself.

"Ain't never supposed to wash these old cast irons—ruins 'em," he'd announce, carefully wiping the cold grease out with paper towels. Her father had loved that pan. Why was it out here? So much else, too. The more she thought about it, the more she realized there was *nothing* important in the new house that came from the old one.

The other boxes revealed even less. Tax stuff, Christmas ornaments.

In the bottom of one box was a strange, swirling pool of liquid studded with colored tubes of paper. It took Nadine a minute to realize it was a bunch of melted crayons. They must have been Sophie's. Nadine loathed crayons, their smeary inadequacy, their resistance to blending, their insufferably low pigment content.

Nadine didn't even bother taping the boxes up again, just tucked the four flaps under one another to effect a closure, like her mother had once demonstrated.

Against the back wall of the garage stood her parents' old dresser. Nadine pulled on the top drawer, but it stuck. She yanked, and the fake bronze drawer-pull came off in her hand, along with a few splinters of veneer. She tugged on all the drawers, but all were stuck. The heat and humidity of the garage, she figured, had swollen the thing. It figured that the plate painting had to be in the very thing to which she had no access. She pulled on a lower drawer. Nothing. She sat on the dirty garage floor, put her feet up on either side of the middle drawer, and pulled with both hands.

The drawer gave way, all at once, and came all the way out, scraping the insides of her knees and landing on her stomach. Nadine yelped, dumping the drawer off herself. It came to rest upside down next to her on the garage floor.

She stood up and inspected herself. The sharp edges of the drawer had drawn blood inside one knee. And she'd hurt her middle finger somehow, but there was no blood at least.

Annoyed, and still in mild shock, Nadine thought about kicking the drawer, whose contents had spilled across the floor. Nadine was about to pick up the drawer and jam it back in the dresser when she noticed an envelope taped to the underside.

She carefully peeled the envelope off. The tape had grown sticky and yellow, and stained the paper so that it was hard to read who it was from or to. It was hard to tell even what the stamp was.

Nadine opened the old envelope.

# CHAPTER SEVENTEEN

# SWIFT

ANGIE KNEW HER DAUGHTER was in the house somewhere, but some psychic field reverberating through Charles Mansion subtly warned Angie to leave her daughter alone for the moment.

Angie wanted to be alone, too. Her meeting with the We Sea people had rattled her, and they had nearly pressured her into writing a very large check, right in their offices. Dougie Sulevitch and Danny Moto had tag-teamed her, at one point even picking her purse up off the ground and handing it to her, along with a Mont Blanc fountain pen. We Sea, Angie thought, was a good organization, doing good things. But there were other causes in the world.

She felt a little sick. She hated this money. It was fun in small doses, but the big numbers were abstract and nauseating. It made her feel the same way to think about weightless neutrinos boring though matter, missing everything.

Angie went down into the wine cellar. She found a bottle of grenache she didn't remember buying. Upstairs in the kitchen, she poured herself a third of the bottle and sat on the couch. She opened her purse and took out her leather address book with the clasp. She opened it and removed her tiny drawing of St. Allison. Angie gazed at her.

Long ago Angie had reached the point where she could no longer look at Shea Babb's painting of Sophie. To her horror, though, Angie realized she wasn't sure where that picture was.

She put down her glass of wine and closed her eyes. Where? The bureau. Her mother's bureau in the garage.

Angie ran to the door at the other end of the house that led to the garage. It stood open. Angie entered.

The bureau. The middle drawer had been yanked out and lay upside down on the floor. Photographs were scattered everywhere. There—Sophie, painted in nail polish on a paper plate. And there—the unfinished, eyeless painting of Nadine.

Angie was about to pick them up when she noticed the underside of the drawer. The remains of old tape. She thought about this for a moment, then remembered.

Angie ran upstairs, knocked on Nadine's door. She knocked again, then went in.

Nadine was not there.


Dean Lee sat in a rented black Camaro in the parking lot of Wolflin Village in Amarillo. The late afternoon sun shone through the windshield. Dean Lee had turned off the engine and air conditioner long ago, and it was getting hot inside the car. Dean Lee liked the feeling of sweat trickling down his neck, of growing warmer and warmer, more and more uncomfortable, but with the power to turn the key and cool off in seconds.

On the first of October 2005, when Dean Lee had been outside sitting in his lawn chair in the front yard of their Fawn Street house, arguing mildly with Lolly Prager about money, he had heard a dull *pup* that he thought at first was a burst bottle, something that happened occasionally at NEK Bottling, where he worked. Too much pressure, some idiot asleep at the carbonator. When the moan came, though, he jumped up and ran inside the house. He was the first to encounter his two daughters, lying on their backs. Nadine was covered in blood. Sophie was on the ground like a busted doll, dots on the wall beyond her. Dean Lee went to Nadine first.

"Daddy," she had said through a lower lip cut so severely Dean Lee could see her little teeth. "Didn't work. It didn't work."

"What happened, honey?" he said, looking at her injury. "Tell your daddy what happened, now."

It was then that Dean Lee saw his revolver laying on the floor against the dirty baseboard. The smell of combusted saltpeter. He looked up to see his wife standing in the doorway of their bedroom, frozen, staring, silent, something caught in her throat. Dean Lee followed her gaze.

Sophie. Her pink cowboy hat on the floor next to her. A darkness spreading through the ribbed fabric of the collar of her yellow Bratz T-shirt.

Dean Lee was barely aware that Lolly was there, on his phone.

Time passed in a meaningless way, then there was a great commotion of police and EMTs.

Dean Lee looked in his rearview mirror at the Wolflin Village shoppers. His flight back to Austin was leaving in thirty-five minutes, and the airport was far outside of town. Dean Lee would have to leave now to make it in time.

Dean Lee took Gringe Bywaters's business card out of the breast pocket of his coveralls, studied the letters and numbers penciled on the back. ABA number, SWIFT code, account number. He placed it on the burning black dash, withdrew his weapon from his shoulder holster, and placed the muzzle against his chest, below his neck. He considered the positioning for a moment. Where had Sophie been hit? He thought it might have been a little farther right. Dean Lee walked the muzzle a half-inch toward the passenger door.

His phone rang. Angie had programmed the ringtone with some song he didn't know. Without moving the gun, he found his phone in his coveralls.

"Grandet."

"Daddy?"

"Sophie?"

"No, Daddy, Nadine. Sophie's gone. It's *Nadine*."

"Nadine. Where y'at, sweetie?"

"I need you."

Dean Lee's gun hand was steady. It always was.

"Well, Daddy's busy right now, honey. Rough luck here, barely playin' even."

"I need you to come home now. Right now."

"Why, I'm up in the panhandle, honey, it's—"

"Please?"

Dean Lee let the revolver fall in his lap.

"You at home? You don't sound like you at home."

"No. I'm downtown."

"Downtown, huh."

Dean Lee slowly turned the ignition key. The radio blared KPUR, the vents burped AC.

"Yeah. Come get me."

"I'll be there in three hours."

And Dean Lee pulled out of Wolflin Village onto Civic Circle, then right on S. Georgia up to I-40 East toward Amarillo International.

# CHAPTER EIGHTEEN

# Drag

NADINE TURNED OFF HER phone. She walked out the front door, leaving it unlocked. She stuck to the alleys in the neighborhood, then ventured out to the sidewalks of the rolling, hilly residential streets of northwest Austin. She made it to Route 2222, wondering idly if her mother was home yet. Probably. Whatever.

There was no sidewalk on this stretch of road, and she had to be careful of traffic. Eventually she made it to Balcones Drive, then Hancock, where traffic was sparse. She paused on the MoPac Bridge for a moment to watch the busy highway below. Then she moved on, arriving at Burnet Road, a busy commercial street, then 45th, then Guadalupe. Her feet hurt; the sunlight fell out of the sky like hot mercury. Twenty more blocks and she'd be on the Drag, at the heart of the University of Texas. She had been walking for more than two and a half hours.

The Drag. Noodle shops, record stores, seedy dorms that suicidal freshmen jumped from with great regularity. The low stone walls lining the sidewalks featured the fossils of ancient seashells.

Nadine had always been fascinated by the small bands of homeless kids that hung out on the west side of the Drag, always dirty, seemingly ever with a mangy, half-blind dog leashed nearby. Crustpunks, she'd heard them called—a terrible moniker, but maybe they liked it. Nadine had always thought she would end up as one of them. How they survived, she didn't know. They couldn't earn enough begging for money, no one ever seemed to give them anything, although her mother always did.

Nadine walked up and down the east side, the university side, where the street kids were not allowed. She spied three groups across the street. The first, hanging out in front of the Scientology building, comprised two girls and two boys, all seemed especially dirty, ragged, ageless, sullen, mean, their dog a pit bull terrier with a tartan kerchief and a large shaved patch above a haunch. One boy was asleep on the sidewalk, the two girls were leaning against each other back to back, the other boy was accosting passersby with an empty Wendy's hamburger sack, begging for change. The second group, two girls and a boy, younger, around fifteen, were camped out in front of the co-op on a big piece of cardboard, reaching out and grabbing at the legs of pedestrians for fun, laughing, throwing trash and cigarette butts, a yippy little black-and-white mutt with a pirate's eyepatch and a Jack in the Box emblem stuck on the tip of its tail nearby. The third group was made up of two young boys and a seemingly much older girl, and they were hanging out in front of the Hole in the Wall, no dog, full punk attire, but ragged, dirty, and hostile. Nadine turned around and walked back to the second group. Feeling fearless behind her full goth mask of makeup, she crossed the street.

"Oooh, scawy," said one of the girls. "Cross my palm with silver, honey?"

Nadine reached into her pocket and pulled out a hundred, one of the banknotes from the envelope sent by Juliette Moorehead to Nadine's mother. Gil's money. She handed it to the girl, who reached out with both hands to accept it. Both palms and her fingertips were callused, dirty; they seemed the hands of a much older woman, maybe even a man. Nadine wondered what this girl had been through to make her hands look like that. Not just a few nights outside. A lifetime. Nadine felt suddenly very young and naïve, and wished badly that she was back home. She wished her daddy was here.

"Jesus Christ, thanks, chica. This fucking thing real?"

"Yeah."

"You shopping?"

"What?"

"Never mind. Why ain't you inside with the air conditioning?"

Nadine realized all at once just how tired she was, what she was doing, what she had done.

"I don't know."

"What, you run away?" said the boy.

"I guess."

"Where from?" said one of the girls.

"Here."

"You rich." She had $900 in cash in her pocket, a couple thousand in the bank. She was rich, compared to them.

"No."

"You look it. You slummin', looking for new friends?"

Again, Nadine did not know what she was doing. She was mad at her mother and had run away, that was it. She'd done it before.

"How much you got on you?"

Nadine said nothing.

"Give what you got to Lonnie."

Nadine dug in her pocket. She felt around, separated another hundred from the folded wad of cash. When she offered it to Lonnie, she realized there were two banknotes stuck together.

"Urch handles the chemicals and the money," said Lonnie, nodding at the other girl, a small Latina with a crude tattoo of a broken heart on her cheek. Dirt seemed to crawl out of the collar of her rugby shirt and up her neck into her black, tangled hair. She held out her hands, cupped, as if waiting for sacrament. Nadine gave her the money.

"Do you want to hang with us?" said the first girl, who was thin, with long, dyed-red hair put up in severe braids. Black leather pants worn furry at the knees clung to her like they had grown right on her body, and a tight, soiled white T-shirt tied off at the midriff suggested she might be for sale.

"Okay."

"Well, you have to pass the Magnusson test first."

"What's that?"

Lonnie slowly got to his feet. Grime coated him like a pelt. He yanked on his combat boots, pulled up his red braces, stuck out his elbow in a mock-gentlemanly manner. Nadine wasn't that naïve. Boys and men had been trying to fuck her in hospitals since she was ten years old.

Nadine crossed her arms.

"Fuck off."

"What'd you say?"

In that instant, a steep memory pressed into her like an atmosphere, or a hug—the moment seven years before when Nadine fired a revolver into her sister, ending her life, watching her tumble backward like a doll in a gust, her little pink straw cowboy hat falling over her face, her deck of cards fanning the air like a magician's trick, the air silent then atomic with the burst of the shell, acrid with the musk of sulfur.

For seven years, Nadine had lived with positively consumptive guilt about her act—shame about her very being.

But in this moment, Nadine felt liberty on her like a rain shower. If she had her daddy's gun right now, she could kill Lonnie. Lay him out on the concrete and watch his life run out in red gusts.

"I said fuck you. Fuck *off*."

Lonnie smiled, the kind of smile where the eyes don't crinkle, a mouth-stretch that animals and poker players recognize as pure deception and hostility. Then he turned and strolled off down Guadalupe, hands jammed in his pockets, one suspender hanging down around his knees.

"Jesus Christ," said Urch. "No one talks to Lonnie like that."

"What's your dog's name?" said Nadine.

"Cutie."

"Cutie," said Nadine, and bent down to scratch the wretched animal under the chin. Cutie blinked, licked her wrist. Nadine felt like a super-hero, a demigoddess.

"You wanna be friends, you gotta pay your way, you understand that?" said the other girl. "Urch sells speed and other shit to college kids. I perform services for gentlemen. What can you do?"

"I can get cash. I have an ATM card and access to a bank account."

"How much?"

"That's my business."

"If you want to be a part of our thing, you'll tell me how much," said Urch.

"You want free money?" said Nadine, not certain what was happening or whether she wanted it to. She had just wanted to punish her mother. Well, joining a street gang would do it. "I'm gonna be in charge of it. I say how much and when."

Urch and the other girl looked at each other. Cutie barked.

"All right, deal," said Urch. "Where the fuck is Lonnie?"

Urch and the other girl looked around, clearly ill at ease without Lonnie around.

"Where do you sleep?" said Nadine.

"Usually under I-35 at 7th Street, but tonight we're staying at Lonnie's friend Mack Straight's house on East 3rd, but we can't go till later. What time is it, Ape?"

"Like two," said Ape, not looking at a watch or a clock or anything. "We can start heading over there. And we can drop by an ATM and get our first daily installment from what's your name?"

"Veronica."

"From Veronica here."

On the walk in the afternoon heat through the east side of town, Nadine wondered who she was. Only fourteen, she had killed two people in her life, one with a gun, the other by neglect. The killing of Sophie had defined her life, the killing of Gil had reified what she had always suspected about herself: she was a kind of human venom. And finding the envelope, Gil's note, hidden from her, made Nadine understand that her mother thought the same thing about her daughter. Well, fuck her.

She needed no one now. She could survive on the streets on her own. She had money. The cops might be looking for her, if her mother had found her note, and she surely had. In all likelihood, they would find her in short order, too, but she would not make it easy for them. She decided to stick with Ape and Urch for the time being, stay at Mack Straight's house. Maybe Mack Straight would try to rape her and she could kill him, too.

"Welcome, all," said the man who answered the door, an old Austin hippie, all grins and carious teeth and loose hemp clothing. "Urch, April, and... who have we here?"

"That's Moneybags Veronica," said Urch, performing a Vanna White–style fingertip merchandise flourish, as though Nadine was a stacking washer-dryer.

"Hello, Veronica, I'm Mack. Can I offer you some tea?"

Mack held out a hand. Nadine took it, squeezed it as hard as she could, like her father had taught her to shake a man's hand, and let it go. It felt like squeezing a frozen gauntlet.

"Okay."

"And where is Lonnie?" said Mack, unfazed by Nadine's death grip.

"We don't know."

"Ah, a free spirit, our Lon."

A kettle boiled somewhere. Nobody moved. It seemed to whistle for a full minute before Mack noticed it. He jumped up and ran off. Presently he emerged with a mug of tea, a carton of half and half, a selection of sweeteners, and a spoon.

"Here you go, Miss Veronica."

"Thanks."

"How did y'all hook up?"

"Lonnie was gonna rape me, but I told him to fuck off," said Nadine.

April and Urch looked at each other, open-mouthed, for a long moment. Urch closed her mouth first, then said: "You're fucking weird, Moneybags."

"You've got a tattoo on your face, and you call me weird? You live on a piece of cardboard on the street, and you call me weird? You whore yourself out, you sell speed to college kids, you walk forty blocks in the middle of the afternoon in the middle of the summer to sleep at some sixty-year-old hippie's house, and you call me weird? Fuck you, Urch. Fuck you, *Ape*. This is good tea, Mack. Thank you."

"Whoa, Moneybags, shit," said April.

"You don't have to prove yourself, bitch," said Urch.

Mack interlaced his fingers and held his tea mug. Something about him seemed perfectly at ease around squabbling homeless teen girls.

"Y'all must be tired. Veronica, do you mind taking the couch in the den?"

"I like sleeping on couches."

Mack closed his eyes and nodded serenely.

"I have a cat, Fitch, that will probably curl up with you. Not allergic, are you?"

Cutie, who was tied up outside, began to yip, as though he'd heard mention of a cat. "How come you're taking a bunch of teenagers in your home?"

"Well, to be honest, Veronica, I'm buying drugs from Lonnie."

"And you're having sex with April?"

"And yes, I'm having sex with April."

Mack sipped his tea.

"Moneybags, you're such a fucking drag," said April.

"I'm going to lie down."

Nadine drank down the last of the tea and found her way into the den. Mack brought her clean sheets and blankets and made up the couch.

"I'm sorry for my behavior," he said. "I need Lonnie. I'm addicted to Vyvanse. And frankly I'm addicted to April."

"Not my business."

"You seem like a nice person, not like them. Are you all right? Do you need help?"

"No."

"Lonnie didn't hurt you, did he?"

Nadine said nothing.

"Do you know if Lonnie's coming? I really kinda need that shit."

Nadine, in spite of herself, was growing concerned about Lonnie. His absence made her a little anxious.

"Don't April and Urch have what you want?"

Mack sat on the couch, put his head in his hands, and groaned.

"I take Adderall," said Nadine. "That's pretty much the same thing. Want some to tide you over?"

"Oh god, really? Veronica, you'd do that for me?"

Nadine reached into her pocket and found her Ziploc of meds. She poured half into her hand and picked out a dozen or so 30-mg extended-release caps. Nadine handed them to Mack.

"Thank you, Veronica. I hope that tea doesn't keep you awake."

"I don't sleep anyway. Where's Fitch?"

"Oh, he'll be along. Goodnight, Veronica. Sweet dreams. And thanks."

"Sure."

Mack Straight turned out the light and returned to the kitchen with Urch and April. She listened to their low voices for a while, until they got into an argument about something. Urch could be heard getting up and leaving, climbing a staircase. Later, April and Mack climbed the same staircase. Somewhere directly above her, Nadine could hear the stresses and exertions of what must be sex. She was sure she never wanted to have sex. It seemed to go on for a long time. Nadine watched the front door for Lonnie.

An electric clock on top of an old console TV audibly ticked away the seconds.

Nadine thought she hadn't slept at all, but every time she looked at the clock, it was further along than she imagined.

At dawn a magnificently large, pasha-like tortoiseshell cat jumped on her stomach and began to milk-tread. It sighed, curled up, and went to sleep.

Around eight, the sex started again. At eight-thirty, Mack Straight came downstairs dressed in a plaid shirt, jeans, and a knit tie.

"Veronica, you're up. Tea?"

"No thanks. Where do you work?"

"State Board of Plumbing Examiners. You and the girls are welcome to stay here today. I'll be home at around quarter to six. Eat whatever you want. I even have two bus passes on the fridge. Say, can you get more Adderall?"

"I'm not a dealer, it's just my own prescription, so no."

"Ah. Well, I'm outta here. Have a nice day."

Nadine lay still on the couch, Fitch snoring on her stomach. She listened to the growing din of traffic on 3rd Street. She realized she hadn't eaten in almost a day.

Noon. Urch came downstairs.

"Lonnie here?"

"No."

"April!" shouted Urch.

"What!"

"We're leaving!"

April came downstairs and turned on the old TV.

"Turn that off," said Urch.

"I never get to watch TV!"

"You could've been watching TV instead of screwing that old dinosaur, but now it's too late."

Urch was going through sets of keys hanging from hooks on the wall by an old yellow telephone with a long, played-out cord.

"Moneybags, get off the couch and tell me what kind of car that is in the driveway."

Nadine scooted out from underneath Fitch, who slid to the couch, scarcely changing position. She peeked out the blinds.

"I can't tell."

"Go out and look."

Just as she stepped outside, a cop car cruised down the street. Nadine immediately ducked back inside, which got Urch's attention.

"What?" She looked out the peephole. "A cop. You got a warrant or something?"

"No."

"So what was that all about?"

"I ran away. I don't wanna go home. So what?"

"So they're gone now. Go tell me what kind of car it is."

Nadine did. "Hyundai."

"We're not walking anywhere today, bitches," said Urch. "First stop, ATM, Moneybags. Then Starbucks, then Taco Bell."

"I wanna buy a swimsuit and go to Barton Springs," said April.

"I'll buy us suits," said Nadine.

"Hear that?" said Urch. "Moneybags is gonna make it so we can all go swimming."

"Thanks, Moneybags!" said April and Urch at once.

Nadine said nothing.

"Everyone go potty," said Urch. "We leave in five."

Urch proved to be a surprisingly careful driver, signaling, checking the rearview, side-views, and over her shoulder when changing lanes, acknowledging gifts of the road with a nod or a wave, obeying speed limits, not once running a yellow or rolling through a stop sign. The trio drove all over Austin, shopping, eating, going to the movies, taking cash advances, all with Nadine's ATM card, preferring to leave her cash untouched. Nadine was careful not to go to the same place twice, because the police might be tracking her movements by her card activity, and likely lying in wait at an ATM she'd already used.

Periodically they drove down the drag to see if Lonnie was at their haunt. Someone had taken their cardboard. There was no trace of their homestead at all.

"Where the fuck is he?" said Urch.

"Probably at Mack's by now. It's past two."

"Let's go see."

Mack was home early and clearly worked up that his car had been taken but was trying to play it cool.

"Hey, you guys! I was worried about you. So glad you're back. Everything okay?"

"Lonnie here?"

"No, no Lonnie. Listen, got my keys?"

Urch handed him the keys and he ran out to check on his car. Nadine sat on the couch. Fitch immediately climbed in her lap. Urch and April went into the kitchen.

Mack Straight came back into the house. He sat on the couch.

"Listen, Nadine, right?"

"Huh?"

"You're all over the news right now. Amber alerts, the whole bit."

"Great."

"Look, I can't have you here. Harboring a fugitive and all. But can I ask a favor? Would you not tell anyone you stayed here? I can't have anyone know about April, you know? I don't know how old she is."

"All right."

"Can I buy the rest of your Adderall?"

"You can have it."

"Thank you, Nadine. I'm sorry about your troubles."

Nadine decided that she would walk to McCandless tonight. She could be there by morning. She would live with Harper and Carrollton from now on. Nadine snuck out the back door. There were no alleys in this part of town, but 3rd Street was relatively deserted. She stopped at a park on the corner of Onion Street and swung on a swing for a few minutes, then headed toward downtown. She would have to be careful because of all the cops. Nadine walked under I-35 at 7th Street. She started across town, cut over to 5th Street to avoid the police station, headed toward MoPac, then cut over to 6th Street. Thousands of people out, no one paid her any attention.

On the other side of Congress Avenue, not far from BookPeople, where her mother used to work, Nadine passed a café-bar with patrons sitting at tables on the sidewalk. She looked up to see a young woman holding a double-size margarita, staring at her intensely. She nearly dropped her glass as she stood and pointed at Nadine, shouting, "Nadine Grandet! I think!"

Nadine ignored her, forced herself to walk and not run. The woman kept shouting. Nadine heard footsteps behind her, then felt a hand on her shoulder.

"Miss?" She turned. The woman, now with a man, said, "Are you Nadine Grandet?"

"Je ne vous comprends pas," said Nadine, happy to use some junior-high school French for the first time.

"I think it's her," said the man. "Call 911."

The woman took out her phone and started to dial. Nadine took off down Nueces Street.

"Hey!"

The man ran after Nadine, catching her easily, tackling her to the ground. She screamed. He was much larger, heavier. He must have been some kind of wrestler—he put her in a hold, immobilizing her. She wanted to cry but couldn't catch her breath to do so.

The police showed up in mere minutes. They put her in the back of a cruiser.

"Are you taking me home?"

"We're taking you to the station to ask you a few questions," said the cop in the passenger seat.

Nadine looked around. The windows were smudged and dirty, as though people had rubbed their faces on them. She tried to imagine needing to rub her face on a cop car window but couldn't.

"Is it illegal to run away from home?"

They said nothing.

In the police station, they left her by herself in a room with a scratched metal table and three plastic chairs. She watched a clock on the wall progress from 4:14 to 5:02 p.m. Two women came in, one in a suit, one in uniform.

"Nadine, I'm Detective Versfelt, and this is Officer Kane. Your mother is on her way."

"I don't want to see her."

Nadine took her phone out of her pocket and turned the power on. Sixty-eight calls and 130 texts from her mother.

She called her daddy.

"Grandet."

"Daddy?"

"Sophie?"

288

"No, Daddy, Nadine. Sophie's gone. It's *Nadine*."

"Nadine. Where y'at, sweetie?"

"I need you."

# CHAPTER NINETEEN

# Free Refills

ANGIE SAT IN THE precinct waiting room. Behind a thick, green glass partition, some cop named Dicerdinek said she had to wait, that her daughter was being resistant.

"You married?" said Officer Dicerdinek, not looking up, writing something on a yellow pad with a stub of pencil shorter than a cigarette butt. It didn't sound like a line.

"Yes, I'm married," said Angie. "How come you let a fourteen-year-old girl have so much control over you? Why can't you just send her out?"

Officer Dicerdinek looked up at a clock. It was nearing 8:30 in the evening.

"Wants to see her daddy," he said, still not looking at her.

Angie sat. She put her head down on her purse and waited.

"Angie," said a voice she recognized, but didn't recognize at all. She turned to behold Dean Lee. There was something different about him. A fundamental change. She was all at once more worried about him than she was about her daughter. And she had been pretty worried. The note on her bed at home had said she would not see her daughter alive again.

She hugged her husband of fifteen years.

Nadine came out, flanked by two cops.

"Those're your parents?" one of them said.

"Yeah."

Nadine ran and hugged her daddy.

"Hug your mama, now, Nadine," said Dean Lee.

Nadine shook her head, turned away, buried her face in Dean Lee's shirt.

"Come, now, honey. Let's all make up."

Angie touched her daughter's shoulder. Nadine shook her off. Then she looked up, gave her mother a quick, civilized hug. Angie began crying. Nadine hugged her mother for real.

"Iron Works is open for thirty more minutes," said Dean Lee. "If we walk fast, we can sneak in before they close."

At a picnic table inside Iron Works Barbecue on Cesar Chavez, the Grandets chewed on pulled pork sandwiches and sucked on Dr Peppers while employees swept around their feet. The last customers were filling little paper ramekins with pickles and ketchup to take home. At a table in the back sat a big man. He was drinking a Lone Star and watching a show about the prospects of the Longhorns, whose season was starting in a few weeks. Dean Lee kept glancing over his shoulder at the man.

"Do you know that man, Dean Lee?"

"Can't say for sure. Maybe, maybe not. Can't place him. Nadine, sweetness, you cain't be runnin' off like that, you heard me? You scared your mother and me to death."

"Nadine wasn't the only one with her phone turned off," said Angie.

"How come you don't ever say *dear* or *sweetie* or *honey?*" Dean Lee asked his wife, without rancor.

Angie knew exactly why.

"My mother objected to terms of endearment. She said that using a surrogate name suggested one was avoiding some kind of truth. Nicknames are an insult."

"I wonder if she had any for me," Dean Lee said, mostly to himself. "Honey, uh, Nadine, you cain't be—"

"Mom, you owe me an apology."

She couldn't look at her daughter, so Angie studied the purse in her lap. Inside were her three portraits. Eyeless Nadine in a slender box that once held a necklace; Sophie in red and brown, glazed in a small, round mahogany frame; St. Allison in silverpoint, encased in thin Mylar and tucked into her address book.

Also in Angie's purse was her checkbook, from which she had, only yesterday, nearly torn off a check with many, many zeroes. It was still there, attached, un-ripped-away, made out to We Sea in precious Mont Blanc ink.

"Nadine, I—"

"Just apologize."

"Wait," said Angie, turning to look at her daughter. Under normal circumstances, Nadine could stare down a hammerhead shark, so there was no way she could look her daughter directly in the eyes. Instead, she focused on her lower lashes. Angie remembered what Harper could do with a lower lash, and this recollection hurt. "I was going to give that letter to you when you were older. I didn't want to upset—"

"I was already upset, Mom. I've been upset since I was six. You kept me away from the only attachment I had to Gil. *The only thing.* And then you forgot about it. What if I lived a whole life without ever seeing his note? What if you died? What if you gave that stupid bureau away on Craigslist? What if there was a fire? I thought about setting one, by the way, squirting lighter fluid all over your wine bottle racks in the basement and lighting a match. Bye, Charles Mansion. You're lucky I just ran off."

Angie had forgotten about the envelope, it was true. It would have stayed where it was and traveled with that bureau wherever it went, whether on its journey through time in the garage, on its way to some Craigslist desperado, or out to the curb, only to wind up in the back of some dilettante furniture refinisher's pickup truck. It would have been gone forever, the envelope found or not, the money pocketed or not, the poem and suicide note found, read, discarded, or left forever in its dark archive.

"Please forgive me, Nadine. I thought I was doing the ri—"

Nadine put up her hand. All was quiet. She rolled up the remainder of her pork sandwich in its butcher paper, wadded it up into a ball, and tossed it, a good twenty feet, into a trash can—all net.

"Okay," she said. "But, as Gil used to say, no one ever forgets where they buried the hatchet."

"You grew up too fast," said Dean Lee. Angie wasn't sure who he was talking to or even about. Maybe himself. He drank the last of his Dr Pepper, then glanced again over his shoulder at the big man.

"How'd it go in Amarillo?" said Angie, just to say something.

"Well," said Dean Lee. "Didn't do so good this time."

Both Angie and Nadine looked up at him. Dean Lee never broke worse than even, at least that he admitted. He reached into the breast pocket of his coveralls and retrieved a light gray business card. He turned it over in his fingers a couple of times, then handed it to Angie.

"What's Gringe Bywaters," said Angie.

"*Who*," said Dean Lee, "is Gringe Bywaters. That is the question."

Only the name was embossed on the card. Nothing else except

some hard-to-read numbers lightly penciled on the back. Angie looked closely. Banking information. Routing number, account number, SWIFT code. Deep in her prefrontal, Angie was beginning to understand.

"You're gonna use them wire instructions on the back there and send ol' Gringe some money."

"Daddy, are you bro—?"

"You know," said Dean Lee, "Gringe's granddad was Jerry Bywaters, that ol' Texas painter with pictures in all the museums. You know *Oil Field Girls?* I always liked that picture. Gringe has a couple of his pictures still, hanging on the walls in his poker room."

"Dean Lee. Your daughter asked you a question. She asked you if you were broke."

Dean Lee smiled, his all-is-merry twinkle.

"I guess to be straight with y'all, I am. Broke. Doing pretty good for a while there, coming home winner nearly every time. Then a bad run of cards, real bad, ran into aces more often than I can c—"

"You... down? Really, Dean Lee? How much?"

Twinkle, twinkle.

"A fair amount," said Dean Lee, not looking Angie in the eyes. He was examining some graffiti long ago scratched into the picnic table.

"All of it? A *hundred million?*"

"So," said Dean Lee. "Like I was saying, you're gonna wanna send ol' Gringe some money."

"How much?"

"Just go ahead and send him what you got."

Angie knew what was happening now, but she catechized her husband anyway. "What I got."

"Ol' Gringe been lettin' me play on credit for the last little while. Those days are over now, Angie. Get your phone out and do it now."

"My phone? I can't—"

Angie realized there was no one in Iron Works Barbecue. No workers, no noise, no country music. The TV was off. The door was bolted. The big man in the back was still there, though, studiously ignoring the Grandets.

"Yes, you can. Done it a bunch of times. Millions, with a goddamn Samsung. Send it all, ever' penny, Angie."

"That's not my debt, Dean Lee. That's yours. We talked about this. You remember Kerbey Lane? The waitress with the... the cute waitress?"

"I'm real sorry, Angie. I'm real sorry, Nadine."

"That's my—"

"Mom, what's happening right now? Daddy?"

"Now, Angie, now, do it now. *Now.*"

Dean Lee looked over his shoulder at the big man.

Angie waited, stared at her husband. She had no trouble staring deep into his pupils. She *watched* her husband. He was watching his daughter, who was looking at the bags of water hanging from the ceiling, placed up there at regular intervals to keep flies away through some visual alchemy that only flies understood.

Angie looked up at the bags, too. Then she took out her phone, signed onto her Wells Fargo account. She clicked on *Transfer Money*, then *Wire Money*, then *Add Recipient*. Angie got a text with a code. She entered the six-digit code into the proper field on her phone.

"Gringe Bywaters, 1514 Lipscomb, Amarillo, 79102," said Dean Lee.

"Mom? What are you doing?"

Angie pressed the *Schedule Wire* button. She entered $101,108,092.42, which represented her half of the lottery money, minus what she'd spent, plus the interest it had earned. She showed it to Dean Lee. After a moment's thought, she showed it to Nadine, too.

"Keep forty bucks back for the wire fee, so you're not overdrawn," said Dean Lee, without apparently realizing the laughable absurdity of the statement. "We're gonna sit here for a minute till the bank calls you to confirm."

"Things are different now," said Angie. "Aren't they."

"No," said Nadine. "They're the same."

Nadine got up to refill her Dr Pepper, which seemed to command the big man's attention. He sat up a bit. Nadine didn't notice this. Neither did Dean Lee. But Angie did. It frightened her.

Angie's phone rang.

"Wells Fargo account services here, regarding your recent online wire instructions. Please confirm amount, recipient, and account details."

Angie did.

"Thank you. Initiate wire?"

"Yes."

Angie hung up. She dropped her phone on the picnic table, put her head in her hands.

"Can we go?" said Nadine.

"Soon," said Dean Lee.

From somewhere in the barbecue joint came the first notes of Merle Haggard's "Okie from Muskogee." The big man shifted at his picnic table, drank down his Lone Star, then answered his phone without a word. He listened, then hung up. He stood, put on a Sooners gimme cap, then walked past, ignoring the Grandets. He unbolted the door to the Iron Works Barbecue and left.

"All right," said Dean Lee. "It's all right. We can go."

# CHAPTER TWENTY

# The Damascus of All Fathers

DEAN LEE WOKE. FOR a full minute, he stared up at the slowly rotating ceiling fan and the glass globe beneath it, trying to recall where he was. Not only could Dean Lee not remember where he was, he could not remember who he was. He remembered his name, that he was born in Pharr, Texas, that he was afraid of his sister, and that he missed his mother. He remembered that hailstorms traumatized him. That he was an exceptional poker player. He was good at frying rib eyes. Something extraordinary had happened, he recalled, and then something else that canceled it all out. What was it?

A beautiful angel appeared. A wavy cascade of auburn hair covered one eye, the other crinkled in a smile. The angel wore deep crimson lipstick, and she was draped in light, sheer periwinkle fabric that suggested she was absolutely available yet inevitably forbidden, like a siren. The angel said something to him in a voice he recognized.

And all at once Dean Lee began to remember.

The angel, Harper DeBaecque, crouched down next to the divan Dean Lee was laid out on: his tacky old leather couch from way back at the old Fawn Street house. He felt it sticking to his shirtless back under the thin blankets. It was a fine feeling, the skin of his back peeling off the cheap cowhide.

"Coffee, Dean Lee," said Harper. "Sit up now, you'll spill."

Dean Lee sat up. He closed his eyes, studied the images coruscating against the insides of his eyelids. A lottery ticket, yes. Cards, yes. Jacks full of nines beating his nines full of jacks. God almighty. The parquet floor of Charles Mansion. The repo men, Travis County Constables in brown and dun, with pistols at their sides. Harper, the angel of the golden age. Carrollton what's-his-name, her pharmacist boyfriend, an all-right redheaded fella generous with his beer. Nadine, his split but indivisible daughter, the adult in all this. Angie, the *mother* in it all.

Dean Lee accepted the mug of coffee, took a sip. The mug read, "Insanity runs in my family…"

"When…"

"It's the fifth of August, Dean Lee," said Harper. "2013. Angie's here, in the spare room, still asleep. Nadine's on the cot in the den, awake, playing on her phone and eating cinnamon toast. She claims to like cots."

"Mm," said Dean Lee. "She always has."

"You like an ice cube in your coffee," she said, dropping a dinghy-shaped cube in his mug, then patting her cheeks and forehead with her damp hand.

"You remembered that?" he said.

"Sure. I remember a lot. What do *you* remember?"

Dean Lee watched the ice dissolve in his caramel-colored coffee. He pulled the thin blanket around his shoulders.

"Chilly for August."

"Carrollton likes his AC icy."

300

"Carrollton. A good man. Are we, uh, *here* now? With you and Carrollton?"

Harper gestured at her little living room, decorated in gray, white, and sepia, the only color the reproduction of Vladimir Tretchikoff's painting *The Chinese Girl* on the brick wall over the fireplace.

"For now, you're here."

Nadine emerged from the hall. A big, threadbare, royal-blue bathrobe hung on her like a gangster's dreadnaught. "Is this Carrollton's?" she said, sniffing at one end of the sash. She grimaced.

"Yep," said Harper, "he left it for you. He sleeps late on Saturdays. But he'll be up when the bacon starts frying. It's thick-cut, takes a while to cook, perfumes the whole house, brings all the boys to the yard."

Dean Lee's mouth watered like Pavlov's dog catching sight of a white lab coat. Dean Lee looked up at Harper like a savior. The savior smiled.

The drive. He remembered the drive now. Dean Lee in the back seat with Nadine, Angie up front, Harper driving them all crammed in her '68 Mercedes 280. Down Far West Boulevard, along Koenig Lane, south down Airport Boulevard, past the Short Stop, past the gross, old Jack in the Crack, past Callahan's, where he used to buy his ammo because they knew him there, welcomed him with smiles, even though .357 cartridges were cheaper at Academy and almost free at Walmart. Then over the Colorado River Bridge.

"Why don't you pull over here for a minute, Harper?" Dean Lee had said.

"What?" said Harper, out-maneuvering a rust-infected Volvo. "No shoulder on the bridge, Dean Lee."

"I'll be quick."

Harper pulled over, stopped, and got immediately honked at by an old, butter-colored K-car. Dean Lee climbed out on the traffic side. He walked round the back of the Mercedes, smiled and waved at the K-car, climbed up on the slender sidewalk, pulled his old Colt Python out of its holder, and skyhooked the weapon into the churning moss-green vortices of the Colorado River fifty feet below.

After an instant's thought, he unbuckled his shoulder holster. He flung that in, too.

Had that been *yesterday?*

Nadine, in Carrollton's blue bathrobe, sat down next to her father, took his mug, and sipped at his coffee. She handed the mug back.

Nadine had brought nothing but a sketchbook, her computer with her writing, and her phone from Charles Mansion. Not even her clothes. When Travis County came to evict them, one of the constables, Marion Altdorfer, had sat down on the roof with Nadine in the folding chairs while they watched a crew of men haul stuff out of the house. Wooden cases of wine, sideboards, paintings. It reminded her of Lolly back in the old days, always looking around the Fawn Street house for something to take and sell. But unlike the dread that hung over Lolly's visits, she felt nothing but relief at seeing the Charles Mansion crap go.

"You can keep your personal things, Nadine," said Marion, shielding her eyes from the late-afternoon sun. "You know, your stuff. Those constables won't take that."

A parade of cutter ants carrying slivers of sycamore leaves marched along the hypotenuse of the rooftop. Marion and Nadine watched them, too. Nadine wondered if Marion saw the parallel.

"I think they're done," said Marion. At first, Nadine thought she meant the cutter ants, which looked like they would parade their julienned leaves until the end of time. It took her a moment to realize she was talking about the movers. "Want to go downstairs?"

Marion folded up the four lawn chairs, threaded her forearm through the handles like it was a big, nylon purse, then plucked Angie's sun-ravaged umbrella out of its sand bucket.

Had that been yesterday, too?

Angie, dressed in tennis shorts, Stan Smiths, and an old, faded green polo shirt, came out of the guest room and found Harper, Dean Lee, and Nadine sitting on the couch. There wasn't room for Angie, but she made some, squeezing between her daughter and her husband.

"So," she said. "What are we going to do?"

"We're having bacon and cowboy biscuits," said Nadine. "Harper's gonna make them."

That wasn't what Angie meant, and her daughter knew it. She knew Harper knew it, too. But Angie wasn't sure about Dean Lee: he lived moment to moment, always had, always would. It didn't matter. None of it mattered.

It would be all right.

BILL COTTER is the author of the novels *Fever Chart* and *The Parallel Apartments*, both published by McSweeney's. He is also responsible for the middle-grade adventure series *Saint Philomene's Infirmary for Magical Creatures*, penned under the name W. Stone Cotter and published by Macmillan. Cotter's short fiction has appeared in *The Paris Review*, *Electric Literature*, and *McSweeney's Quarterly Concern*. An essay, "The Gentleman's Library," was awarded a Pushcart Prize. When he is not writing, Cotter labors in the antiquarian book trade.

## ACKNOWLEDGMENTS

*THE SPLENDID TICKET* would have sunk long ago if not for persistent propping-up and cheerleading, as well as occasional emergency triage, from the following people: Sam Anderson-Ramos, Aaron Bergman, Wayne Alan Brenner, RJ Casey, Marcio Coello, Bob and Cathy Cotter, Albert "Bug" Cotton III, Missy and Brian Dempsey, Adam Eaglin, Karen and Joe Etherton, Elizabeth Frengel, Rodger and Kiki Friedman, Nancy Gore, Madison Grant, P.J. (Tricia) Hoover, Britta Jensen, Sara Kocek, Karen Krajcer, Masha Krasnova-Shabaeva, Michael Laird, Kate Dillon Levin, Jody Lockshin, John McMurtrie, Carly Nelson, John and Lenka Norris, Krissy Olson, Bryan Sansone, Dave Spears, Raj Tawney, Sunra Thompson, Alvaro Villanueva, Eric Cromie, Dan Weiss, Amanda Uhle, Amy Sumerton, Rudy and the crew at Batch Coffee in Austin, and so many others I will later feel terrible about having neglected to include here. I'm forever indebted to you all.